Anastasia

AND

HER SISTERS

CAROLYN MEYER

Anastasia

AND

HER SISTERS

A PAULA WISEMAN BOOK
Simon & Schuster Books for Young Readers
NEW YORK • LONDON • TORONTO • SYDNEY • NEW DELHI

SIMON & SCHUSTER BOOKS FOR YOUNG READERS
An imprint of Simon & Schuster Children's Publishing Division
1230 Avenue of the Americas, New York, New York 10020

SIMON & SCHUSTER BOOKS FOR YOUNG READERS
is a trademark of Simon & Schuster, Inc.
For information about special discounts for bulk purchases,
please contact Simon & Schuster Special Sales at 1-866-506-1949
or business@simonandschuster.com.
The Simon & Schuster Speakers Bureau can bring authors to your live event.
For more information or to book an event, contact the Simon & Schuster Speakers Bureau
at 1-866-248-3049 or visit our website at www.simonspeakers.com.
Jacket design by Lizzy Bromley
Interior design by Hilary Zarycky
The text for this book is set in Centaur.
Manufactured in the United States of America
2 4 6 8 10 9 7 5 3 1
Library of Congress Cataloging-in-Publication Data
Meyer, Carolyn, 1935–
Anastasia and her sisters / Carolyn Meyer. — First edition.
pages cm
Summary: A novel in diary form in which the youngest daughter of Tzar Nicholas II describes
the privileged life her family led up until the time of World War I and the tragic events that
befell them. Includes bibliographical references.
ISBN 978-1-4814-0326-9 (hardcover) — ISBN 978-1-4814-0328-3 (eBook)
1. Anastasia, Grand Duchess, daughter of Nicholas II, Emperor of Russia, 1901–1918—
Juvenile fiction. [1. Anastasia, Grand Duchess, daughter of Nicholas II, Emperor of Russia,
1901–1918—Fiction. 2. Princesses—Fiction. 3. Sisters—Fiction. 4. Diaries—Fiction.
5. Russia—History—Nicholas II, 1894–1917—Fiction. 6. Soviet Union—History—
Revolution, 1917–1921—Fiction.] I. Title.
PZ7.M5685Am 2015
[Fic]—dc23
2014003498

FIRST
EDITION

For Tony

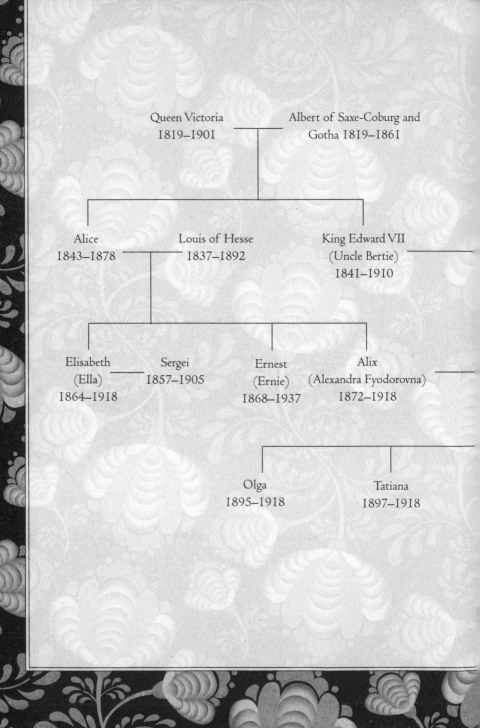

FAMILY TREE

Alexandra
1844–1925

Dagmar
(Maria Fyodorovna)
1847–1928

Tsar Alexander III
1845–1894

King George V
(Georgie)
1865–1936

Nicky
(Tsar Nicholas II)
1868–1918

Georgy
1871–1899

Mikhail
(Misha)
1878–1918

Maria
1899–1918

Anastasia
1901–1918

Alexei
1904–1918

Xenia
1875–1960

Alexander
(Sandro)
1866–1933

Olga
1882–1960

SIBERIA, APRIL 1918

am Anastasia Nikolaevna Romanova, age seventeen, and I am trying not to show how afraid I feel.

Four days ago a string of peasant carts lined with filthy straw drove off through half-frozen mud and slush with Papa and Mama and my sister Marie. A handful of servants went with them, along with our own Dr. Botkin. They are being taken to Moscow, where Papa, once known to the world as Tsar Nicholas II, Emperor and Autocrat of All the Russias, will be put on trial by the evil men who have seized power. Our brother, Alexei, is too ill to travel, and that forced Mama to make a wrenching choice: to accompany Papa or to stay here in Tobolsk. In the end she decided to go, taking Marie and leaving Olga and Tatiana and me here with Alexei.

"We'll send for you, and you'll join us when Lyosha is well enough," Papa said. His face was drawn and haggard, but he smiled so bravely that I cried, even though I said I wouldn't.

We watched them go. Four days, and so far there has been no word.

We call ourselves "OTMA," a name made up of our initials: Olga, Tatiana, Marie, and Anastasia. Olga and Tatiana, the two older sisters, are the Big Pair; Marie and I are the Little Pair. I miss Marie awfully. We have never been separated like this. We've always done everything together.

Alexei—Lyosha, as he prefers to be called—lies in bed and stares at the wall. He is thirteen, the only son and, until the terrible events of a year ago, the tsarevich, the future tsar. Wherever he went, the Russian people worshipped him, begging for the chance to touch him. They adored the tsar, too, and even kissed his shadow when he passed. He was their *Batiushka*, "Little Father," and Mama was *Matushka*. But that was before everything went so horribly wrong, before the people who call themselves Bolsheviks took over the government and forced Papa to abdicate. Now there is no tsar, present or future.

"Someone will rescue us," Tatiana reassures us as the hours crawl by. "Our friends will see to it that our whole family is saved."

I want to believe her.

From the window I stare down at the road, deserted now and bleak. The shutters are closed at the house across the street where Dr. Botkin's son Gleb and daughter, Tatiana, wait for word from their father. I turn away.

"Grandmère Marie promised to take me to Paris last year for my sixteenth birthday," I remind my sisters wistfully. "But she couldn't because of the war. Maybe that's where we'll go, when we've been rescued."

Alexei says no, we will probably go to England, where both Papa and Mama have cousins.

"England has already refused to offer us asylum," Olga says. "I despise them for that. Our relatives have no concern for us."

"I wish we'd be allowed to stay in Russia, at Livadia," Tatiana says. Livadia is our beautiful palace on the Black Sea.

"You're wishing for a miracle," Olga says, and shakes her head. I know what she's thinking: *There will be no miracle. No one will rescue us.* Olga is such a pessimist. What's wrong with dreaming of Livadia? Or Paris?

Another gloomy day passes, and the guard delivers a telegram from Mama. They have not been taken to Moscow after all, but to Ekaterinburg. Mama does not explain why they are still in Siberia, why this change. MORE LATER, she wires.

The waiting goes on. It feels as though it will never end. Easter comes and goes. We pray and pray. It's all we can think to do.

At last a letter from Mama. We must be ready to leave soon, she's written, and she instructs us to "dispose of the medicines." This is our secret code and refers to the jewels we packed in a great rush during our last hours at Alexander Palace, concealing them among the things we were bringing with us—religious icons, family pictures, albums of photographs, trunks stuffed full of mementos collected over the years. The jewels were not found then, but we may not be so lucky, or our guards so careless, the next time.

Alexei and his dog, Joy, take positions by the door to alert us if anyone comes up the stairs while we're "disposing of the medicines." Tatiana is in charge. She is always the one in charge, the organized one—we call her "the Governess." Three of our ladies help us to sew the jewels into our clothing. We work industriously, almost cheerily, under Tatiana's direction, covering diamonds with cloth to disguise them as buttons, stitching rubies and emeralds between the stays of our corsets, hiding ropes of pearls in the hems of our skirts. Trina, our real governess, sews gems into the flaps and pockets of Alexei's jacket.

Olga is sitting quite still, staring morosely at her idle hands. Trina notices and places a velvet bag in Olga's lap. When she opens it, out tumbles an exquisite pearl and diamond necklace. It was a gift from Papa and Mama for Olga's sixteenth birthday.

Olga pulls off her old, worn sweater, and in her chemise she struggles to fasten the gold clasp behind her neck. I jump up to help her. She walks to the mirror above the bureau. Her image stares back, face pale and gaunt, eyes ringed with dark circles.

"Remember this?" she asks dreamily. In the dim lamplight the gems glow against the pallor of her skin. "Remember my pink gown?" She turns to us and smiles, a rare thing for her these days, and I'm struck by how beautiful she still is, in spite of everything that has happened. "Remember the ball at Livadia?"

Of course I do. Our beautiful new palace at Livadia, November 1911, six years ago: I remember as though it were just last night.

At precisely a quarter to seven, the great carved doors of the state dining salon swung open and the master of ceremonies announced in a sonorous voice, "Their Imperial Majesties!"

Mama in a regal satin gown and diamond tiara and Papa in his pristine white naval uniform appeared at the top of the broad marble steps. Gathered in the salon below, the gentlemen bowed and the ladies sank into deep curtsies. Alexei, with the sailor-attendant who always accompanied him, followed our parents, drawing polite applause. Tatiana came next, tall and confident on the arm of her escort, Lieutenant Pavel Voronov, a junior officer on the imperial yacht. Marie, twelve, and I, just ten years old then, entered together, wearing pretty white lace dresses and ribbons in our long hair. I was very excited. I loved parties. I always wished there were more of them.

We joined the others at the foot of the stairs, waiting expectantly. Then Olga appeared and hesitated for a moment in the doorway. She wore her blond hair up for the first time, and she was dressed in her first ball gown, pale pink lace over darker pink silk, embroidered with tiny crystal beads. In the low neckline of her gown gleamed the pearl and diamond necklace that Mama had fastened around her neck an hour earlier. Papa had slipped a sparkling diamond ring on Olga's finger. "You're a young lady now," he'd said, and kissed her cheek. She'd smiled, delighted.

Oh, I did envy her! *Six more years*, I thought. *Then it will be my turn, and Grandmère Marie will take me to Paris.*

"The Grand Duchess Olga Nikolaevna!" cried the master of ceremonies.

The orchestra began to play, and Olga descended the steps, clutching the arm of her escort, Papa's aide-de-camp, Lieutenant Nikolai Pavlovich Sablin. She smiled a little nervously and nodded to the dozens of guests and Romanov relatives who had come to celebrate at her birthday ball. I thought she looked very beautiful.

Mama and Papa, Olga and Tatiana and their escorts, and Marie and I were seated at a round table in the center of the dining room, the guests assigned to smaller surrounding tables. The dinner went on for a long time, with many courses presented: *Sterlet au Champagne, Selle d'Agneau, Filets de Canetons, Faisans de Bohême.* All Mama's doing, for Papa was not fond of elaborate French meals. He preferred plain Russian dishes. *Shchi*, cabbage soup, was one of his favorites, or suckling pig with horseradish. None of these were on the menu.

After the sturgeon in champagne and the duck with truffles and the other dishes, my favorite part of the dinner finally arrived: a dessert especially created for Olga's birthday, miniature scoops of several flavors of ice cream presented in individual pastry baskets decorated with candied violets. But Olga hardly noticed it—she was gazing at Lieutenant Voronov. When she caught me watching, she blushed deeply and turned to her escort for the evening, Lieutenant Sablin. "My Hussars have received permission to wear the white pelisse!" she exclaimed. "Such an honor!"

Olga was the chief of the Ninth Hussar Regiment, and they did look dashing in their white jackets trimmed in black fur and worn thrown over the shoulder, but I was more interested in another long look that passed between her and Lieutenant Voronov. Marie, sitting beside me, was too busy with her ice cream to notice.

Papa rose, signaling that the meal had ended, and

announced, "Gentlemen, in honor of the sixteenth birthday of my daughter Olga Nikolaevna, you may ask the grand duchesses for the pleasure of a dance without first requesting special permission."

The change from the usual formality made everyone smile. This was not to be as stodgy as most imperial balls! While servants swiftly cleared the dining room for dancing, the guests lined up to kiss their sovereigns' hands. That took quite a while, as those things always did, but when it was finally done, the master of ceremonies announced a quadrille. Lieutenant Sablin asked Olga for the honor of the first dance, Lieutenant Voronov led Tatiana out on the floor, and two of the youngest officers from our yacht, the *Standart*, appeared and invited Marie and me to dance. Mama settled into an armchair to watch. Alexei, who had probably eaten himself into a stupor, was with her, and after a few minutes Papa joined his friends in another room to play bridge.

It was a beautiful autumn evening, and the glass doors to the terrace had been thrown open. The breeze was warm, there was a scent of flowers everywhere, and silvery moonlight glittered on the sea. Until two o'clock the next morning, the band played spirited quadrilles and energetic mazurkas and lively folk dances, and I danced every one of them. It was wonderful. I would have been happy to attend such a lovely ball at least once a week.

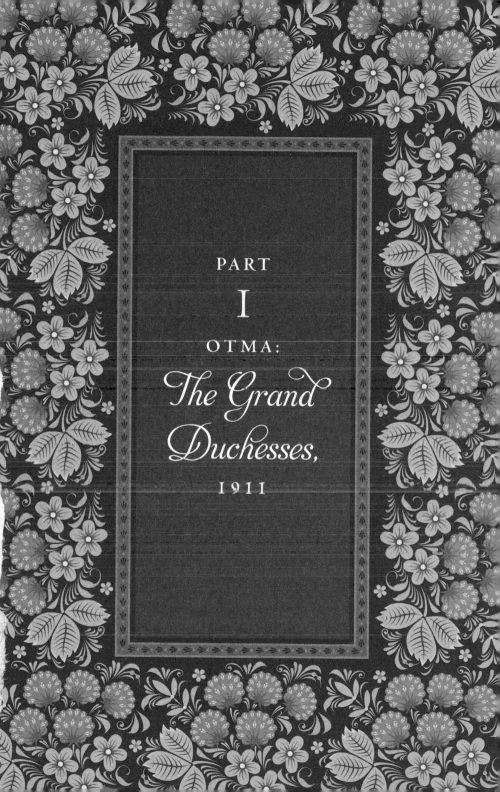

PART

I

OTMA:

The Grand Duchesses,

1911

CHAPTER 1

Olga's Secret

LIVADIA, 1911

very year, from winter to spring to summer to fall, our family—the seven of us—moved from one palace to another, traveling either on the imperial train or on the imperial yacht. It does seem odd now, looking back, that I have no idea how many Romanov palaces there were. A dozen? Several dozen? *Too* many, our enemies would claim. But our main residence, the one we always went home to, was Alexander Palace in Tsarskoe Selo, the small, quiet "Tsar's Village" a half hour's journey from Russia's capital city, St. Petersburg. But no matter where we were, we followed more or less the same routine. Papa had meetings with government officials and members of the imperial court, my sisters and my brother and I had lessons with our tutors, and Mama had her friends.

The autumn of 1911 was different, because it was our

first visit to the new palace at Livadia, our estate in Crimea on the Black Sea. The old palace where our grandfather, Tsar Alexander, died, long before we were born, had been torn down. We adored this new one, much more than any of the other imperial palaces that had belonged to generations of Romanovs. Nearly every day, we went for a hike along mountain paths or took an excursion in one of Papa's motorcars. He kept several French vehicles in the palace garage, and I loved riding in the big open Delaunay-Belleville with the wind in my face. In the afternoons Papa played tennis with officers from the *Standart*. Lieutenant Voronov was usually one of them, which must have delighted Olga.

The commandant, Admiral Chagin, often came, too. He was a particular friend of Papa, and Mama was very fond of him, but he was gray-haired and portly and didn't play tennis. He and Tatiana sat with Mama in the pavilion next to the court and watched. After Papa and Lieutenant Voronov had played one set, Marie and Olga were invited to play mixed doubles, the lieutenant and Olga on one side of the net, Marie and Papa on the other. Marie played poorly, but Papa made up for it. I wasn't included, because I was still taking lessons and my shots always went completely wild.

"Keep practicing, Nastya," Papa advised, but I was deeply irritated at having to sit and just *watch* while the others played.

Meanwhile, Mama and Admiral Chagin discussed plans for the charity bazaar Mama was organizing for the benefit of the poor people of Yalta, the port near Livadia where the *Standart* was docked. Mama's friend, Lili Dehn, helped with the planning, and Lili's husband, an officer on the *Standart*, was assigned to recruit other officers to carry out Mama's orders.

The bazaar was being held at the boys' school in Yalta. Commodore von Dehn and his fellow officers set up display tables. Mama, assisted by Lili, had her own huge table in the center of a large hall, displaying a vast assortment of things she had created—pretty cushions and fancy boxes and framed portraits of OTMA and especially of Alexei—plus items made by OTMA that were deemed nice enough to be sold. We were to act as "salesgirls," while Lili handled the money. All the important ladies of Yalta wanted to have tables close to Mama's, to make them feel even more important.

On the day of the bazaar, people came by motorcar, carriage, horse, mule, or foot from surrounding estates and villages to buy items made by the imperial family. Ordinary Russians and poor peasants, even the rugged-looking Tatars coming down from the mountains, flocked to the bazaar for a look at the tsar and tsaritsa and their children. Papa was there, smiling and chatting, and Mama smiled and chatted, too, though she felt ill. The most popular person, drawing the biggest crowds, was of course Tsarevich Alexei.

There was even a bit of scandal, when a pretty young girl named Kyra Belyaevna, daughter of a good family, asked to take part in the event with a table of her own, selling fine linen handkerchiefs bordered with delicate lace. Some of the older ladies didn't like her, saying that she dressed too daringly, was too friendly, and attracted too much attention with her bright eyes and musical laugh. When several of the ladies insisted that she not be given a table, she begged Admiral Chagin to intervene. The admiral gallantly took her request to Mama, who thought Belyaevna was being judged too harshly and sent word that she must be allowed to stay. A number of gentlemen and naval men suddenly found themselves in need of a lace-trimmed handkerchief, and crowded around her table. Even the old admiral seemed to be enchanted. I decided the ladies must be jealous.

The bazaar went on for three days and raised lots of money for Mama's cause, but Mama herself was so exhausted that she spent the rest of the week in bed. Even Lili Dehn, who was always full of energy, looked weary.

None of us wanted to leave Livadia, but early in December we said good-bye to the officers of the *Standart* and boarded the imperial train for the long, monotonous journey north into winter. The great black locomotive moved s-l-o-w-l-y—a horse could run almost as fast—across the flat, treeless steppe, a distance of a thousand miles. I was always excited at the start of a train trip but thoroughly tired of it by the end.

Our train was a rolling palace in miniature. Mama and Papa's private car contained a bedroom, a sitting room for Mama, a study for Papa, and a bathroom. My sisters and I and our brother shared bedrooms and a bathroom in another car; the bathtub was specially constructed so that water didn't slosh out when the train rounded a curve. A third car was for Mama's ladies-in-waiting and Papa's aides and our governesses. The dining car seated twenty at a long, narrow table; at one end were a kitchen and a little room where Papa and his friends gathered before dinner for *zakuski*—hors d'oeuvres, Mama called them, preferring the French term—while the train chuffed through the darkness. A car for the servants and a baggage car completed the train.

A second train that looked exactly like the first—dark blue cars with the double-eagled Romanov crest embossed in gold on the sides—traveled either ahead of us or behind us. It was actually a dummy train. A revolutionary or an anarchist planning to throw a bomb would not know on which train the tsar was traveling. I had no idea then what a revolutionary or an anarchist was, but I did understand there were men who hated my father because he was the tsar, and who might cause something terrible to happen to him, just as they had blown up Papa's poor uncle Sergei a few years earlier. What I did not understand then was why they hated Uncle Sergei enough to kill him. I simply could not fathom why all of us had to be guarded wherever we went—four girls and a little boy who had nothing to do with the government. And how could anyone possibly hate Papa, the kindest man in the world?

No one could answer any of those questions to my satisfaction.

Keeping a diary, making an entry every single day, was something all of us were expected to do. Mama kept a diary, and so did Papa. I therefore assumed that everyone did. At some time during the summer of 1911, I had become curious about what my sisters were writing in their diaries. Marie's lay on a shelf near her bed, and in less than a minute I had leafed through it and discovered there wasn't a thing in it that wasn't almost exactly like mine. Tatiana's was hidden but easy to find—under her pillow—and it was full of lists of things to do, birthdays and name days of family and servants who might require gifts, various projects she had dreamed up and intended to organize. Olga's, lying in plain sight on her desk, included notes about books she was reading—she was particularly interested in English writers, like Jane Austen and the Brontë sisters—and the latest piano piece she'd been working on. Hardly worth the trouble of reading.

Boring. Every single one of the diaries was boring. I didn't bother to look at them again for months.

But then, just after we'd returned from Livadia to Tsarskoe Selo, I needed an address book that I thought one of my older sisters had left somewhere. Olga was practicing in the music room and Tatiana was with Mama in her boudoir, and not wanting to disturb them I went alone into their bedroom to look for it. On a shelf among Olga's prayer books I noticed a book with a black leather cover stamped with a gilt cross. I thought it was a book of devotions. I have no idea what led me to open it, but what I found was a notebook disguised to *look* like a book of devotions. It was not. It was another kind of diary. The rest of us kept diaries so dull that anyone could read them without finding anything the least bit shocking. But the first few lines were enough to tell me that Olga's notebook was not for the eyes of anyone but Olga. I began to read.

Livadia, 4 November 1911

What happiness! I am sixteen, and last night at my birthday ball I danced three times with Pavel Alexeyevich. For a few moments we stood on the balcony, and he took my hand. We were

surrounded by people, we dared not kiss, but I was happy. For one
perfect night I could allow myself to be in love and to know that
Pavel returns that love. For one perfect night we danced and let
our eyes speak the words that we could not say aloud.

Pavel Alexeyevich was Lieutenant Voronov, and Olga was
in love with him!

I knew I should not read the diary. The contents were private. I worried that I would be caught and she would be very
angry. It was *wrong* to read it!

I closed the book and returned it carefully to its place
among the prayer books, promising myself that I would not
look at it again.

Within days I had broken my vow. I found Olga's secret
notebook, and from then on I could not stay away.

Livadia, 10 November

We will be here for another month, and it is pure bliss! I see Pavel
nearly every day, and we have even had a few moments alone to
talk when everyone was busy at the bazaar. P. gave me a lovely
lace handkerchief as a gift—of course I know that he bought it
from that girl everyone was making such a fuss over.

Livadia, 12 November

Tanya has noticed. We were in our bedroom dressing for dinner,
when she asked suddenly, "Do you think I don't see how you look
at him?" I pretended not to know whom she was talking about.

She calls him "your lieutenant" and says I gaze at him like a sick puppy! She also reminded me that there's no future for me with him. "You won't ever marry Pavel Alexeyevich or anyone else of his class." Her words exactly.

I asked who had said anything about marrying him, and assured her I am not contemplating marriage at the age of sixteen, any more than she is at fourteen.

She said that if my crush on Pavel is obvious to her—she insists on calling it a "crush"—then it is surely obvious to Mother as well.

I asked if Mother had said anything. Tanya said no, but then she said, "I'm warning you—if she does take notice, you can be sure it's the last you'll see of him. Lieutenant Voronov will be transferred to Vladivostok before you can snap your fingers."

I know that Tanya is right, and I have resolved to be more careful.

Livadia, 14 November

The afternoon tennis matches continue, and I follow darling P. with my eyes and ache for a few minutes alone with him. But that does not happen. I hate the thought of leaving here, for it will be spring until I see him again.

I put the notebook back where I had found it. I could hear Olga practicing on the piano, but there was a chance that

Tatiana might come in and find me. I wondered if she knew about the notebook-disguised-as-prayer-book. When did Olga even have time to write in it?

A little further investigation revealed that she slept with the lace-trimmed handkerchief under her pillow. Poor Olga! I worried about her and how her heart might be broken.

CHAPTER 2

Family Secret

The snow lay deep at Alexander Palace, and the Neva River, winding toward the Baltic, was thick with ice. Days in Tsarskoe Selo were short and bitterly cold. We settled in for the long winter, dreaming of spring, of returning to Livadia and cruising again on the *Standart*.

In the meantime we looked forward to Christmas. My sisters and I knitted scarves and embroidered handkerchiefs to give as gifts to servants and friends. The palace was decorated with huge fir trees trimmed with ornaments and lit with tiny candles, a German tradition. There was one tree in our playroom, another in Mama's sitting room, a third in the dining room.

Everyone else might be having a cozy Christmas at home, but not the Tsar of All the Russias, whose obligations never end. Papa had to attend several Christmas celebrations—at the military hospital, the nursing school, the home for disabled soldiers. The biggest celebration was for the men of our family's personal guard—those Cossacks who were always following us around! Mama wasn't feeling well, but Papa's younger sister, Olga Alexandrovna, came from St. Petersburg and took her place. Aunt Olga, who was cheerful and fun-loving, never seemed to mind filling in for Mama when she was feeling out of sorts. Alexei looked adorable in his white uniform and white fur hat. A gigantic tree had been set up in the horse ring and decorated with hundreds of little electric lights.

Next to the tree, tables were piled with Christmas gifts. Each Cossack saluted Papa, took a numbered slip and presented it to Aunt Olga, kissed her hand, and accepted the gift from the pile, a silver spoon or cup with the imperial seal. A balalaika orchestra played, followed by a chorus of Cossacks in their brilliant red coats, singing "Absolute Master of our great land, our tsar," followed by Cossack dancers leaping and whirling and throwing their daggers. This went on for three long hours! The Cossacks were splendid, but still! And then, after we'd had tea, there was yet another Christmas tree party for the officers, this one at our palace.

"I can't bear it," my sister Olga muttered.

"It's our duty," Tatiana, "the Governess," reminded her.

Daughters of the tsar couldn't argue with duty. Duty was duty, and we had no choice.

When the official obligations were over and the first star gleamed in the sky, we gathered by the light of a single candle for our own quiet Christmas Eve supper. The table was spread with the twelve traditional Russian dishes—bowls of *kutya* made with wheat grains mixed with honey and nuts, mushrooms served in several ways, almond soup, pickled herring, and roast carp stuffed with buckwheat—but it was the last of the forty days of fasting, and there was no meat or eggs or cheese, and no sweets. Papa loved the meal, and we ate it because Papa did. Mama hardly touched it.

A crowd had gathered, as they always did, in front of Alexander Palace to wish our family a joyous Christmas. We stepped out onto Mama's balcony to acknowledge their joyful shouts and cheers, as we always did. At midnight we attended Mass in the chapel, and the next day, the Great Feast of the Nativity, we exchanged gifts and presented our handmade presents to our servants and friends.

Papa believed in a strict routine—rising at a certain hour, eating at set times, working and studying and exercising during certain periods. In Tsarskoe Selo we rose at seven and joined Papa for breakfast at eight. He always had the same thing, tea and two rolls, buttered. After breakfast he disappeared into his study to receive visitors and read reports and do whatever else a tsar does, and we dragged ourselves to our schoolroom to spend the morning at the mercy of our tutors. Our tutors arrived at nine o'clock. Alexei was taught separately. Hour after tedious hour we were at our lessons.

An Englishman, Charles Sydney Gibbes—we called him Sydney Ivanovich; I'm not sure why—instructed us in English. When I was seven, our family made a summer visit to England as the guests of King Edward VII. He was an uncle of both Mama and Papa—it's a very complicated family tree; you really need a chart to keep it all straight—and we called him Uncle Bertie. He informed our parents that their daughters spoke English with "atrocious accents." Papa speaks English beautifully, almost as though he was born and raised there, and Mama does also but with a German accent. They must have agreed with Uncle Bertie, because when we arrived home in Russia, Mama hired Sydney Ivanovich to correct the problem.

Monsieur Pierre Gilliard, a Swiss with an upturned mustache and a well-trimmed beard, taught French. We called him Zhilik, our Russian version of his name. My sisters read French rather well, but I'm the only one who actually spoke it well. I may not have gotten the grammar right, but my accent was impressively good. Gilliard's explanation: "Anastasia is a born mimic. She imitates perfectly what she hears."

Dear Trina—Catherine Schneider—tried valiantly to teach us to speak German. When Mama had come from Germany as a girl engaged to marry Papa, Trina was hired to teach her Russian. Poor Mama struggled; she had a terrible time with it. "It's very hard to learn a foreign language when one is an adult," Mama told us. "And that's why you girlies—and Baby, too—must learn while you're still young." She always called Alexei "Baby" or "Sunbeam."

We spoke English with Mama, Russian with Papa, French with Grandmère Marie, a mixture with each other, and German with nobody.

Dear old baggy-eyed Pyotr Vasilyevich Petrov, our Russian tutor, also attempted to instill in us some knowledge of geography. He had mounted a large map of the world on the wall of our schoolroom. "First, Your Imperial Highnesses, let us look at the Russian Empire," he announced at the beginning of each day's lesson, taking up his pointer. It made me laugh when he called us by our formal titles, since he saw us every day and we had known him for most of our lives, but Pyotr Vasilyevich was a traditionalist, and traditionalists don't change. He swept his pointer from west to east, from central Europe to the Pacific Ocean—"Fifty-four hundred miles! More than eight thousand *versts!*"—and then from north to south. "The tsar's mighty empire covers one sixth of the land surface of the world!"

It was, I thought, truly impressive: Russia was much bigger than all the countries of Europe put together, bigger than China, bigger than the United States. Our papa was the tsar, the emperor, the autocrat—whatever you wished to call him— and ruler of more than one hundred seventy million people: the most powerful man in the world.

After that stirring introduction, Petrov droned on interminably about mountain ranges and river systems and natural resources, and the many different nationalities living within Russia's distant borders. Olga took a particular interest in geography, although I could not understand why. I yawned and sketched flowers in the margins of my copybook. Only when the lessons were in art, dancing, and music did I truly apply myself.

In early January Alexei, racing around the palace in his usual rambunctious manner, took a tumble and was hurt. For days he did not leave his bedroom. These were the times we dreaded. A gloom settled over the entire palace, surely noticeable to everyone. Papa constantly wore a worried look. For days at a time Mama hardly left Alexei's bedside, and we scarcely saw her. Meanwhile, we were expected to carry on as though nothing was wrong. My brother had an illness that was a closely guarded secret. We had been instructed by our parents never to speak of it outside the circle of our family and a few close friends. "It is our burden to bear," Mama said.

The secret was that Alexei has hemophilia. His blood doesn't clot. He could die from a minor cut or a nosebleed. When he bruises himself, he bleeds inside his body. The blood has nowhere to go and collects in his joints, and that causes him great pain. It's an inherited disease. Only males suffer from it, and only females carry it. Mama's grandmother, Queen Victoria of England, was a carrier, and many of her descendants are bleeders. Alexei is one of them.

Our parents learned of this terrible illness when Alexei was still a baby, but they never spoke of it because they didn't want the Russian people to know that the tsarevich might not live to become their next tsar. The doctors could do nothing. There is no treatment for it. Two sailors from the imperial navy, Andrei Derevenko and Klementy Nagorny, were assigned to stay with him constantly to keep him from injuring himself and to carry him when he couldn't walk.

Mama and Papa were in despair, until they met Father Grigory.

To us, he was always Father Grigory or Our Friend, but to others he was known as Grigory Efimovich Rasputin. He was a *starets*, a holy man. He prayed with Mama, and when he did, Alexei got better. The swelling went down, and the pain went away. Mama came to believe in Father Grigory completely and loved him devotedly, because of the effect he had on Alexei. He had only to bow his head and take my brother's hand, and

Alexei immediately became calmer. When Father Grigory visited my parents, he usually came to our rooms and spent time with my sisters and me, talking quietly and praying with us in front of our holy icons.

Father Grigory was a big man, taller than Papa and much broader and heavier. He dressed in the rough clothes of a *moujik*, a peasant—baggy trousers and loose blouses and muddy leather boots, as though he had just come in from working in the fields. He looked as though he never changed those filthy clothes, or bathed, or even washed his grimy hands, and he smelled worse than Alexei's pet donkey. His thick, scraggly black beard was stuck with bits of food, and his long, stringy hair hung down to his shoulders.

Bad as he looked and smelled, there was something deeply mysterious about Father Grigory. His brilliant blue eyes were so magnetic that I could not look away when he gazed at me, and I felt sure that he could see into my very soul. His voice was so compelling that when he spoke my name, I shivered, but it wasn't a shiver of fear—it was something I couldn't name. My sisters, too, felt his powerful spell. Strangely, his animal smell didn't bother us when he bent close to us and placed a gentle, fatherly kiss on our foreheads.

Mama believed that God had sent this holy man to her and to all of us. She was convinced that he possessed miraculous powers that would save Alexei from his terrible illness—not cure him, but heal him and let him live without suffering. "If God does not hear my prayers, I know that He hears Father Grigory's," she said.

But not everyone loved him. Our governess at that time,

Sophia Ivanovna, mistrusted him. "Holy man or not, Grigory Rasputin should not be going into your bedroom while you girls are in your nightgowns. He should not be sitting down beside you on your beds, and touching you in a most familiar way. It's simply not proper for him to be there with you unchaperoned."

Sophia expressed her disapproval to Papa, and Papa spoke to Father Grigory. His visits to our bedrooms stopped, but he was still a regular visitor to Alexander Palace. Then one day our dear nurse, Maria, upset and weeping, told Sophia that Father Grigory had done something very wicked to her. Sophia reported Maria's story to Mama. A few days later Maria was sent away. When I asked Sophia what had happened and where our nurse had gone, our governess just shook her head and grimaced. "It's too shocking. I shall say no more about it," she said, and changed the subject.

I didn't know what to think. Papa and Mama believed Father Grigory was a saint, and Sophia Ivanovna thought he was a devil. She said no more to us, but she must have spoken to others, because Mama heard about it, and suddenly Sophia Ivanovna, too, was dismissed.

Mama instructed us not to speak of Father Grigory to anyone outside our little family. "They don't understand," she said.

Lyosha is much better, and we are grateful for the help we've received from Fr. G. But Mother allows no criticism of him. Everyone is afraid to say a word.

Today Zhilik came to the music room while I was practicing and listened with his eyes closed until I finished. Usually so calm, he paced nervously and asked if he could speak frankly. I said he could. In the three years he has served our family, he said, he has observed that Lyosha suffers from physical problems, but the cause has never been explained to him. At times Lyosha seems quite well; then, without explanation, the lessons are suddenly suspended. A fortnight later the boy is racing through the palace again——or one of the sailors carries him about as if he were an invalid. Could I explain it? Zhilik asked.

What to tell him? We've been told never to speak of it. I decided on the truth, and described the nature of the disease and the reason for secrecy. Then I revealed another secret: Only Fr. G is able to help him.

A look of distaste crossed our tutor's face, though he tried to hide it. He said he'd met Fr. G only once but has heard much talk about him. "And how does this man Rasputin help?"

I explained the effect the starets has on Lyosha and told him that Fr. G is a holy man who prays with Mother, and then Lyosha gets better. No one can deny it, and no one is allowed to question it. Then I begged Zhilik not to let anyone know what I told him.

The truth is that I find Fr. G completely revolting, but for Mother's sake and Lyosha's, I must be careful never to let anyone know how I feel. I feel guilty for saying as much as I did, because Mother instructed us not to——especially not to Zhilik, who is Swiss and not of our religion and wouldn't understand.

I was shaking when I put away Olga's notebook. I wished that I did not know what she thought of Father Grigory. Mama would be furious if she found out.

Tsarskoe Selo was only a half hour's journey from the gaiety and excitement of St. Petersburg, but ours was a different world. Our family occupied the west wing of Alexander Palace, which was very small—only a hundred rooms—compared to the enormous Catherine Palace nearby that my parents used only for formal occasions, and there weren't many of those. The east wing had quarters for our tutors, for our physician, Dr. Botkin, and his children, Gleb and Tatiana, and for Mama's ladies-in-waiting and Papa's gentlemen. Between the two wings was a huge semicircular hall with a giant dome, filled with busts and portraits of important people.

OTMA shared two large bedrooms (Big Pair in one, Little Pair in the other), slept on camp beds with thin mattresses, endured cold morning baths, and kept diaries in which we recorded the events of our day. I thought the diaries were a waste of time, because every day was almost the same as the previous one, even when we'd moved to a different palace. Sometimes we bargained for a change: Olga finally persuaded Mama to persuade Papa that warm evening baths were more beneficial for young girls than cold baths in the morning. We thought the biggest treat in the world was having Papa's permission to use his huge marble swimming bath.

Our bedrooms, schoolroom, and music room were on the floor above our parents' rooms, connected by an elevator because Mama tired easily and could not use the stairs. Our maids and governesses and nurses occupied the rooms across the hall. Beyond the palace was a Chinese village, built by Catherine the Great, who liked Chinese things, and a small traditional Russian village called Feodorovsky Gorodok that Papa had had built. There was also a zoo with an elephant, a favorite with Alexei, who especially loved to visit when the great animal was bathing. When we weren't imprisoned with our tutors and punished with interminable lessons, we went boating in summer and skating on an artificial lake and sledding down the ice mountain that the servants built for us in winter. There was an island with a playhouse, as well as lots of parkland that would have been a fine place to wander. But there really was no such thing for us as just *wandering*—we always had to be guarded. I amused myself by trying to escape from the huge, black-bearded Cossack whose duty was to guard me. I was never successful.

When Papa went out for a walk at half past eleven, our tutors set us free and we went with him. At noon there were more visitors and more reports for Papa and more studies for us, until luncheon at one. We joined Papa and whatever visitors he had invited—Mama usually chose to eat with Alexei in her boudoir. Father Vassiliev in his long black robe was there to pronounce the blessing in a loud, cracking voice. The chef prepared three courses, but Papa stuck to his borscht and his cabbage soup.

Chef Kharitonov drew up several menus each morning. The menus were then presented to Mama by Count Benckendorff, a dignified man with snowy whiskers and a monocle, the grand marshal in charge of managing almost everything that went on in the palace. Mama decided on the meals for that day, and the grand marshal carried the orders back to the chef.

Mama also decided what we would wear. She preferred matching outfits: one day we might all dress in black skirts and white silk blouses, and on another day she'd pick white dresses with pale green sashes. Some days it varied a little: Big Pair wore blue sashes and Little Pair wore yellow. Only once did I announce that I did not want to wear the blue dress with the sailor collar, which I disliked. Mama reacted with such shock at this act of rebellion that I never did it again.

Mama seldom rose from her bed before noon, claiming that she felt too tired or ill to speak with us. Instead, she wrote us long letters in which she lectured us on our behavior. She sent a maid to deliver them.

I hated getting one of those letters. I had been sent quite a few, usually about something I had said, rather than something I had done. Marie burst into tears whenever she received one, sobbing, "I don't believe Mama loves me!" When I tried to tell her that I loved her, all of us loved her, she was the best sister in the world, and of course Mama and Papa loved her, she wailed, "No, Nastya, they love you best—Papa calls you *Shvibzik*, the imp, because you always make him laugh. Tanya is always so well organized, she's our governess, and she's so close to Mama, she knows how to keep Mama happy. And Olya—"

"It's Olya we should feel sorry for," I interrupted. "You're sweet-tempered, everyone loves you, even if you don't believe it, Papa goes on and on about what an angel you are, that you must have wings hidden somewhere. But poor Olya! Nothing she does pleases Mama—that's why they argue."

Olga was always the quiet one—unless she and Mama were arguing. Mama didn't call them "arguments" or "disagreements." Instead, she said, "Olya is having another of her sulks."

Olga was our best musician. She could play almost anything by ear and sight-read pieces easily. I practiced as little as possible, but Olga willingly spent hours in the music room next to our schoolroom, playing scales and arpeggios and going over a piece until it was perfect. That was the best time to have a look at her secret notebook. I had only to worry about being caught by Tatiana, but since Tatiana spent most of her free time with Mama, I often decided to risk it.

When I played a Liszt Hungarian Rhapsody at my lesson yesterday, my teacher said, "If you were not a grand duchess, you would certainly become known as a fine concert pianist."

I think about what she said and wonder if it might be true.

I skipped ahead a few pages and read this:

I lose myself in books. English novels like Wuthering Heights, Jane Eyre, *and* Pride and Prejudice *are my favorites. From them I've gained a fair idea of what life is like among ordinary English people. I probably know Heathcliff and Rochester and Mr. Darcy better than I know Pavel Voronov. How would Elizabeth Bennet behave if she were the daughter of the tsar of Russia instead of an English country gentleman? My books substitute for a life beyond the narrow, suffocating restrictions endured by a grand duchess.*

Suffocating restrictions? Did Olga feel suffocated?

I put the notebook back on the shelf, reached for Miss Austen's novel, and turned to the first page:

It is a truth universally acknowledged, that a single man in possession of a good fortune must be in want of a wife. However little known the feelings or views of such a man may be on his first entering a neighbourhood, this truth—

"She's a fine writer, isn't she?"

I hadn't heard Olga come in. "Oh!" I exclaimed, and nearly dropped the book. "I didn't think you'd mind if I looked at it." I must have had guilt written all over my face.

"Of course not, Nastya," she said. "I'm not sure you'd find life in an English country village of much interest. Maybe when you're older."

That remark truly irritated me: *Maybe when you're older.* I shut the book and returned it to her stack of English novels.

The notebook was certainly more interesting, but it was more upsetting, too.

CHAPTER 3

Our Social Life

ST. PETERSBURG, WINTER 1912

 was gazing out the window at the swirling snow, thinking about "the narrow, suffocating restrictions" of life as a grand duchess, when Shura, my favorite of all our governesses, bustled in carrying an armful of clothes.

"Time to dress for tea," she reminded me. "Tanya says your mother wants you all to wear the gray flannel jumpers today."

She laid out the clothes on my bed, everything needed for the prescribed outfit—jumper, blouse, belt, stockings, underclothes, shoes. Everything Shura did, she did quickly, but she never made me feel rushed.

I took off the dress I'd been wearing and washed my face and hands. Marie waited outside the bathroom door, urging me to hurry. Shura checked my fingernails for cleanliness and helped me put on clean stockings and the rose-colored silk blouse and the jumper, a proper outfit for tea, and inspected my shoes, wiping them with a cloth to be sure they were shined perfectly.

"Shall I brush your hair, or shall you?" Shura asked, taking the barrettes from my long hair.

"You do it, please, Shura."

This was our usual routine. "Will you be checking my nails and shining my shoes and brushing my hair when I'm married?" I once asked her.

"Of course I will, Nastya," she answered.

"And when I'm an old lady, will you do it then, too?" I couldn't imagine life without Shura.

"Even then," Shura promised.

We had tea in Mama's mauve boudoir. Everything in the boudoir was done a particular shade of purple that was Mama's favorite color. The chairs were covered in flowered chintz, the curtains were flowered chintz, family pictures and religious icons hung on the walls, and objects she treasured crowded the tables. Vases of flowers from her greenhouses filled the air with their sweet scent, even in the middle of winter. No other room in the palace was as comfortable as Mama's boudoir.

Alexei was sitting with Mama and playing with a little windup Cossack, marching him back and forth. Water simmered in the gold samovar, and the tea concentrate sat in a small teapot balanced on top. Glasses were lined up in their silver holders. Plates were arranged on the linen cloth, along with a platter of bread, already buttered. The menu was always the same: bread, butter, and tea. When Papa walked in, greeting everyone, a servant poured tea concentrate into the glasses, added hot water, and handed them around. After two cups of tea and one slice of bread and a little conversation about our day, Papa returned to his study. Mama could not bear to have us idle and expected us to find something useful to do until dinner. I had no talent for embroidery as the others did, but I could knit woolen stockings at top speed.

Dinner was served at eight. Sometimes all seven of us ate together, but often Mama and Alexei dined alone in the boudoir, and my sisters and I ate with Papa in our family dining room. There were no guests at dinner.

Afterward, we sat around a large table and pasted photographs into our albums or did needlework while Alexei played with his toys and Papa read aloud, something pleasantly soothing, until bedtime. Mama and Papa gave us each a blessing and kissed us, and our governesses escorted us upstairs to our bedrooms and made sure our teeth were brushed and our rooms were tidy, and they listened to our prayers before we lay down on our camp beds.

It was a quiet life, the way Mama and Papa wanted it. Mama did not enjoy social evenings with formal dinners and receptions and balls that went on until dawn. We saw few people other than my parents' closest friends—Anya Vyrubova, Lili Dehn, Dr. Botkin, Baroness Buxhoeveden and Countess Hendrikova, who were two of Mama's ladies-in-waiting, Papa's friend Prince Dolgorukov, a few others—and we rarely had an opportunity to be with young people. We didn't even see much of Gleb Botkin and his sister. They were close to our age and lived in the palace, and I would have liked to see more of them.

Mama was fond of Gleb, a serious twelve-year-old with unusual green eyes that Mama said allowed you to see into the

depths of his soul. Gleb wrote poems and drew amusing pictures to illustrate his stories about talking animals, and he had
decided that he would one day become a priest.

"Does that mean you'll be a *starets* and wear dirty clothes
and smell like a goat?" I once asked him. I thought Gleb would
know that I was joking.

"No, Anastasia Nikolaevna," he said, his beautiful green
eyes glittering with tears, his lip trembling. "I shall worship
God and pray for you and your family every day of my life."

I felt so terrible that I apologized over and over and begged
Gleb to forgive me. He said he had. I think he did, eventually.

Tatiana Botkina and my sister Tatiana were friends, but not
close. "Our lives are too different," our Tatiana explained with
a shrug. "I suppose it's hard to be a friend of a grand duchess."

Our dear aunt Olga Alexandrovna, Papa's youngest sister, rescued us. Every Saturday during the winter, Aunt Olga, who was
also my godmother, came out from St. Petersburg to Tsarskoe
Selo. We watched from our window for the sleigh that would
bring her from the train, arriving at the palace entrance with
bells jingling, and for Aunt Olga to emerge from under the fur
robe and hurry into the palace. We ran down to greet her, to
kiss her cold cheeks and help her off with her sable coat and
handsome fur-lined boots.

Our aunt spent the day with us, doing whatever we wanted
to do: playing piano duets with us in the music room or teaching us a new dance or applauding a song Alexei had learned
on his balalaika. Sometimes we painted still lifes—bowls of
fruit or Mama's flowers—or we made sketches of one of the

Ethiopian guards who stood stiffly outside Papa's study and Mama's boudoir, ready to open a door or announce a visitor. Our favorite wasn't an Ethiopian but an American Negro named Jim Hercules, who brought us guava jelly from his visits home to a place called Alabama. Jim willingly posed for us in his crimson trousers, jacket embroidered in gold, shoes with turned-up toes, and a white turban.

After lunch we went skating on our lake. Papa often joined us. Aunt Olga skimmed over the ice as graceful as a bird. She even went tobogganing on our ice mountain in the park, tumbling off into the snow and seeming not to mind at all. We returned to the palace with rosy cheeks. Ice crystals sparkled in Papa's beard.

Teatime didn't vary—that bread-and-butter-only custom must have dated back to Tsar Peter the Great—but the evening was livelier when Aunt Olga was there. We all had cameras and loved to take pictures, and she never failed to comment on the most recent photographs we had pasted in our albums. When I first got my Kodak Brownie, a man from the camera shop in St. Petersburg came to Tsarskoe Selo and showed me how to use it. I snapped roll after roll of film, annoying my sisters by catching them in undignified poses that I hoped might turn out to be slightly embarrassing. The palace photography staff developed our film and gave us prints, and I learned to tint them with watercolors.

I would have hated for Saturday to end, except that I knew Sunday would be even better. After Mass in our chapel, Aunt Olga shepherded four excited girls to the imperial train. At the St. Petersburg station, a beautiful sleigh drawn by sleek black horses waited to carry us to Anichkov Palace for luncheon with our grandmother, Dowager Empress Marie. The palace covered an entire block on the Nevsky Prospect by a branch of the Neva River, but we seldom ventured beyond our grandmother's suite.

Our father's mother was a lively woman with bright, dark eyes and a warm smile. She didn't seem *old*—not like some of the ladies of the court, with their wrinkled faces and too much rouge. We'd been taught to call her "Grandmère Marie," and she greeted us in French. She asked first after *"mon très cher Alexei,"* and when we had to report, as we often did, that he was not well, she murmured, *"Quel dommage!* What a pity!"

Then she inquired politely, "And your mother? Not feeling quite well, as usual?"

It was up to Tatiana to explain that Mama was indeed rather tired and begged to be remembered to Motherdear—that was what our grandmother had insisted Mama call her when she and Papa were first married. I guessed that Grandmère Marie was not fond of Mama, and that Mama didn't have much affection for her mother-in-law. Anyone could feel the coolness between them.

The table was set for our luncheon in the small formal dining room with rose-colored silk damask on the walls and carvings of little cherubs everywhere. The porcelain dishes were so delicate that, if I held a plate up to the light, I could see the shadow of my hand through it. (I did this once and was told it was bad manners and I must not do it again.) A collection of knives, forks, and spoons was lined up on either side of the plate. We never had this much silverware laid out at luncheons at Tsarskoe Selo, but Grandmère Marie believed we should know what each piece was for and how to use it expertly.

A uniformed footman stood stiffly behind each chair and served each dish as if we were taking part in a solemn ceremony. First came the consommé, followed by little patés, followed by cold trout that swam in a quivering jelly. I pondered the jellied fish unhappily and tried to think of some way to make it disappear from my plate without actually having to *eat* it. Grandmère Marie kept a sharp eye on us, and when I failed to use the fish knife correctly, she frowned. I received a firm lecture, and then I had to show that I understood and, worst of all, had to eat the fish. I made a horrid face that only Marie was meant to see, but my grandmother noticed that, too.

"No need to behave badly, my dear Anastasia Nikolaevna," she said, frowning, but I knew that I was her favorite and that she would not be truly angry with me, even if I failed to swallow the dreadful fish and hid it in my napkin instead.

During the meal, which proceeded slowly, we spoke French as well as we could, but not well enough to satisfy Grandmère Marie. "My kind regards to Monsieur Gilliard," she said, "but tell him, *s'il vous plaît*, that your command of the past perfect must be improved."

Once we'd survived our grandmother's critical lessons and played something for her on the piano—she preferred Chopin, so I always had a nocturne ready—or recited a poem we'd memorized for the occasion, we kissed her hand and she embraced us warmly and sent us off with a cheery order: "*Amusez-vous bien, mes chères jeunes filles!*"

Aunt Olga called for the sleigh, and we drove to the palace

on Sergievskaya Street that Papa had given her. Her husband, Duke Peter Alexandrovich of Oldenburg, lived at one end of the two-hundred-room mansion, and Olga lived at the other end. "Petya sends his warmest greetings," she told us, but we rarely saw him.

Our aunt had an artist's studio, and it was the first place I wanted to see whenever we came for a visit. Canvases were stacked along the wall, some blank, others with paintings of religious icons or landscapes exploding with color. The half-finished painting of a church surrounded by autumn trees rested on an easel. "I'm not satisfied with the sky," she admitted. "Something is wrong with the clouds."

I thought the sky was splendid, the clouds exactly right, and I hoped that some day I would learn to paint as beautifully as my aunt Olga.

She ushered us out of the studio and into her sitting room and instructed us to lie down on a divan or a chaise longue and close our eyes. "One hour only!" she said. "This gives your lunches time to digest, and your complexions time to regain their glow and your eyes their sparkle."

Tatiana and Marie promptly drifted off, but Olga's eyelids quivered and I knew she was faking. I didn't bother to pretend. Sundays were too exciting for sleep.

When the hour was up—it seemed longer—our aunt rang a little bell, and we rose and changed into the dresses Mama had sent from Tsarskoe Selo with our maids. Aunt Olga had arranged an afternoon party and had invited lots of young people, the sons and daughters of members of the court. Down we went to an elegant salon just as the guests began to arrive.

Some of them were our cousins. Papa's other sister, Xenia, and her husband, Sandro, had seven children: one daughter, Irina, who was a close friend of my sister Olga, and six sons. I was not fond of those boys, who were noisy and rough and ill-mannered. Andrei, the eldest, was seventeen and unbearably arrogant. Feodor, fifteen, apparently never brushed his teeth. Nikita, who was about to turn fourteen, once accused me of biting him, but that was a lie and typical of him. The younger three could usually be ignored. Aunt Olga spoke sharply to the boys, and they settled down.

We began by playing games—my favorite was charades, because I loved to act and I was good at pantomime. Later we wound up Aunt Olga's gramophone to hear some music. The party ended with tea, the kind of tea I loved—platters of *blini*, tiny pancakes filled with smoked salmon and cheese; pickled herring on rye toasts; *pirozhki*, little meat-stuffed pastries; and all kinds of delicious cakes and sweetmeats. So much more delightful than our bread-and-butter teas!

That winter, another cousin attended one of Aunt Olga's Sunday afternoon parties: Dmitri Pavlovich, the son of Papa's uncle Pavel Alexandrovich. Dmitri's mother had died when he was born, and Papa had exiled Dmitri's father to Paris for then marrying an unsuitable woman. Dmitri and his older sister, Maria Pavlovna, grew up in the home of Uncle Sergei (another of Papa's uncles) and Aunt Ella, Mama's older sister. After Sergei was killed by a revolutionary's bomb, Maria Pavlovna married a Swedish prince and moved to Stockholm, and Dmitri came to stay in the east wing of Alexander Palace. Papa was very fond of him—they passed evenings playing billiards in Papa's study and often went out riding together. Dmitri was an excellent equestrian, and he planned to represent Russia at the 1912 Summer Olympics in Sweden, competing in dressage and jumping.

Dmitri was twenty-one, older than most of the other guests. He flirted with the older girls (Olga and Tatiana, and our cousin Irina) and teased the younger ones (Marie and me). He put a recording on the gramophone and invited my sister Olga to dance with him. "Come, Olya, let me teach you the Boston. It's like the waltz, and I hear it's all the rage in America. You'll be the first girl to do it in St. Petersburg."

Olga blushed and shook her head. "No, no, it wouldn't be proper."

Dmitri turned to me and grabbed my hand. "Then Nastya and I will demonstrate the Boston," he announced, and everyone stopped to stare at us. I had never waltzed. Mama said I wasn't old enough, and besides, I tended to be clumsy. But Dmitri put his hand on my waist and grinned at me. The gramophone produced a waltz tune. "Just follow me," he said. "I promise not to drop you when we dip. Here we go!"

We went spinning away. It was slower than a waltz, and I did not stumble but felt rather graceful. It was almost like floating, until he tipped me over backward. That was the "dip." I let out a startled squeal.

Abruptly the music stopped. Aunt Olga was glaring at us. "That will be enough, Dmitri," she said sternly.

"I thought Nastya would find it amusing," Dmitri said, with a charming smile and a shrug. He was right. I was grinning like a fool when he bent over my hand and kissed it.

"Thank you, Your Imperial Highness," he said, without even the hint of a smile.

That was, without question, the best party I had ever been to at Aunt Olga's or anywhere else. I also believed I might be a little bit in love with Dmitri. He was the first boy—the first *young man*—who had ever paid any attention to me, and that was exciting. And I was the first girl in St. Petersburg to dance the Boston!

Afterward Tatiana said to me, "I think we'd better not tell Mama anything about this. She might be upset that Aunt Olga allowed Dmitri to dance with you like that."

"Like what?" I asked with feigned innocence.

"In such an inappropriate way, Nastya! You're far too young for such dancing—especially as a grand duchess. We must always remember that we're the tsar's daughters, and our behavior must be above reproach."

"She was just having fun, Tanya," Olga said. "But she won't do it again—will you, Nastya?"

I promised I wouldn't, but secretly I was hoping I'd have the chance. I was sure I'd take it.

We all wrote about the tea dance at Aunt Olga's in our diaries. I reported that Dmitri was going to the Summer Olympics, but in case someone should read it, I did not mention that we had danced the Boston. Tatiana wrote, "Such a lovely time playing Aunt Olga's gramophone." Marie wrote, "I had a game of dominoes with our cousin Vasili, and he cried when he lost. The food was delicious."

And Olga wrote, "Irina was paid a great deal of attention by Dmitri Pavlovich." But in the secret notebook she wrote, *I thought only of P. and wished he could have been with me at Aunt Olga's.*

Dmitri had paid attention to Irina? And all the time I'd believed he was paying attention to *me*.

On a cold and bitter Sunday in February, our aunt announced that there would be no party that afternoon, but before we could be disappointed, she added, "My darlings, today we are going to the Passage!"

The Passage was a long arcade under a glass roof on Nevsky Prospect, the main boulevard in St. Petersburg. On even the grimmest winter day the Passage was brightly lighted. Crowds of people in fine clothes and others more humbly dressed strolled from one elegant shop to the next, gazing in the windows at displays of jewelry and furs, leather purses and ladies' hats the size of serving trays. As always, a half dozen stony-faced Cossacks in bright blue coats, red shirts, and tall black fur hats hovered close by us.

"I hate being followed around," I grumbled. "Now everybody recognizes us. Wouldn't it be nice just to wander where we please without anyone knowing who we are?"

"Being followed around is part of what it means to be a daughter of the tsar," Tatiana said. "You should be used to it by now."

"I'll never get used to it," I said glumly. "And I don't see why we need protection. Why would anyone bother to shoot us?" I thought of poor Uncle Sergei.

"Not shoot us, but kidnap us and hold us for ransom," Tatiana said, "or to force Papa to do something—release prisoners or some such."

Now, that was an interesting idea. How much ransom would they demand for me? How many prisoners' lives was I worth?

Another part of being a grand duchess, I learned that day, was that we knew very little about handling money. We each received a monthly allowance of twenty rubles' pocket money, from which we were expected to pay for little gifts for our friends and for our own small wishes. Other than notepaper and perfume or an occasional scented sachet for a governess, we hardly ever bought a thing, and never in a shop. We just asked Shura or one of the governesses to order it for us.

Marie begged to stop at a flower shop. The owner flitted from one end of her shop to the other, chattering all the while. "Smell this lovely rose, just coming into bloom! And this orchid—have you ever seen one more beautiful?"

I would have bought flowers to take home for Mama, but it would have taken all four of our entire monthly allowances to afford even a small bouquet! I'm sure the flower lady was disappointed when we left without buying anything, but she would certainly tell her friends and the other shopkeepers that she had received a visit from the grand duchesses.

"I'd forgotten," Aunt Olga said as we strolled through the Passage. "You have no idea of money, do you?" She opened her purse and gave each of us a handful of gold coins with Papa's profile on one side and the Romanov double-headed eagle on the other. "Each gold coin is worth ten rubles," she explained, and added a warning: "When the shopkeeper rec-ognizes you, he may try to make a gift to you of some item you've admired, but you must not accept it. Insist upon pay-ing. When you learn the price, hand him a little more than he asked. You'll receive change—silver coins and perhaps a few copper kopeks—but don't count the change in front of him. That makes him feel that you believe he may have cheated you. Take the parcel, thank him, smile, and leave. It's as simple as that."

"And that's how it's done?" Marie asked, her big blue eyes—"Marie's saucers," we called them—even wider. "Always?"

"Always," Aunt Olga assured her. "If you're a poor peasant buying eggs for your family's supper, or you're the tsar ordering a jeweled egg as an Easter gift for the tsaritsa, you find out the price, and you pay."

We visited a glove maker's shop and a perfumery, a shop that sold elegant soaps, another with hand-painted silk scarves, still another with silk stockings as delicate as spider webs, and a confectionery. I insisted on stopping at a tobacconist's to buy Turkish cigarettes for Papa, his favorite. We bought and bought, for ourselves and for our favorite servants, and for Mama and Papa and our tutors, enthralled with the idea of shopping. When we ran out of money, as we soon did, our aunt laughed and gave us more. But she made us keep an account of every ruble, every kopek we spent.

We passed a cinema, a wax museum, and a concert hall where poets were giving readings of their work, but those would have to wait for another visit. When our arms were too full of parcels to carry any more, we stopped at a coffeehouse. We never had coffee at home—only tea. "Oh, dearest Aunt Olga," Marie begged. "Please may we come here again?" She sported a small mustache of whipped cream from the coffee she thought she wouldn't like.

Aunt Olga laughed and promised that we would indeed return to the Passage another time. "But now I'm sending you back to Tsarskoe Selo. You're like gamblers who don't know when to quit."

It was our last visit to St. Petersburg that winter. The Great Fast was about to begin—seven weeks of doing without cheese, milk, eggs, meat, fish, and everything good. March in Tsarskoe Selo was still snowy and cold, and the sky was dark and cheerless. There would be no more performances at the opera house or ballets in St. Petersburg, no balls or parties. No festive Sunday luncheons at Grandmère Marie's Anichkov Palace, no Sunday afternoon gatherings in Aunt Olga's salon, no marvelous shopping trips.

The week before the start of the Great Fast was called Butter Week, seven days of indulging in all the things we'd be denied, but especially cheese-filled *blini* swimming in butter. Mama barely tasted them. Olga and Tatiana enjoyed them, but Marie and I stuffed ourselves, butter dripping down our chins. Tatiana said, "It's not a contest, Nastya. You don't have to prove how many *blini* you can eat at one sitting."

And then it was over, and there was no sour cream on the borscht, no sausage in the cabbage soup, no butter on our tea-time bread.

But we didn't mind. In a few days we would board the imperial train and set off on the journey toward the sunshine and warmth of Livadia, where spring had surely arrived. No one seemed more excited about going than my sister Olga.

CHAPTER 4

Lieutenant Voronov

LIVADIA, SPRING 1912

The imperial trains—the real one and the dummy—
rumbled slowly southward, leaving winter behind.
I played checkers with Alexei. Marie worked on
an embroidery project, Tatiana was organizing
something—I'm not sure what—and Olga stared dreamily out
the window, a book open and neglected on her lap. Our tutors
emerged from their car every morning and attempted to give us
our lessons, but it was futile. Occasionally the train stopped, we got
out and walked around a little, and then we were on our way again.

My first mission when we arrived in Livadia was to figure out
where Olga was keeping her secret notebook. This was important, because soon Lieutenant Voronov would come to play tennis and stay for tea, and he might even go on excursions with us,
and I wanted—needed—to know what Olga was thinking.

But the notebook was not among her devotional books,

because, with the exception of those having to do with the Great Fast and Holy Week, she hadn't brought them to Livadia. As I searched without any luck, I noticed among her music books one I'd never seen, covered in green moiré silk with a picture of Mozart ornamented with gilt. The notebook was wearing a new disguise!

I skimmed through recent entries and found this, written a week earlier:

Anya Vyrubova will of course go with us to Livadia, along with her collection of ludicrous hats. I marvel that Mother can put up with it. She wears one of these ghastly monstrosities for every occasion, even when she and Mother are singing duets together, which Anya loves to do. Papa always gets up and leaves the room. Who can blame him! Anya's soprano vibrato rattles around like a can of dried peas. But I will be glad to have her there, because then I won't have to keep Mother company while everyone else is out enjoying themselves. I know this sounds as though I'm an unfeeling daughter, but whenever it's my turn to sit with her, we end up in an argument. Nothing I do pleases her. Anya, on the other hand, never fails to please her.

This was not at all like what Olga had written just the day before in her "regular" diary, the one she left lying around for anyone to read:

Anya and Mother entertained us this evening, singing duets.

That was all. Period.

• • •

Anya Vyrubova had introduced Father Grigory to Mama and Papa, and that made her a very important person in our household. I once asked Aunt Olga if Anya had always been with our family, and my aunt replied, "Not always, but for a very long time. She managed to have herself appointed one of the empress's maids of honor and became her closest friend, although she's much younger than your mama."

Here's what else Aunt Olga told me: Believing every woman should be happily married, Mama had decided early in their friendship to find Anya a husband. But Anya was very buxom—that is to say, she was *fat*—and red-faced and frumpy, and Mama had a hard time finding a suitable man for her. Finally, when Anya was twenty-three, Mama was successful.

Alexander Vyrubov, a naval officer, proposed, Anya accepted, and Mama began to plan the wedding. Around this time, Anya first met Father Grigory and asked him what her marriage would be like. According to my aunt, he looked deep into her soul with those piercing eyes and told her, "It will be far from happy." Anya couldn't bear to disappoint Mama, and she decided this was her destiny. Anya and Vyrubov were married, and as a wedding gift Mama gave them a little yellow cottage close to Alexander Palace, so that she and Anya could continue visiting every day.

Father Grigory was right. Anya was unhappy from the start, and a year later the marriage was dissolved. Anya settled permanently into the yellow cottage, and Mama went there often in the afternoons, taking one or sometimes all of us with her. Soon Anya was going everywhere with us. Wherever we went, there was Anya, keeping Mama company, singing duets.

Life was much more exciting at Livadia than it ever was at Tsarskoe Selo. People on the estates near ours gave parties and went out sailing and organized elaborate picnics, and they often invited OTMA. Mama allowed us to go, with Anya or Aunt Olga or one of our tutors as chaperone. Also, we had lots of guests at Livadia. Army regiments were stationed nearby, and the officers sometimes were invited to lunch with us.

My favorite guest was the emir of Bukhara, a small, mountainous region in Central Asia that was a Russian protectorate. He arrived with his entourage of ministers and his personal doctor, driven from his palace to ours in a line of black carriages drawn by white horses. And this was just for luncheon! The emir was very tall and very fat, with a hearty laugh, and he dressed in brilliantly colored robes embroidered with gold and a white turban glittering with diamonds and rubies. He presented us all with extravagant gifts. Aunt Olga received an enormous gold necklace with tassels of rubies that quite astonished her.

The only man in the entourage who did not have a beard dyed bright red and was not wearing embroidered robes was the emir's translator. The emir had been educated in St. Petersburg and spoke Russian as well as anyone, but a Bukharan rule forbade him to speak to another sovereign in any but the Bukharan language, a Persian dialect. He would say something in Persian, his translator would repeat it to Papa in Russian, Papa would reply in Russian, and the translator would repeat the reply to the emir in Persian. Back and forth it went. The emir liked to tell jokes, and it took a long time to get to the laughter.

Alexei didn't want to miss the luncheon with the fascinating emir who handed out such wonderful presents. But when the conversation in two languages went on too long, Alexei got bored, and when Alexei was bored, he was a spoiled brat. Alexei could be charming, but he could also behave badly, and he was allowed to get away with it because he was the youngest, he was a boy, he would be the next Tsar of All the Russias, after Papa, and—this was most important—he suffered from a terrible, incurable illness that caused him great pain and placed a huge burden on Mama, and on Papa as well.

The only one he obeyed without question was Papa, and often Papa was too engrossed in a conversation to notice his misbehavior.

Alexei was sitting by Olga, but slouching in his chair, toying with the food on his plate, eating with his fingers, and finally—this was the last straw—picking up his plate and licking it. Papa turned away deliberately, saying nothing, concentrating on the emir's translator. Olga murmured, "Lyosha, please behave like a gentleman."

"I'm not a gentleman, I'm the tsarevich, and I can do whatever I please!" he shouted.

Mama, sitting across the table, scowled—not at Alexei, but at *Olga*. "Olga, why are you not paying attention to your brother? It's your duty as his eldest sister to speak to him, to make sure that he doesn't embarrass himself, or his father or me."

My sister stared at Mama. "*My* duty, Mother?" she said, too loudly. "And what about the embarrassment he causes the rest of us, his sisters?"

Now it was Mama's turn to stare, open-mouthed, as Olga jumped up from her chair. "I beg to be excused," she muttered, and hurried out of the pavilion.

I felt terrible for Olga, I was sure she felt guilty, and I could guess what would happen next. Mama would write another of those dreaded letters.

Later I found the expected letter tucked in Olga's notebook:

You must be an example of what a good, obedient girlie ought to be. You are the eldest, and you must always do your best to show the others how to behave. I count on you to think of every word you say and everything you do. I expect you to be responsible for Baby's behavior. That is your duty. Above all, learn to love God with all the force of your soul. Remember He sees and hears everything.

I refolded the letter and put it back where I'd found it. Poor Olga! I was glad that nobody expected me to be perfect, or anything other than what I was. I was the *shvibzik!*

This was the first Easter we would celebrate at Livadia. On Saturday my sisters and I had watched women from Yalta at work decorating eggs. They first poked a small hole in each end of the egg and blew the contents into a bowl, and then, their pots of paint and fine brushes lined up in front of them, they painstakingly painted a traditional pattern on the fragile shell. One old woman dyed eggs with onion skins and glued bits of straw to the shell in delicate patterns. Another offered to teach us how to paint eggs with a simple design, but even very simple designs were hard to do well. We made them for Papa and Mama, and I honestly believed mine were the best, because I was the most artistic one in the family.

As midnight approached on Saturday, our entire household filled the chapel, holding lighted candles. It was so quiet I could hear my heart beating. At twelve o'clock, the doors swung open and we followed the priest out into the clear night air, a solemn procession in search of the Christ. We circled the palace and returned to the chapel, and when we reached the doors again, the priest turned to us and shouted, "Christ is risen!" We shouted back joyfully, "He is risen indeed!" Bells rang out, and we entered the chapel amid clouds of incense ascending toward heaven and the sound of the men's choir singing the ancient Easter liturgy.

This scene was being reenacted all across Russia, in every great cathedral and humble country church, exactly the same way as every year before. Mama always wept at this moment, overcome with emotion. Papa, too, had tears in his eyes.

After the long service finally ended—it was the custom to stand through it all—Mama and Papa led us across the courtyard to the palace. Tables were laden with all the delicious dishes we'd been denied for the past seven weeks. At the center was an enormous *paskha*, made of farmer's cheese, raisins, and almonds and molded into a kind of topless pyramid decorated with the letters *XB*, which stand for "Christ is risen." Bowls of red-dyed eggs and tall cylinders of *kulich*, a sweet bread, surrounded the *paskha*. Everyone in the household came to receive the traditional three kisses from their tsar and tsaritsa and to share in the feast.

Every year Papa ordered Fabergé, the court jeweler, to create special "eggs" for Mama and Grandmère Marie. The tradition had begun with my grandfather, who'd ordered a jeweled egg for my grandmother every year until he died. Papa continued the tradition, making a little ceremony of presenting Mama with hers. Each exquisite egg opened to reveal a surprise inside. Papa never knew what the newest eggs would look like, or what was hidden inside. He left it up to Monsieur Fabergé.

One year, before I was born, the jeweler created the Great Siberian Railway Easter Egg. The route of the railway across Russia from Moscow to Vladivostok was outlined in silver on the surface of the enameled egg. Inside was a scale model of the train, only a foot long. The locomotive, made of gold and platinum with a ruby for a headlight, pulled five cars, accurate to the tiniest detail. We loved all the fabulous Easter eggs, but that was a favorite.

The egg Papa gave Mama this year was enameled in blue, overlaid with the Romanov crest, the double-headed eagle, in gold. When you pressed a little button, the egg opened to reveal a miniature portrait of Alexei in a frame studded with diamonds and a tiny crown, orb, and scepter. Monsieur Fabergé called it the "Tsarevich Egg." It wasn't as exciting as the Great Siberian Railway, but it was beautiful and Mama loved it.

On the Monday after Easter, children from the village of Yalta and surrounding farms came to Livadia, and my sisters and I handed out miniature *kulichi* made by our bakers. The little boys bowed and the little girls curtsied, and they kissed our hands. Marie, who always adored children, was in heaven.

• • •

One fine sunny day, Olga and Tatiana made plans for a motor-car excursion through the mountains to a waterfall, with a stop by the road for a picnic. Chef Kharitonov and his assistants packed wicker baskets of food and drink along with linens, silver, and crystal goblets. Several officers of the *Standart*, including Commodore von Dehn and Lieutenant Voronov, were invited. Lili, Aunt Olga, and Monsieur Gilliard were eager to go. Mama declined, but Papa was agreeable, as always. A caravan of motorcars would drive to an designated stop. Servants would prepare the picnic while we climbed to the falls.

Olga was almost giddy with excitement when we set out mid-morning in a light fog. By the time we reached the stopping point, the fog had lifted. Papa and Aunt Olga found a suitable clearing in a grove of trees not far from the motorcars for the picnic. We started up the dirt path through the pines, Papa leading the way. He always walked much faster than the rest of us. The sound of the falls became louder as we climbed. Olga, usually as agile as a cat, seemed to need help getting over rocky parts of the path and lagged behind. Fortunately, Lieutenant Voronov was there to offer his hand. Marie and I gathered pink and white wildflowers just coming into bloom, and I took advantage of these pauses to glance back at the laggards. Olga frowned when she saw me looking.

By the time we caught up to Papa and whoever had managed to keep up with him, we were out of breath and ready for a rest, but they had finished smoking their cigarettes and were ready to start off again. Gilliard had his camera ready when we reached the roaring falls, the spray capturing rainbows in the sunlight, and he snapped pictures of us balanced on the rocks with the falls in the background. Olga required even more assistance from the lieutenant when we started down again.

The servants had prepared a fire, threaded cubes of lamb on green sticks, and roasted the *shashliki* over the hot coals. Count Smolsky, Lili Dehn's father, who had an estate near Yalta, was waiting with a hamper full of wine from his vineyard. Out of the wicker baskets came vegetable salads, dumplings stuffed with mushrooms, and black bread to spread with fresh cheese. I was ravenous, as usual; Marie, too. Olga didn't sit with Voronov—that would have been too obvious—but she could hardly take her eyes off him, and she barely noticed what she was eating.

The men's conversation turned to politics, as it often did. I watched Olga watching Pavel Voronov, who was listening to the talk when he wasn't gazing back at Olga. Commodore von Dehn asked if anyone had had any news of the strikes that were spreading across Russia, workers walking off their jobs.

"And who knows just whom some crazed anarchist will target next!" Count Smolsky grumbled. "I do hope, Nikolai Alexandrovich, that you are doing everything possible to protect yourself and your family."

"I have an excellent security guard," Papa said mildly. "The best in the world."

I thought of the stone-faced Cossacks who even now were lurking nearby.

"Nevertheless, one must take every precaution. These are dangerous times."

Aunt Olga, who had been listening silently, joined the conversation. "It isn't just the workers and anarchists we must be afraid of," she told them. "I'm acquainted with a cavalry officer who says he's observed rising unrest among the peasants as well."

"I don't fear the peasants," Count Smolsky said. "I treat mine well. They're devoted to me."

"You'll see that everything will be fine," Papa said. "We're planning to celebrate three hundred years of Romanov rule next year. I expect a demonstration of loyalty to the crown as it's never been seen before."

Aunt Olga sighed. "I hope you're right, Nicky."

Late in the afternoon, as we boarded the motorcars for the drive back to Livadia, Papa called out, "Next time, we'll ride horses to the falls!" Everyone but me seemed to think that was a fine idea. I was not an especially talented equestrienne, and I often believed that horses had taken a dislike to me.

I was sure Olga would try to arrange it so that she rode in the same motorcar as Pavel. When it didn't work out—that was really too much to hope for—I knew she was disappointed, but she was happy that he would stop at Livadia for tea.

Admiral Chagin of the *Standart* was waiting with Mama when the motorcars arrived. He bowed and kissed Papa's hand.

"Your Imperial Majesty, I regret to bring very sad news," the admiral said. "The British luxury liner *Titanic*, four days out of Southampton on her maiden voyage to New York, struck an iceberg in the North Sea just before midnight Sunday. She sank in less than three hours."

"But she was believed to be unsinkable!" Papa exclaimed.

"Alas, she was not. The loss of life is thought to be great. Of the more than two thousand aboard, well over half have been lost."

Papa sat down suddenly, his head in his hands. "It's difficult to grasp what has happened," he muttered. Then he said that we must all pray for the souls of those who had lost their lives.

The tea was brought, and the conversation continued about the tragedy—how it could have happened, which ship had answered the SOS and picked up the survivors in lifeboats, what was known of the captain.

"How terrifying that must have been!" said Anya, helping herself to more buttered bread. "Like the time several summers ago when the *Standart* struck a rock while we were at tea!"

Though I was only six when it happened, I remembered very well how frightened I was. It had felt as though we'd smashed into something. There was an awful noise, teacups and teapot and plates flew through the air, and alarm bells sounded, a horrible racket that made us even more frightened. The crew immediately lowered the lifeboats and helped us into them, Derevenko carrying Alexei, other sailors looking after Mama and us girls, Papa staying as calm as could be. Mama was terribly upset, and although Papa pretended he was not, he did seem short-tempered, and that was unusual for him.

We were taken to another ship and waited to find out what had happened. "I really thought it might be an assassination attempt," Papa said now. "Of course it turned out to be nothing of the kind. A submerged rock tore a hole in the hull."

"As the iceberg did to the *Titanic*," Mama said. "Imagine the terror of those people."

We grew quiet again. There seemed to be nothing more to say. Admiral Chagin promised to bring any further news of the fate of the passengers of the *Titanic*, and he and the other officers took their leave and were driven back to the *Standart*.

In Olga's notebook I read this:

An excursion today to a beautiful waterfall, hiking up a steep and rocky trail that required dear Pavel's assistance. He took my hand and even squeezed it several times. He is so handsome, so intelligent and kind! I was VERY bold and suggested that we might slip away for a few minutes after tea when the others were discussing politics, or whatever it is they talk about, and look at the new gardens just coming into bloom. It would have given us a chance to speak privately and would not have been improper, though Mother might have thought otherwise. But no—Chagin was here with awful news about an English passenger ship that sank, so many dead, and it was so sad and depressing that the tea ended more like a funeral. It was a very great tragedy and I pity the victims, but I'm disappointed that I did not have even one moment alone with P. all day! I tell myself that we will be here in Livadia for another month, and perhaps something good will happen in that time.

We celebrated Tatiana's fifteenth birthday at the end of May with a luncheon in the pavilion. Many neighbors were invited and came. I hoped that the emir of Bukhara might also come, but he did not. Then there was a rush to pack up and take the train back to Tsarskoe Selo. I watched Olga closely, but unless she was cleverer than I think she was, she never did get that moment alone with Pavel Voronov that she yearned for.

CHAPTER 5

On the Sea and in the Forest

BALTIC AND BIALOWIEZA, 1912

For the few weeks we were at home in Tsarskoe Selo, Papa was kept busy with official duties. Years earlier, after peasant uprisings, he had allowed the creation of an elected assembly, called the Duma, with a prime minister that would take part in governing Russia. Even though he'd permitted it, Papa hated the whole idea. He believed that as tsar, he was the appointed representative of God in Russia—the autocrat, the emperor, the Little Father of all the Russian people. It was God's will that the tsar and the tsar alone must rule. Now the men of the Duma wanted to meet with him to discuss certain matters. This had him fuming.

"I want nothing like the Parliament the English have," he told Mama. "I don't see how my cousin George can possibly rule as king of England with Parliament constantly interfering."

Mama completely agreed with him. "Being the king of England is not at all the same as being the Tsar of All the Russias," she said. "It doesn't begin to compare."

Even so, the prime minister had finally persuaded Papa to meet with the members. Papa was so busy with his meetings that my eleventh birthday was almost ignored—just a luncheon for the family. Grandmère Marie came from St. Petersburg, but I noticed that she and Mama didn't have much to say to each other. Nothing had changed there.

At last his duties were finished, Papa gave a speech to the assembly as he had been asked, and at the end of June we boarded the *Standart* for our summer cruise in the Baltic Sea.

First we sailed to meet Kaiser Wilhelm of Germany on his yacht, the *Hohenzollern*. We called him Cousin Willy, because he and Papa were distant cousins, and he and Mama were first cousins—their grandmother was Queen Victoria. Mama had been very close to her mother's mother, and it annoyed Mama to no end that Willy loved to brag tearfully about how the queen had died in his arms. After Papa and Cousin Willy had a long talk together, the rest of the family—except for Mama, who was feeling tired and ill and didn't much like Cousin Willy anyway went over to the German yacht. The *Hohenzollern* was a little smaller than the *Standart* but larger than our other yacht, the *Alexandria*, which we used in places where the water was not deep enough for the big yacht. Cousin Willy told Papa that he'd be happy to get the *Standart* as a gift, and Papa laughed as though he must be joking. But I didn't think Willy was joking at all—I thought he really meant it. It wasn't always possible to tell if Willy was serious or not.

Cousin Willy had pale gray eyes—cold as ice, I thought—a loud voice, a barking laugh, and an amazing mustache with ends that turned up like the handlebars on a bicycle. Papa told us that a barber went every morning to Kaiser Wilhelm's dressing room and waxed his mustache to make the ends stand up properly. I couldn't help staring at it.

"It's rude to stare!" Tatiana scolded.

"But Cousin Willy *wants* to be stared at," I said. "Why else would he have a mustache like that?"

I did know better than to stare at his left arm, which was small and undeveloped. He had his jackets designed with a special pocket so he could hide it.

The conversation was odd because Cousin Willy spoke German to Papa, Papa answered in French, and they both spoke English to the rest of us. Cousin Willy joked with me, telling me that he thought every day should be celebrated as his birthday. "Then you must be very old indeed, Cousin Willy!" I said, and that made him laugh: *Har har har!*

After dinner he handed out gifts to each of us: silver dresser sets for Olga and Tatiana, porcelain dolls (as though we were *children!*) for Marie and me, and a miniature of the *Hohenzollern* for Alexei. Then we had to watch a boring film showing Kaiser Wilhelm, dressed in tall black boots, a white cloak, and a helmet with a fierce-looking spike on top, marching back and forth in front of a regiment standing at attention, Kaiser Wilhelm on a battleship with sailors standing at attention, and Kaiser Wilhelm in a very large motorcar.

Marie and I were falling asleep as our launch took us back to the *Standart*, but when I heard Olga whisper to Tatiana, "Can you imagine, Cousin Willy once courted Aunt Ella!" I was instantly wide awake. "He used to send her love poems when he was a student."

"Ugh!" Tatiana said. "He's a pig! How could she even bear to be around him?"

"She couldn't! She once told me that," Olga said. "He was so insulted when she rejected him that he vowed to marry some other princess as soon as he could."

I scrambled to sit closer to my older sisters. "So did he?" I asked. I loved this kind of gossip.

"He did," Tatiana said. "A German girl, even though his family said she was a nobody. And Aunt Ella married Papa's uncle, Grand Duke Sergei."

"But after Uncle Sergei was blown to bits by a revolutionary's bomb, Aunt Ella became a nun and founded the Convent of Mary and Martha in Moscow," Olga whispered. "You were only three when that happened, Nastya. You wouldn't remember."

I hated it when Olga and Tatiana talked about things that I was too young to remember. But I would learn that some things were better *not* to remember.

After the visit with Cousin Willy, we cruised near the coast of Finland, dropping anchor in a small bay we'd named the Bay of Standart, near a special island where we went for long hikes and had picnics on the beach, Alexei played in the sand, and Papa swam in the icy water and played tennis on the court he'd had built. Mama stayed on the *Standart*, reading and embroidering and chatting with Anya. A few times, she was carried ashore and made comfortable in a shady spot, where she continued with reading and embroidering and chatting with Anya.

Grandmère Marie arrived on her yacht, the *Polar Star*, for the celebration of her name day in July. She and Mama politely ignored each other, but the rest of us were happy to see her and glad of an excuse for a party. The balalaika orchestra played, and we danced the mazurka and the polonaise on the deck with the ship's officers as our partners. Olga tried, not very successfully, not to show just *how* happy and glad she was.

She finally got what she had wanted all along: Lieutenant Voronov kissed her! I, naughty child that I was at age eleven, had made it my mission that summer to spy on them. Olga must have known what I was doing and simply decided to ignore me, thinking I would tire of the game. Generally I didn't like being ignored, but in this case it served my purpose. I was lurking in the shadows by one of the great funnels when her big moment came.

All the proof I needed was recorded in one brief sentence in her secret diary:

P. kissed me. Not once, but three times. Oh, what joy!

I had witnessed only a single kiss. When and where, I wondered, were the other two?

Later that summer when we had finished cruising and left the *Standart*, Papa and Mama traveled to Moscow for the hundredth anniversary celebration of a great battle against Napoleon, and we were left at home in Tsarskoe Selo to annoy our tutors.

Olga moped, because her happy days of kissing Pavel were over for the season, probably until Livadia in autumn.

Counting the days when I'll see P. again. Sometimes I feel so miserable, surrounded by people, never really alone, but lonely! I think Mother has some notion of my feelings for P., though she has not said anything. It's possible that A. saw us together, but I don't think she'll tattle. I dread Bialowieza and Spala in the fall—such gloomy places, and the weather is sure to be rotten! But Papa loves them, and so we'll go.

I can't get rid of the feeling that something terrible is going to happen. What is it?

"A." of course referred to me, and Olga was right—I wouldn't tell Mama what I saw. Why would I? But I didn't understand why Olga felt so lonely. Or why she believed something terrible was going to happen. Alexei had a disease we were not allowed to talk about and something awful could happen to him at any time, but other than that, it seemed to me our life was almost perfect.

When Papa and Mama came back from Moscow, we went by train to the royal hunting lodge deep in the Polish forest of Bialowieza. With its turrets and steep roofs, the lodge looked like something that belonged in a fairy tale. Mama scratched the date of our family's arrival with a diamond on a balcony window: *1 September 1912.* The last date she'd marked was in 1903, the summer before Alexei was born, when I was only two.

My sisters and I were half frightened of the huge, shaggy stuffed beasts that loomed in the entry hall and the stuffed heads with murderous tusks we had to pass every time we climbed the stairs to our bedrooms. Those terrifying beasts were aurochs, long-horned wild oxen that had become almost extinct. Papa said there used to be countless bears and wolves and even lions prowling the forest, until our grandfather, Tsar Alexander, had them killed off in order to protect the aurochs. The idea was to bring the aurochs back from the brink of extinction so that he and his friends could hunt them—and, I guess, stuff them and put them in the entryway to scare his grandchildren. Now there were lots of them roaming the forest, and they were known to be extremely dangerous. I hoped I would never see a live one.

It rained almost every day in Bialowieza, but that didn't stop my sisters and me from venturing into the forest with Papa on horseback and hunting—not for animals, but for mushrooms. Armed guards rode with us, just in case. Alexei couldn't go on these excursions, because the doctors would not allow him to risk injuring himself. His sailor-attendant Derevenko tried to find safe ways to keep him entertained, but the precautions didn't always work. One day while we were away with Papa, Alexei somehow hit himself on something, and when we got back with our mushrooms, the bleeding inside his body had begun. It hurt badly, and Alexei was suffering. Mama and Papa pretended nothing serious was wrong, as they always did, but anyone could see how worried they were.

Dr. Botkin made Alexei stay in bed and rest—the only treatment he knew. Alexei hated that, especially when the rest of us were out enjoying ourselves, and so one of us always took a turn staying with him. After a week, Dr. Botkin decided he was well enough to be moved, and we left the royal lodge in Bialowieza for another royal lodge in Spala, where the Polish kings used to hunt before Poland was made part of Russia two centuries ago.

The Spala lodge was dark and gloomy, and it always felt damp and smelled moldy. The hallways were narrow, and the rooms were small and cramped. The electric lights were kept burning all the time. This was my least favorite of all the imperial palaces, but Papa loved to hunt there for stags. He and his guests, Polish noblemen whose names I could not pronounce, went out hunting every day. We could hear the stags bellowing from early morning on, and in the evening the corpses of the deer the men had shot were laid out on the lawn with greenery woven in their antlers. Between *zakuski* and dinner, the noblemen, dressed in their belted greatcoats and tall fur hats, and the ladies, wrapped in cloaks and furs—all except Mama—went out to admire the poor dead beasts by torchlight. I felt sorry for the stags, and I didn't understand what pleasure the men got from killing them.

"It's an old custom," Olga said. "And you know how Papa loves old customs."

At Spala, Alexei seemed to be getting better—so much better that Mama, thinking he needed to get out of the dismal lodge and into the fresh air, took him for a carriage ride with Anya. The bumping of the carriage over the rutted roads made the bleeding begin again, and Alexei had to be put back to bed. Dr. Botkin did what he could, but nothing eased the pain. Papa sent to St. Petersburg for another doctor who might be able to help—Dr. Vladimir Derevenko. While we waited for him to come, Papa reminded us, "We must continue to act as normally as possible. There is nothing we can do until the doctors arrive, and Alexei's condition must not become public."

To distract our parents and entertain their friends, Marie and I decided to put on a play. With Monsieur Gilliard's coaching, we rehearsed two scenes from *Le bourgeois gentilhomme*, "The Middle-Class Gentleman," by the French playwright Molière. In one scene, Marie played the part of the daughter of the man who wants to be recognized as a gentleman, and I took the role of Cléonte, the man she loves. Her father refuses to let her marry him because he's only a commoner. In the other scene, Marie played the father. When Cléonte appears in disguise, passing himself off as the son of the sultan of Turkey, the father approves the marriage. I loved being the Turkish prince in a turban, and I enjoyed seeing Olga's face turn pink at the idea of a girl in love with a man beneath her station.

We had a lively audience that evening for our little theatrics, and no one would have guessed from looking at Mama as she chatted with her guests that she was worried sick about Alexei. His pain was terrible, his fever soared, and he was delirious. You could hear his pitiful cries and heartrending moans even through closed doors. For days Mama never left Alexei's side, sometimes sleeping a little on the sofa next to his bed. Papa stayed with him, too, but once I saw him rush out of Alexei's room, weeping. It was hard for all of us to bear.

My sisters and I had no idea what to do. It seemed so odd—Mama and Papa were afraid Alexei might die, they were

nearly mad with worry and grief, and yet the hunting lodge
bustled with guests who laughed and talked and helped themselves to caviar while liveried servants kept their champagne
glasses filled.

Finally, the new doctor, along with Dr. Botkin, convinced Papa and Mama to inform the Russian people that
their beloved tsarevich was gravely ill. My parents reluctantly
accepted this advice and sent out a notice to the newspapers.
Papa ordered a large tent to be set up in the garden at Spala to
serve as a chapel. Polish peasants from nearby villages as well
as Cossacks and soldiers and our household servants crowded
the tent night and day, all praying for Alexei's recovery. Soon
all of Russia was praying for the tsarevich. OTMA, too, cried
and prayed and cried some more. The priest gave Alexei the
last sacrament.

I was sure my brother would not survive. Alexei was going
to die.

But I was wrong. Mama had sent a telegram to Father
Grigory, who was at his home in Siberia, and begged him to
pray for Alexei. Then came a reply.

We were with Mama when she received Father Grigory's telegram, and I saw a change come over her as she read it. She no longer looked stricken. She was calm now, and she sounded hopeful
when she read his message aloud to us: "'God has seen your tears
and heard your prayers. The illness is not dangerous. The Little
One will not die. Do not let the doctors bother him too much.'"

"You see?" she said. "Baby will not die! Father Grigory says
so. We must have faith!"

The next morning she was smiling as she told us, "The

doctors don't see that Baby is better, but they're wrong. He is certainly no worse, and I believe he may have turned the corner."

Slowly, very slowly, Alexei began to improve. The doctors couldn't explain it, but Mama could: it was all because of Father Grigory and his prayers. Nobody could possibly disagree with her. From far away Siberia, Father Grigory had performed a miracle. He had saved my brother's life. Alexei wasn't in mortal danger now, but he was very weak and tired, and so was Mama.

We stayed another month at Spala while Alexei recovered. Kharitonov outdid himself preparing tempting dishes to coax him to eat, and little by little he regained some of the weight he had lost. Bit by bit Mama got her strength back. The rest of us followed our usual routines—French lessons with Monsieur Gilliard, English lessons with Mr. Gibbes, Russian lessons with Pyotr Petrov, held in one of the few rooms at Spala where a little daylight leaked in for an hour or two each day. Papa hunted with his Polish friends and played tennis with the army officers. Olga pined for her lieutenant.

I was ready to die of boredom, when we learned of a family scandal. Papa got a telegram from his brother Mikhail— our uncle Misha—announcing that he had married Natalia Brassova. We hardly knew our uncle, and we had never met Natalia Brassova. We did know that Uncle Misha had been the cause of much scandal in the family, falling in love with "unsuitable" women. Papa had refused to grant him permission to marry those women and then sent him far away to keep him out of the public eye and, it was hoped, to put an end to the affairs. But now Uncle Misha had defied Papa and married

Natalia without permission—after making a solemn promise to Papa *not* to marry her.

Anya Vyrubova happily told us all about it. "A completely unsuitable woman!" Anya announced gleefully. "Twice divorced! Everybody says Brassova is beautiful and dresses very stylishly, but, my dears, she's had two husbands! She was still married to the second one when she took up with Grand Duke Mikhail. He asked your papa for permission to marry her, but of course the tsar couldn't allow that—it would have been scandalous!" Anya lowered her voice to a hoarse whisper. "They even have a child together, I hear. A little boy." She paused to let us consider that shocking bit. "Then, when your darling brother was so terribly ill, they ran off to Vienna and were secretly married. Only after the deed was done did they inform your poor papa. What could he do? Why, he banished them, of course! The grand duke is forbidden ever to return to Russia!"

We sisters looked at each other. Tatiana agreed that it was shameful. "Papa had no choice but to forbid them to marry. And I think it was very selfish of Uncle Misha to go against Papa's wishes and break his promise."

"But they're in love!" Olga protested. "It would be too cruel not to allow people who love each other to marry, just because she's not *appropriate*—whatever that means."

"It means she's a commoner. A twice-divorced commoner," Tatiana said sharply. "And Uncle Misha is second in line to become tsar."

"One must always obey the tsar's wishes," Anya said piously. "And I hate to think what the Dowager Empress Marie has to say about it."

I thought I knew exactly what my grandmother would say. "'I shan't be able to show my face in public,'" I said, mimicking Grandmère Marie's haughtiest tone. "'It should have remained a *secret!*'"

My sisters stared at me, and then burst out laughing. Anya, though, pursed her lips. "I do not find that at all amusing, Anastasia Nikolaevna," she said.

Anya had another bit of gossip to pass on. Admiral Chagin, the commander who had assigned Derevenko and Nagorny to be Alexei's sailor-attendants, had come all the way from St. Petersburg. "He was terribly upset! He was in charge of your brother's safety, and he'd chosen two of his most reliable sailors to look after Baby. He takes it very personally and blames himself for the tsarevich's injury. But the tsar, with his usual kindness, assured the admiral he was not at fault, and sent him home."

"Poor Admiral Chagin!" Marie sighed. "Such a good man."

"Yes," Anya agreed, "a good man, but rather foolish at times."

We looked at her, waiting to hear more. "What do you mean, Anya?" Olga asked.

"Oh, you know—that business with the girl at the tsaritsa's bazaar in Livadia last year. He did make a fool of himself, flirting with her."

"You mean Kyra Belyaevna, with the lace-trimmed handkerchiefs?" Tatiana asked. "Half the men there were flirting with her, and all the women loathed her for it."

"Scandalous behavior," Anya sniffed.

• • •

Normally in late autumn we would have been in Livadia, but because of Alexei's condition, those plans were canceled. We would stay at Spala until the crisis was over, return home to Tsarskoe Selo for the winter, and then go to Livadia for Easter as usual.

Olga had been looking forward to celebrating her seventeenth birthday at our palace by the sea—and with a certain lieutenant coming nearly every day for tennis and no doubt more stolen kisses. Instead, Mama decided, we would have a small dinner for her at Spala with the family and a few friends—Anya, Dr. Botkin, our tutors, and others who were close to us. Olga tried not to look disappointed. We all were, but no one protested. We would make the best of it.

We had dressed and gone down to the small anteroom for *zakuski* when Marie paused, head cocked, and asked, "Nastya, do you hear music? Coming from somewhere outside?"

We slipped away from the anteroom and went to peer out through the narrow windows in the entrance. It had been snowing off and on all day, wet, heavy flakes. A small crowd, some carrying torches, had gathered on the lawn, and, surrounded by our Cossack guards, they were singing. I stayed to listen while Marie went to find Papa.

A footman had gotten to Papa first, and he and Marie came to peer out the window at the singers. "It seems that some of our neighbors have heard that it's the birthday of the grand duchess, and they've come to offer greetings to Olya," Papa said. "These are the same people who came here to pray for the tsarevich's recovery. I've invited them to join us."

The front door opened, and the neighbors—peasants

from nearby farms and villages—crowded into the entrance hall, stomping the snow from their boots. Some were carrying balalaikas and other stringed instruments, and there was even an accordion.

The entrance hall couldn't hold them all, and Papa suggested that everyone move into the dining room, which was now set for dinner. A small raised platform at one end could be used as a stage, and after a hurried discussion among themselves, a dozen musicians climbed onto the platform and began to play. Several others performed a lively dance while the "audience" clapped in rhythm. The hearty singing resumed. Mama, who was frowning at first, actually seemed to be enjoying the unplanned entertainment.

The sailor Derevenko stood nearby holding Alexei, pale and very thin and still not able to stand on his own. The musicians saluted him and presented him with a handsome balalaika they'd made especially for him. One of the singers, an elderly woman with a gap-toothed grin, stepped forward and gave Olga a white linen shawl embroidered all over with pale yellow flowers. One of their party who spoke Russian explained that it was to be worn at her wedding. That made her blush.

Our Polish guests produced bottles of plum brandy, a gift for Papa, who proposed the first toast, *"Na zdrowie!"* ("To your health!" in Polish), and then everyone began drinking toasts, tossing back glasses of the strong spirits and shouting, *"Na zdrowie!"* Meanwhile, Mama had sent a message to the kitchen, and soon servants were passing platters of *pierogi*—little pastries filled with wild mushrooms or farmer's cheese.

Nothing like this ever happened at Tsarskoe Selo. It was

great fun, much more fun than it would have been at the usual stuffy dinner, with the ladies making curtsies so low you'd think they'd fall over, and the gentlemen bowing almost double. Alexei, who only a short time earlier had been on the verge of dying, was laughing and making everyone cheer—even Mama—when he picked out a tune on his new balalaika.

Things did get a little out of hand after all the plum brandy. Our unexpected guests began dancing, first with each other, and then—strictly against all the rules—they asked my sisters and me to join them, not knowing—or not caring—that only under certain special circumstances were men permitted to invite grand duchesses to dance.

I saw Mama frowning and shaking her head and looking to Papa to put a stop to this improper nonsense, but Olga, usually so reserved, was skipping merrily around the dining room in the arms of a tall, bearded peasant as though she'd been practicing for just this moment. It didn't take long for Marie and me to have partners as well, young boys with pink cheeks. Only Tatiana held back, shaking her head, until an older man with a gray-streaked beard stepped forward and swept her away, too.

I loved swirling past the members of the imperial suite, the noble ladies and gentlemen who traveled with us, and seeing how aghast they looked, as though they smelled something slightly off. Papa, standing to one side with an amused smile, signaled the leader of the group when he must have felt it had gone on long enough, and the music and clapping stopped. Papa thanked everyone, and our visitors bowed again, quietly gathered their cloaks, and filed out into the snowy night.

I thought it was the best party we'd ever had. Mama

complained that these guests were not particularly clean and their manners were rough. I did not mention that they were a lot like Father Grigory.

Now it was time to go home. Papa wanted to be at Tsarskoe Selo for Christmas. Mama ordered the road from the hunting lodge to the train station to be made smooth as glass, so that nothing would jolt Alexei. Our train, which always traveled slowly, now crept along even more slowly. The new doctor, Vladimir Derevenko, stayed with him for every mile of the journey.

New Year, 1913. I have not seen P. since August. I'm thinking of sending him a letter. I've written it over and over in my head and even put it on paper, tearing up the paper and burning the pieces until I was satisfied with the result. I've thought hard about whom I could trust to deliver it. It would be terrible if it fell into the wrong hands and it was found out that we are in love. Such yearning I feel in my heart, the ache of wanting to be near him, even for just a moment! It's nearly unbearable.

How sad for my poor sister! I could not think of a single person Olga could trust to take a letter to Lieutenant Voronov. Maybe one of our Russian maids knew someone who could deliver a letter, but how would Olga arrange it? Who would bring Olga a letter from Pavel Voronov? How would she get it? I loved my Shura and I knew that she was devoted to me, but I could not imagine asking her to deliver such a letter—she would feel it was her duty to inform Mama or Papa. Poor Olga! It must have been very hard for her.

And then something terrible happened. Admiral Chagin killed himself.

Mama told us soon after Papa was given the news, but she would not say much. No one did. On our way to Anichkov Palace for our Sunday luncheon with Grandmère Marie, we asked Aunt Olga if she'd heard about it.

"Of course I've heard about it. The newspapers say it was because he felt guilty about Lyosha's injuries, but that's not the case. He did it because of that stupid girl."

We stared at our aunt, open-mouthed. Mama would never have told us such a thing.

"Here's what really happened. His flirtation with Belyaevna began at the bazaar and continued after we returned to Livadia for Easter. By the time we left, the girl had fallen madly in love and she followed the admiral to St. Petersburg. He decided that the honorable thing was to marry her, but as an officer in the imperial navy he needed the tsar's permission. By then it was October and you were all in Spala. When Chagin finally arrived at Spala, he found Lyosha deathly ill, and he decided to return home without speaking to the tsar about his problem. The girl was waiting for him, insisting that he marry her. But he could not bring himself to go on, and he killed himself. When she found out what he had done, she tried to kill herself, too." Then Aunt Olga added, "Best if you keep this to yourselves, my darlings. Don't let your mother know what I've told you."

I glanced at Olga, who was studying her hands and did not look up. What was she thinking? I waited for the chance to read her notebook, but when it came, I was not prepared for what I read there.

I am so wretchedly unhappy. Father and I had a confidential talk today. He and Mother are very worried that Lyosha, because of his illness, may not live to adulthood——we were both in tears as we discussed this——and this leaves an enormous problem: Who will become tsar after Father? The son of Catherine the Great changed the rules and women are no longer allowed to inherit the crown. By law I cannot succeed Father. I am deeply grateful, because I can't begin to imagine the burden he must bear! The logical person to become the next tsar is Uncle Misha, but he removed himself from the line of succession by marrying Mme. Brassova, a commoner and twice divorced.

Father then asked if I would consider marrying Dmitri Pavlovich. Father is fond of him, and he believes the Russian people would accept Dmitri as the next tsar if he married me, because he's the son of Papa's uncle, Grand Duke Pavel Alexandrovich.

"Please think about it, Olya," Father said, and I said I would.

Mother strongly opposes the idea. She says Dmitri is fast living and has already been involved with many women. She intensely dislikes his friend Prince Felix Yussoupov; she calls him dissolute and says the two of them go to disreputable places and do unspeakable things. Father admits that Dmitri's reputation is bad, but he believes all that would change if we were married and he were under Father's guidance. "Remember, Alicky," he said, "I was no saint as a young man, before you agreed to marry me." Mother blushed and rejected that argument.

It doesn't matter. The gossips are already saying that I am, or will soon be, engaged to Dmitri Pavlovich. But I will not marry him, not even for the sake of the succession. And I have decided that I must not try to contact darling Pasha. No letters, nothing. Father would never consent to the marriage, and if we continue with this, it will only end in more heartache.

I was sorry that I had ever begun to read Olga's secret notebook. But how could I possibly stop now?

CHAPTER 6

Celebration

 n January, our family moved to the Winter Palace in St. Petersburg to get ready for the huge tercentenary celebrating three centuries of Romanov rule.

Every Russian knows the story, going back to the year 1547 when a seventeen-year-old prince named Ivan proclaimed himself tsar of Russia and announced that he was looking for a wife. Ivan ordered two thousand young girls to appear before him, and out of the crowd he chose Anastasia Romanovna. That was the first Anastasia! When she died ten years later, Ivan went crazy and did such awful things that he became known as Ivan the Terrible.

After Ivan's death and a period of unrest, a national assembly chose a new tsar—one of Ivan's distant relatives, a sixteen-year-old boy named Mikhail Romanov. On the twenty-first of February, 1613, Mikhail was informed that he'd been chosen. The first

Romanov tsar was crowned in Moscow on the eleventh of July. Now, three hundred years later, Russia was going to celebrate.

None of us wanted to leave Tsarskoe Selo, because none of us liked the huge and drafty old Winter Palace. It was supposed to be the tsar's main residence, though no tsar had actually lived there for years and years. We did not look forward to the ceremonies and religious observances and dinners and receptions we'd have to endure—Mama especially dreaded them, but it was her duty, and ours.

The morning of the twenty-first of February in 1913 dawned cold, windy, and rainy. We climbed into motorcars, trying to keep our court gowns from being splashed with mud, and were driven slowly down Nevsky Prospect, past wet flags and drooping banners. It looked so different from the fashionable avenue where my sisters and I loved to stroll with Aunt Olga on our Sundays in St. Petersburg. Guns boomed a salute from the fortress. Huge, enthusiastically cheering crowds ignored the foul weather and had to be held back by cordons of soldiers. Red-coated Cossacks rode at the head of the procession, escorting Papa and Alexei in the first motorcar. Mama and Grandmère were in the second.

"I wonder what they're talking about," I said.

"Mother is probably grinding her teeth," Olga said. "It just kills her that Grandmère Marie will take precedence at all the events."

"They're probably not talking at all," Tatiana said. "You know how it is, Olya. The dowager empress always goes ahead of the empress, Grandmère Marie takes it for granted, and Mother resents it."

"It's a stupid rule," I informed them. "Mama should go first. She's the wife of the tsar."

"It may be stupid, but it's tradition," Tatiana said. "In Russia, you don't challenge tradition."

"Our mother resents a lot of things," Olga said, peering out the rain-smeared window. We were nearing the Cathedral of Our Lady of Kazan. "She resents calling her Motherdear. She really resented it when Grandmère Marie wouldn't turn over the crown jewels when she and Papa were married. Mama embarrassed her into doing it."

"You can't blame Mama for being upset! How do you know that?"

"Gossipy servants. How else do we get to know anything?"

"Well, I think it's all very exciting," said Marie the peacemaker, trying to change the subject. "Just listen to all those church bells ringing and everyone cheering like mad!"

The cathedral was thronged, everyone standing with no room to move. Mama and Grandmère Marie maneuvered into position with Papa between them at the very front. They wore gold-embroidered court gowns with huge trains and long open sleeves, jeweled *kokoshniks* on their heads, and gobs of jewels on their fingers, wrists, waists, and necks. My dress didn't have a train, but I did wear a *kokoshnik*, and when I posed for a formal photograph I thought I looked wonderfully *Russian*.

Marie nudged me. "There's Father Grigory, and he's standing at the front among all those noblemen!" she whispered. "I've never seen him so dressed up!"

I recognized the crimson silk blouse that Mama had spent hours embroidering for him, and the fine gold cross Mama had given him on a chain around his neck. Mama and Papa, their eyes on the Orthodox patriarch at the high altar, didn't see the shocking thing that happened next. One of the officials decided that Father Grigory didn't belong there and quietly ordered him to leave. When he refused, the official grabbed him by his shirt and literally shoved him out. I gasped. How could they do such a thing? I was glad that Mama hadn't seen it, because it would have upset her very much, but she would certainly hear about it later and be absolutely furious.

The service went on and on—they were always very long—but in the afternoon after it was over, we rested while Papa went off to deliver a speech to the members of the Duma. He was in a bad mood when he left, as he always was when he had to meet with the Duma. Mama thought he should have refused even to go speak to them. He was the tsar!

"I won't be telling them anything they want to hear," he growled, and marched off.

That was the first day of the tercentennial. The days that followed were a blur of boring ceremonies and dinners and receptions. At events where my sisters and I required escorts, Dmitri Pavlovich was assigned to be mine. He wore the uniform of his regiment and looked very dashing. I was thrilled to be with him, remembering how we had danced the Boston at Aunt Olga's and shocked everyone, and I hoped he wouldn't find me dull and tedious.

I could not believe that Dmitri was as awful as Mama said, dissolute and fast living, consorting with loose women and disreputable men, because he was always so nice and polite to me. He didn't treat me like a child but spoke to me as though

I were a grown-up lady, and I tried hard to behave like one.

When I asked him about the Olympics in Sweden where he'd competed the previous summer, Dmitri rewarded me with that gleaming smile.

"I'd hoped to bring home a gold medal for Russia," he said. "But the Swedes took all three medals in dressage, and a Frenchman and a German took the medals in jumping. I did place seventh in the combination, where a rider has to be good at everything."

I congratulated him, and he promised that someday he would give me lessons in dressage. "It's like ballet on horseback," he said.

That was such a fascinating idea that I decided not to confess that I wasn't much of a rider and horses seemed to dislike me. I would try to overcome that before the dressage lessons began.

On the third night, the Romanov grand dukes and grand duchesses—Papa's sisters and aunts and uncles and cousins, close and distant, and their respective husbands and wives— gave a grand ball in honor of Mama and Papa. Hundreds of people would attend. Marie and I were not invited, but Olga and Tatiana were, even though they were not yet eighteen and weren't officially out in society. I was disappointed to be left out. I had never attended a grand ball and begged to be allowed to go, not mentioning that I hoped Dmitri would be my escort.

Mama said no. "You'll attend enough balls in your life, Nastya. Be glad you can miss this one."

Watching my older sisters being laced into their corsets, I told myself that I was just as happy not to be going. Olga and Tatiana had bosoms, and Marie and I did not. It seemed that having a *bosom* was a requirement for being allowed to attend big, formal balls.

Tatiana admonished me not to use that word—"Much nicer to say *figure*, Nastya."

Their white satin gowns were trimmed with pink velvet and gold. I envied them the gowns, not the corsets, which looked awfully uncomfortable. Marie and I weren't yet allowed long ball gowns and jewels; Mama thought short white dresses and pearls were quite enough for girls who did not yet have *bosoms.*

Mama hated the big formal balls, but of course she had to go, whether she wanted to or not. I saw her before she and Papa left. She was wearing dark blue velvet with pearls and diamonds, and I thought I had never seen her look so beautiful. But she felt so miserable, so tired and ill, that she nearly fainted. One had to pity Mama—she always felt so poorly. Papa got to her just in time to help her out of the huge ballroom before she collapsed, and they had all come back to the palace before the supper was served.

"You've never seen so many jewels," Tatiana told us as the maids undressed her and Olga. "So much glitter that they hardly needed to turn on any lights."

"Was Dmitri Pavlovich there?" I asked, trying not to sound overly interested.

"Oh yes, of course," Olga said. "He was paying a great deal of attention to our cousin Irina. She is quite beautiful, with those big blue eyes, and she looked absolutely ravishing! Her rose-colored gown positively shimmered with tiny pearls."

I wished I hadn't asked. I didn't want to hear about Dmitri's attention to blue-eyed Irina.

• • •

The next night all of us went to the Mariinsky Theatre. The opera was *A Life for the Tsar* by Mikhail Glinka, a famous composer, and in the second act the dancers came on stage and performed a polonaise, a waltz, and a mazurka.

"Look who's the principal dancer," Olga murmured to Tatiana. "Kschessinskaya."

I knew who they were talking about. Kschessinskaya had once been the prima ballerina assoluta at the Mariinsky, the highest position a dancer can achieve.

"The one who was Papa's mistress," I whispered knowingly. I'd heard Aunt Olga and my older sisters talking about her, but I didn't know exactly what a mistress was.

Tatiana gave me her fiercest frown. "Don't call her a mistress," she scolded. "She was Father's good friend, and that's all you need to know about her."

Mistress was apparently a word like *bosom* that I was not to use.

I made up my mind to ask Aunt Olga. She always explained things to me that no one else would. Days later, when the celebrations in St. Petersburg were over, I had a chance to speak with her. "Why must I not call the dancer Kschessinskaya a mistress?" I asked.

My aunt looked startled. "Where did you hear that?" she asked, and I told her.

"Well, it's not a good word to use," Aunt Olga explained. "Mathilde Kschessinskaya was your papa's friend, but she was also in love with your papa."

"Was he in love with her as well?" I wanted to know everything.

"He was certainly fond of her. But they both knew it would end, because she was not an appropriate wife for the future tsar, because she's not of noble birth and your grandfather would never have given his approval. Besides, your papa had already met your mama and fallen in love with her, and that was the girl he wanted to marry."

"Was Kschessinskaya's heart broken when he and Mama married?"

Aunt Olga smiled—sadly, I thought. "Probably, for a while. But he gave her a beautiful house in St. Petersburg as a gift. Now, shall we talk of other things? Have you some lovely drawings for me to admire?"

I wasn't ready to let go of this subject. There was so much more I wanted to know. "What if one of us wants to marry a man who isn't of noble birth? Could we?"

Aunt Olga studied me thoughtfully. "I'm sure your mama and your papa want all of you girls to marry young men you love, and they wouldn't force you to marry someone you don't. But they would not allow you to marry someone below your rank. It would not be appropriate," she added, "for one of you to fall in love with one of those magnificent bearded Cossacks."

Then she did change the subject and asked me if I had taken any new photographs. I showed her some I'd taken of Olga and Pavel Voronov on the *Standart*—when my sister saw the pictures, she asked me to give her two: one for her, and one for "my friend," as she called him.

Aunt Olga looked at them and smiled, and said nothing. But I guessed what she was thinking: *Not appropriate. Too bad.*

• • •

At Easter we were still in St. Petersburg, still at the cold and dreary Winter Palace. Spring refused to come. Tatiana had fallen ill with typhoid from drinking contaminated water. She was so sick that her hair began to fall out and had to be cut. There had been no visit to Livadia. The days crept by slowly with only our sessions with our tutors.

I hadn't read Olga's secret notebook for weeks. What could there be for Olga to write about? But one day when she had gone to visit our cousin Irina and I had nothing else to do, I searched for the notebook.

I'm worried and frightened. We keep telling ourselves that the Russian people love us, yet everywhere we go there are so many guards, so many soldiers, all because they're afraid of revolutionaries determined to kill any Romanov—especially the tsar. I'm not sure why. Hasn't Father given them what they said they want?

I have begun to realize that many people dislike Mother. They call her Nemka, "German woman." That is so stupid! Hardly any of the past tsaritsas have been Russian. Catherine the Great was German! Everyone adores Grandmère Marie, yet she was born in Denmark. I see the way Mother looks, always frowning, her mouth set in a tight line, wishing she was anywhere but where she is. With a few exceptions—Countess Benckendorff and Countess Hendrikova—the so-called ladies of the court wait for her to say or do something they decide has offended them. Anya is her closest friend, but I find Anya awfully tiresome. Mother is devoted to Father Grigory, because he's the only one who helps Lyosha, but

Irina says he is deeply distrusted. Many believe he has too much influence on Mother, and on Father, too. All of this dislike and distrust makes me feel that something terrible is going to happen. Maybe not right away, but someday soon. I pray that I'm wrong.

I was shocked by what I read. Could Olga be right about this? Did people really dislike Mama so much? Was something bad going to happen? I didn't understand it, and there was no one I could ask—not even Aunt Olga.

Late in the spring we made a journey to places in the country-side important in the early life of Mikhail Romanov, the first Romanov tsar. We traveled by imperial train from Tsarskoe Selo eastward to Nizhny Novgorod. There we boarded the steamer *Mezhen* and journeyed up the Volga River to visit Kostroma, the village where Mikhail Romanov was born. Aunt Olga and a crowd of other Romanov relatives traveled with us. We stood on the deck in the chilly wind and waved to the cheering peasants crowded along the riverbanks. "God save the tsar!" they shouted, and "May he live forever!" Some even waded into the freezing water to get a glimpse of their tsar and the tsarevich.

Olga must have been wrong. This was so different from St. Petersburg! Here was proof that the common people truly loved Papa, and Mama, too, and maybe it was just some of those wicked noblemen and their snobbish wives in St. Petersburg who delighted in criticizing. Or maybe the rainy, cold weather had put them in a sour mood.

We boarded our train for the final leg of the journey to the outskirts of Moscow. Our destination was the cathedral where the first tsar had been crowned. Papa rode into the city on horseback, alone and in advance of his Cossack escort, the rest of us following in open carriages: Mama and Grandmère Marie in one carriage, Alexei with Nagorny in the next, followed by OTMA, and then all the other Romanov relatives in the procession behind us. People cheered and the bells of dozens of churches began to peal when we reached the Kremlin. I hoped that Olga would see how thrilling it was, that our parents were indeed loved.

But Olga didn't see.

I'm not the only one afraid something terrible will happen. I sat next to Father in the dining salon of the train on the way to Moscow. General Spiridovich, who's in charge of his security, sat across from us, drinking vodka and eating zakuski. The general pleaded with Father not to go through with his foolish idea of riding ahead of the Cossacks into the city. Hundreds of thousands of workers are on strike, he said, and the mood is ugly and growing worse. At any moment a revolutionary could throw a bomb or fire a gun at the tsar, and there would be no one to protect him. Two years ago during a visit to Kiev, Papa took Tanya and me to the opera and a revolutionary walked up to Prime Minister Stolypin and shot him. We were watching from the royal box and witnessed the whole thing. Tanya cried the whole night after it happened.

But Father told General Spiridovich that the Tsar of All the Russias must show himself to his people and he would ride unprotected into Moscow. Thank God nothing happened.

*I saw Fr. G standing near the entrance to the Kremlin. I'm sure
it was the starets, but when I tried to point him out to Tanya,
he had melted into the crowd. It seemed to me a bad omen, though
Mother would think just the opposite.*

Olga seemed determined to see the dark side of everything. Marie, on the other hand, always saw the bright side. I
felt stuck in the middle. How could we be so different?

Two thousand people attended a grand ball at the Hall of the
Nobles in Moscow the night after our arrival. Aunt Olga said
the hall was the finest ballroom in all of Europe. Marie and I
were not invited, but Olga and Tatiana were. Mama wouldn't let
them wear ball gowns, just the usual white dresses and pearls.
Tatiana's hair was growing back after her illness. She tied it
with a velvet ribbon.

"We look like schoolgirls," Olga complained, studying her
image in a tall mirror. "Mama still wants to dress us like children."

Marie and I were waiting for them when they came back.
"Tell! Tell! Tell!" we begged.

"Mother and Father opened the ball with a polonaise,"
Tatiana reported, stripping off her long gloves.

"They weren't actually dancing," Olga said. "They just
walked in a stately kind of way through the ballroom. It was
quite splendidly decorated—lots of ferns and huge urns filled
with flowers."

"Ferns in urns," I said, enjoying the sound of the words,
"and urns of ferns. Who were your partners?"

Tatiana wrinkled her nose and flung herself down on her bed. "Army officers. My captain waltzed rather well, but he smelled of cigars."

Olga laughed. "Mine, too. And his hands were clammy. So, you see, you two didn't miss anything."

At the end of May we went home—at last!—to Tsarskoe Selo. Tatiana's sixteenth birthday came two days later, but there was no celebration like Olga's. Mama had decided that another formal ball was not necessary.

Tatiana agreed. "I've had enough balls. I'd rather have a party on the *Standart,*" she said. "Or a picnic on our special island."

Olga would be happy no matter which Tatiana chose. Pavel Voronov would be there.

I'm counting the days until I see Pasha again. It has been nine months since we were together and that magical night when we kissed THREE TIMES.

I would have to keep a close watch, or I would miss everything.

CHAPTER 7

Olga in Love

he *Standart* cruised along the coast of Finland. Papa and Mama were both tired from all the balls and receptions and dinners and ceremonies and happy not to have any official duties.

Tatiana celebrated her sixteenth birthday on the *Standart*, just the way she wanted. Mama decreed white dresses, pearls, and colored sashes—Olga was right, we did look like little girls instead of *young ladies*. Tatiana received her pearl and diamond necklace. It was a tradition in our family that each of us was given a diamond on our birthday and a large pearl on our name day, so that when we turned sixteen, we would each have a complete necklace of thirty-two beautiful gems. Chef Kharitonov produced a delicious meal, the balalaika orchestra played, and we danced on the deck with the officers, including Lieutenant Voronov.

I turned twelve on the fifth of June (twelve each, diamonds and pearls, kept in a velvet case), and nine days later Marie was fourteen, with more treats and dancing (and one more diamond). I was the only sister who did not yet have a bosom, but Marie promised that I would very soon. "Madame Becker is likely to make her appearance, Nastya," she said. "Madame Becker" was their name for their monthly cycles.

Everyone was in a happy mood. Mama kept remarking on how successful the three hundredth celebration had been, how people had cheered and applauded wherever we went, especially the peasants in the countryside. "The *real* Russians," she said, "not like those overstuffed, overdressed counts and countesses who look down their noses at everyone, at us, and at each other. How I despise them!"

Every day there were chances for Olga to see her Pasha. So often during the long winter and spring Olga had seemed sad and distracted, as though she wished she were somewhere else, or maybe even *someone* else. But that summer she was lighthearted and gay, laughing and joking, and not just when Voronov was around, but with all of us.

We went ashore for picnics and hikes, we swam, and I tried to improve my tennis. In the evenings we danced mazurkas and polonaises on the deck with the officers. Tatiana was good at flirting. So was Marie. You could see it was just a game with them, a merry way of passing the time, and the young officers played along. But Olga was a serious girl, and you had only to look at her face. It was as though somebody turned on a light switch the minute Lieutenant Voronov appeared.

I was sure Mama and Papa knew very well what was

happening. Olga tried to pretend that nothing was going on with Pavel Voronov, but too often I heard her slip and call him "Pasha." Voronov was much better at acting reserved and formal when others were around.

I felt sure her notebook would reveal what was happening out of my sight.

After so many months apart, we are at last together for a few precious weeks—except that we're not! My darling P. fills my heart and my dreams but it's so hard to find a place where we can be alone, to kiss and speak privately. I yearn to be with him, but he is cautious, and I must be, too—especially around Tanya. My sister and I share every secret except this one, but she is the perfect daughter, closer to Mama than I could ever be. If she notices anything at all, she'll feel she must report it to Mama. And so I say nothing.

I also said nothing. I remembered what Aunt Olga had told me about "inappropriate" marriages and crossed my fingers for Olga.

Alexei injured himself again. The poor boy had to wear a brace to try to straighten the leg he'd hurt the year before at Spala. He got around by hopping on one foot, and they let him take off the brace only when it was just too awfully hot. Then, after a month of cruising, we left the *Standart* in the port of Kronstadt and were taken to Peterhof on the *Alexandria*, a smaller yacht that could maneuver in shallow water. We had barely settled in at our summer dacha before Alexei somehow hurt his elbow and was in the most horrible pain. His pitiful moans were more than anyone could bear.

Mama sent a telegram to Father Grigory, begging him to come to Peterhof. He arrived the next day and went immediately to Alexei's room with Mama. Our room was near my brother's, and Marie and I could hear the *starets's* low, quiet voice. Alexei's moans quickly subsided.

"Is it better now?" we heard Father Grigory ask. Alexei answered calmly, "Yes, yes, much better."

Mama and Father Grigory came out of the room, closing the door softly behind them. Right there in the corridor Mama fell on her knees, weeping, and kissed Father Grigory's hands. Assured that the tsarevich was sleeping and in no pain, Papa left with them to talk and drink tea.

Father Grigory stayed for a few days in Peterhof before we traveled back to Tsarskoe Selo for a short time and then continued to the hunting lodges in Poland. Mama really didn't want to go back to Spala; she had such terrible memories of Alexei's injuries the previous year. Father Grigory did not travel with us. He never did, and I didn't understand why. Aunt Olga tried to explain it.

"Your father and your mother, especially, are very fond of the *starets*. She truly believes he's a holy man and the only one who can help Alexei. But there are many others who dislike him and mistrust him. Some even think he is a devil—Grandmère Marie, for instance, believes he is somehow playing tricks. And so your parents have decided it's better not to make too much of him in public."

"What do you think of him, Aunt Olga?" I asked.

"It's not for me to say," she replied, but she was not looking at me as she spoke.

"You think he's a devil, don't you?"

"If he helps your brother, who suffers so very much, then it doesn't matter what I think."

She refused to say more.

The hunting season in Poland passed without much happening, except to the poor stags, and OTMA counted the days until we would board the train for Livadia. The *Standart* would be there, and Lieutenant Voronov. Mama would be more relaxed, and there would be lots of interesting visitors, like the emir of Bukhara and his red-bearded court.

But once again Papa had to deal with Romanov family problems. Our cousin Maria Pavlovna, Dmitri's older sister, had left her Swedish husband and gone to live with her father in France. Her father was Papa's uncle, Grand Duke Pavel Alexandrovich, who asked Papa's permission to arrange for Maria Pavlovna's divorce, explaining that she was ill.

I scarcely knew Dmitri's sister, and I wasn't much concerned with whether or not Papa would allow her to divorce her husband. It seemed odd, though, that Papa should have to decide who was allowed to marry or get divorced, even if he *was* the Emperor and Autocrat of All the Russias and God's representative on earth. Didn't Papa have enough to do without that?

When I told Aunt Olga what I thought, she smiled and said, "I understand why you think as you do, my dear little Nastya, but that's simply the way it is. When you're older, I will tell you my own story."

"Why not tell me now, dear aunt? I'm twelve, and I think I'm quite old enough to hear it."

But she shook her head and hugged me, whispering, "Someday, but not quite yet."

Being told that I was too young to hear something obviously very important and interesting was maddening—and made me determined to find out what it was.

Then in October, while we were at Livadia, we learned that our cousin Irina was going to marry Felix Yussoupov.

We hadn't seen Irina since the previous spring, when Dmitri was my escort at the celebration but flirted madly with Irina. Felix was Dmitri's best friend—they were often together—and Felix had also been flirting with Irina.

Mama was horrified when she heard about Irina's plans. "I would never allow any of my daughters to have anything at all to do with Felix," she said firmly. "And certainly not marry him!"

Olga did not want to talk about it.

The more I see of these engagements, the less I want one. I'll soon be eighteen, and I know my parents are thinking of a suitable husband for me. But I am more than ever in love with my dear, sweet friend. I don't need to name him. And he has made clear his love for me. He knows as well as I do that marriage is impossible, Father would never consent to it, but we have promised ourselves and each other that we will cherish each day, each hour, that we can be together until it is no longer possible. How I dread that day.

Olga celebrated her eighteenth birthday in Livadia at a party with a splendid luncheon with dancing afterward, not in the palace but on the quarterdeck of the *Standart*. Naturally, Lieutenant Voronov was among her partners, but she danced with him only twice. I know they would have danced every dance if they could, but they behaved prudently and danced with others. I could see that he was always searching for her, and her eyes followed him wherever he went, but unless I missed something, there was no chance for them to slip out of sight.

I wondered who else in our family knew about her real feelings. Surely others must have noticed how she glowed like a dozen candles when he was nearby. I should have guessed it would be Aunt Olga.

The only person in whom I can confide is Aunt Olga. She brought it up herself just yesterday. She said that Mother and Father are aware of my "attachment." I asked if they want to end it, and she said it is very likely. I began to cry, and she was so kind and understanding and told me something I didn't know about her marriage to Petya. She has never loved him, but Grandmère Marie insisted on the marriage, because she didn't want Aunt Olga to leave Russia. It was a disaster from the beginning. "Our marriage is unconsummated," she said, and that shocked me. I didn't know what to say.

I wouldn't have known what to say either, because I didn't know what *unconsummated* meant. It was probably another word to add to my list of words not to be used.

Possibly, I thought, it had something to do with what happened between married people, and that was a totally forbidden subject. Whenever I asked a question—and I had lots of questions—Mama always told me the same thing: "Time enough for you to know all that, my girlie, when you are grown up and ready to marry." Don't even say the word! Better not even to think it!

Shura, my nurse, had explained to me the changes that a girl's body goes through as she becomes a woman, the "visits from Madame Becker," but nothing beyond that. Marie was also completely uninformed, and our older sisters were not much help. Tatiana explained how babies grow inside their mothers, because she remembered when Mama was expecting Alexei, but not even Olga would say how the babies got there.

Expecting was a proper word, according to Tatiana, but *pregnant* was not to be used, along with *bosom* and *mistress*. I made up a little song: "If a *mistress* has a *bosom* she might be *pregnant*." It had the desired effect—Tatiana turned red and called me *Shvibzik*.

Now I had a new word to spring on her: *unconsummated*.

Alexei, doing something silly and reckless, fell off a chair. This time he hit his knee, it began to swell all the way down to his ankle, and he couldn't walk. The pain was even worse than usual. The new doctor, Derevenko, prescribed hot mud baths, and eventually he did get better—whether it was the mud or Father Grigory's prayers, I couldn't say—but we stayed in Livadia longer than usual.

Olga, of course, didn't mind at all that we lingered in Livadia, because that meant she would see more of Pavel Voronov. She didn't even bother to pretend that she was not in love with him, and I was a little embarrassed to read in her notebook such romantic stuff as *My tender darling smiled, and I could read the love in his eyes,* and *My dear, sweet friend rejoiced when I told him we could meet for a walk in the rose garden.*

But the roses soon faded, and we left Livadia to return to Tsarskoe Selo when Alexei's pain was somewhat better. Then something went awfully wrong for Olga. Her eyes were red and swollen from weeping, and she wouldn't say what had happened. I was sure it had something to do with Pavel.

Marie asked me, "What do you think has upset Olya?" I shrugged and said I didn't know. Marie said, "Well, let's ask her."

I was with Marie when she spoke to Olga. Tatiana was there, too, also waiting for the explanation.

"It's quite simple," Olga said sadly. She sat on the edge of her bed, smoothing her dress over her knees, pressing a row of lace that would not lie flat. "Mother and Father have informed me that I must break off my friendship with Lieutenant Voronov. He has become engaged to Olga Kleinmichel."

"Olga Kleinmichel!" Marie exclaimed. "She's one of Mama's ladies-in-waiting, and she's not half as pretty as you, Olya!"

I nudged Marie and whispered for her to hush. Tatiana bit her lip.

Olga tried to smile and ended up choking back tears. "It really doesn't matter. They're friends. Her aunt has an estate near Livadia, and he's been spending time there. He isn't in love with her, I know that much, but I don't know if she loves him or not. They're to be married at the beginning of February, and then he is being given a leave of two months, for them to travel.

They're to live in St. Petersburg, I understand. Pasha"—she corrected herself—"Lieutenant Voronov has been reassigned to the yacht *Alexandria*. No more *Standart*. I think he's sad about that. He loves the *Standart!*"

She stopped and dabbed at her eyes with a handkerchief. Marie, who hated to see anyone crying and unhappy, ran to Olga and hugged her. Tatiana, arms folded across her chest, frowned and said sternly, "You didn't think Mother and Father would allow it to go on any longer, did you? And you didn't exactly keep it a secret."

"Oh, I knew we'd never be allowed to marry!" Olga said. "But Aunt Olga has never been allowed to marry the man she loves, and no one seems to be terribly upset about that."

"But she's married to Uncle Petya!" Marie said, wide-eyed.

"The marriage is unconsummated," I said, pleased that I knew something Marie didn't. I instantly regretted it. All three of my sisters stared at me.

"It's what?" Marie asked innocently.

"How do you know that?" Tatiana demanded.

"How do you even know the word?" Olga asked, and I could see that she might have caught on how I learned it—by reading her notebook.

"It's just one of those words," I said, shrugging, and quickly changed the subject. "Anyway, what were you saying about Aunt Olga?"

"We're not supposed to talk about it," Tatiana said.

"But we *are* talking about it, aren't we?" Olga said. "So let's just say it: Aunt Olga doesn't love Petya, and she never did. Grandmère Marie wanted her to marry him, and so she did. But they never—" Olga hesitated and looked helplessly at Tatiana.

"Lived as husband and wife," Tatiana said, completing her sentence. "More like brother and sister."

"You mean they never kissed?" Marie asked.

"Exactly," said Olga, sounding relieved. "They never kissed."

"And that's what 'unconsummated' means?"

"Well, yes," Tatiana said—unconvincingly, I thought.

"Who is it she really loves?" Marie wanted to know.

"A cavalry officer," Olga said, sniffling. "Nikolai Kulikovsky."

"But you said Aunt Olga isn't allowed to marry the man she really loves and wants to kiss," I said, determined to get to the truth of the matter. "Why not?"

"Because she's still married to Uncle Petya, and he won't give her a divorce."

"So Uncle Petya and Aunt Olga live separately," Tatiana explained.

"And she sees Nikolai Kulikovsky as much as she wants," Olga said. "Mama says it's shocking."

Marie sighed. "I wonder if she kisses him."

Olga started to say something, but Tatiana gave her a sharp look and Olga kept silent.

"I'm confused by all of this," I announced.

"Good," Tatiana said. "I'm glad to hear that, Nastya. This is not a proper subject for a girlie your age, and I suggest we talk about something else."

I hated it when Tatiana called me a girlie. That's what Mama called us. Tatiana is only four years older than I am, and we nicknamed her "the Governess" because she is so bossy. I did not think that gave her the right to call us girlies. I decided to say nothing but gave her a *look*. As for kissing and being unconsummated, I would have to wait for my next chance at Olga's notebook for more information on the subject.

CHAPTER 8

Out in Society

ST. PETERSBURG, WINTER 1914

apa took my sisters and me to spend Christmas Eve with Grandmère Marie. Aunt Xenia and Uncle Sandro came to Anichkov Palace with their daughter, Irina, who was planning to marry Felix Yussoupov in February, and their six uncivilized sons.

Preparations for Christmas had exhausted Mama. "Baby and I will stay at home and have a cozy supper together, and the rest of you can have a gay time and come back and tell us all about it."

I knew that exhaustion was just an excuse. She and Grandmère were extremely polite to each other, but the chill between them seemed to have increased another few degrees. Olga said it was because each felt she should be the most important woman in Papa's life. "Mother thinks that Grandmère Marie treats Father as if he was still a boy, and

Grandmère thinks that Mother has too much to say about how Father rules Russia."

Also, Mama could not bear to be around Aunt Xenia and "her brood," as Mama called all those big, noisy boys, when she herself had produced only four daughters and one sickly son.

When Olga was born, cannons boomed one hundred times to announce to the Russian people that a daughter had been born to the tsar and tsaritsa. Mama and Papa were happy to have such a healthy daughter. A year and half later Tatiana arrived, and again the cannons boomed one hundred times. Our parents were happy to welcome a second daughter. Two years later, Marie appeared, and they were grateful for another daughter, but they must have thought, *Surely the next time.*

But when the next time came two years later, it was a fourth daughter, *me*, Anastasia, and everyone stopped pretending to be happy or grateful. Poor Mama! It was her duty to provide a male heir to the throne. She cried and cried—one of my nurses told me this—although Papa didn't show how disappointed he was. Mama must have felt that she absolutely *had* to have a baby boy the next time. There had to be a *next time!*

So when Alexei was born, the cannons boomed three hundred and one times, and the whole country went mad with joy. But Alexei was not strong and healthy like Xenia's sons. Every time he hurt himself, Mama feared he might die and there would be no heir. No one blamed Mama for feeling envious of Aunt Xenia, no matter how oafish those boys were.

Anichkov Palace was beautiful, the Christmas tree was lovely, the twelve traditional Russian dishes were served, and lots of French dishes, too, including another awful jellied fish that I managed to avoid. Irina and her fiancé, Felix, were there early in the evening. Felix was certainly handsome, but in my opinion not as handsome as Dmitri. After they had gone on to the Yussoupovs' palace for another gathering, Aunt Xenia told us about the plans for Irina's wedding in February. They'd decided to have it there in Anichkov Palace. Aunt Xenia was delighted that they had somehow gotten hold of a lace veil that once belonged to Marie Antoinette. I don't know why that made her so happy, considering what happened to the French queen in the end.

Before we left for Tsarskoe Selo, Grandmère Marie reminded us of the Winter Ball she was giving in our honor—as though we could forget! She'd been planning it, and we'd been talking about it, for weeks.

"You young ladies need to get out into society more than you do," she'd said, and Papa winced, because it was Mama who didn't like going out into society. "I shall expect you to dress in elegant gowns for this occasion, and to wear your finest jewels."

"We'll all have on our glass slippers," Tatiana said, laughing.

"And I'll be sure that their coach doesn't turn into a pumpkin at the stroke of midnight," Papa said.

I wanted to wear a real ball gown, like Olga's and Tatiana's, but I was sure Mama would insist that Marie and I dress like "girlies" and wear our usual white dresses. Tatiana was "out" now, sixteen and allowed to wear her hair up and gowns to her ankles. But when I complained to Mama, she said, "Don't be in such a hurry to grow up, Nastya. There will be plenty of time for ball gowns and dancing and midnight suppers as you get older, I promise you."

That's what she *always* said.

But Grandmère Marie, without telling Mama, ordered beautiful dresses for all four of us. Marie's and mine were ivory satin, and Olga's and Tatiana's were deep rose with more sophisticated necklines. We loved our dresses, and Mama pretended she wasn't annoyed that Grandmère had gone around her and got us dresses she liked.

Invitations to the Winter Ball were delivered to hundreds of people—"All the court society of St. Petersburg," Aunt Olga told us—and almost all accepted the invitation. Everyone loved our grandmother, because the dowager empress was always lively and gay and loved parties and balls and everything social. Mama didn't enjoy these things at all, preferring to stay at Tsarskoe Selo with Anya, playing piano duets and chatting and embroidering.

I had always said that I hated dancing, but that wasn't exactly true. Dancing a mazurka on the deck of the *Standart* with an officer was one thing. So was swooping through the Boston with Dmitri. But trying to follow a clumsy boy who managed to step all over my feet was something else entirely. All six of Aunt Xenia's barbarians were present. I was disappointed that Dmitri hadn't come. He might have wanted to dance the Boston, and I would have had to refuse or risk causing a scandal.

Mama came with us to Anichkov Palace, but just before the supper was served she said she had a headache and felt too ill to stay longer, and she was taken back to Tsarskoe Selo. Papa stayed on until the ball ended. It was well after midnight when we were driven in a sleigh to our train. Papa sipped tea and listened to Marie and Tatiana and me discussing our dancing partners—the ones with sweaty hands, the ones wearing too much cologne, the elderly gentleman with the dyed mustache. Olga said hardly anything.

I tried my best to act happy, for the sake of Grandmère Marie, but it was impossible. I think of him night and day. I know that I must try to forget him but I cannot, and I don't want to. May the Lord grant happiness to my beloved Pasha. He and Olga Kleinmichel are to be married in February. It is painful and sad. May he be happy, but I cannot.

The ball at Anichkov Palace was the beginning of the winter season in St. Petersburg, and that meant Sundays with Aunt Olga and her lovely parties. The rest of the week we were at Tsarskoe Selo with our tutors, going out every day for walks with Papa no matter how cold it was, bundled up in our warmest woolen stockings and fur jackets and mittens.

I did as little as I possibly could with Monsieur Gilliard and Mr. Gibbes and Pyotr Petrov. Now that she was eighteen, Olga no longer had to endure classes, except to practice her languages. Mama insisted that she be fluent in three languages: French, English, and Russian. "And you may have to acquire a fourth some day," Mama explained. "All of you may."

We understood what was implied: When we married, we might have to learn the language of our husband's country. The very day Olga turned eighteen, everyone began gossiping about a possible engagement. There had been suggestions that perhaps the English boy, Edward, Prince of Wales, would be a good match. He was a great-grandson of Queen Victoria, and for that reason Mama rather liked the idea. Mama had been very close to the queen.

"Father called me to his study," Olga told us. "I tried to tell him that I could not imagine ever living in England. And I remembered meeting Edward when we visited Uncle Bertie six years ago, and I didn't think much of him then."

"Ugh," said Tatiana, making a face. "I remember him, too. He was very unlikable, I thought. He had a string of names, but everyone called him David."

"He was nice looking, though, wasn't he?" asked Marie, who was inclined to find something good about almost everybody. "And smiled a lot and had straight teeth."

"He was a pig," I announced. "He snorted like this when he laughed at his own stupid jokes." I demonstrated an English pig-snort.

"How can you remember that, Nastya? You were only six or seven."

"I always remember people who make bad jokes."

Olga wore a pained smile. "Father probably agrees with you. He finally admitted that the more they heard about Edward, the less they believed he would be appropriate. Anyway, the Prince of Wales is no longer a candidate. And neither is Prince Arthur of Connaught, because he married someone else in October! And Sergei Georgievich, eighth Duke of Leuchtenberg, seems to have been taken off the list, but I'm not sure why. At least he's Russian!"

The problem was that there weren't many appropriate husbands for grand duchesses. We were not supposed to marry

men of a lower rank, and it was not possible to marry someone with no rank at all, no matter how wonderful, intelligent,
and kind he might be—like Pavel Voronov. Olga would be
the first OTMA to marry, and she had to follow the rules. I
was glad that I would be the last. Maybe the rules would have
changed by the time my turn came. Maybe by then no one
would care—I could marry the court juggler, if we had one.
Or not marry at all.

We drove in two motorcars from Tsarskoe Selo to Anichkov
Palace for Irina's wedding to Felix Felixovich Yussoupov. She
refused to wear a traditional Russian court dress with long,
split sleeves, the style that my sisters and I have been photo-
graphed in dozens of times. Instead, she chose a modern wedding gown, a long white satin dress embroidered in silver with a
train, very simple and elegant, and a diamond and crystal tiara
that was Felix's gift to her. Irina arrived at the chapel looking
so beautiful I could not stop admiring her.

But where was Felix? No one had seen him. Had he changed
his mind?

"It's the lace veil," Aunt Olga said. "The one that belonged
to Marie Antoinette. I warned Xenia that it was bad luck." I
didn't know if she was serious.

At last the missing bridegroom was discovered, stuck in
the old palace elevator. Papa and the always practical Tatiana
finally managed to free him. He looked elegant, too, but in a
more traditional way: white trousers with a black frock coat,
the collar stitched with gold, and a row of nine gold buttons
marching down the front.

Papa escorted Irina to the chapel. As a wedding present he gave them a bag of twenty-nine diamonds, each as big as a cherry. Felix was probably the richest man in Russia, even richer than Papa—he owned fifty-seven palaces, four of them in St. Petersburg—and now he was twenty-nine diamonds richer. Being so wealthy apparently made up for the fact that Felix had no rank. None at all! Irina was the granddaughter of a tsar, but now none of her future children would inherit titles.

This was the society wedding of the season. Every detail was perfect. Grandmère Marie, delighted to be at the wedding of her eldest granddaughter, charmed everyone. Aunt Xenia seemed tearful, which I suppose mothers are when their daughters marry. Aunt Olga was her usual merry self, making sure everything went off flawlessly. Mama wasn't smiling, but then she hardly ever smiled at big public events. Olga looked sad— she must have been thinking again of Pavel. I wished she would get over him. Tatiana attracted quite a lot of attention from the young men, because in my opinion she was even more beautiful than Irina. And Marie, who loved weddings, announced, "When I am grown up, I want to marry a Russian soldier and have twenty children!"

Her enormous blue eyes—"Marie's saucers"—were shining with the vision of all those little ones clinging to her skirts, squalling for attention. I thought she must be crazy. Where could she have gotten such an idea?

On the last Sunday before Butter Week and our last afternoon party until after Easter, I lay in Aunt Olga's sitting room with my eyes closed. When my sisters were breathing deeply, or pretending to, I got up quietly and tiptoed into my aunt's bedroom. She sat writing at a little desk, her pen racing across the paper.

"My dear Nastya!" she said when I appeared. "You're supposed to be resting your eyes."

"I'm too restless to rest my eyes," I explained. "And I suspect that you don't really rest yours, either."

She smiled. I loved my aunt's smile, because she smiled with her eyes and not just her lips. "You're right. But when I need a little time alone, I get it by sending everyone to bed! Now sit, please, and we'll talk." She patted the chaise longue beside her desk. "Put your feet up. You may be dancing quite a lot this afternoon."

I leaned back in the white velvet–covered chaise piled with silk pillows and gazed around. I loved this room—simple, but rather romantic. On her desk was a small, framed portrait of a man in a uniform. When she saw me looking at it, she picked up the portrait and handed it to me. I didn't recognize him; but it wasn't Uncle Petya. The man was very good-looking, and a lot younger than Petya.

"Who is it?" I asked, although I was fairly sure it was the cavalry officer.

"That's my friend Nikolai Kulikovsky," she said. "Though I believe your mother would disagree, I think you're old enough for some frank talk, and you're unlikely to get it from your parents. I adore Nicky and I'm very fond of Alix, but there are subjects I suspect they avoid. They want to protect you and your sisters, to keep you innocent. I can't fault them—maybe if I had daughters, I'd do the same. But . . ."

She shrugged, watching me closely. "Kolya is my lover."

No one had ever said such a thing to me. "Your lover?" I stammered. "But what about Uncle Petya?"

"Petya is a decent man, but he prefers men to women," she said. This made no sense to me, but I nodded as though I understood. "I had no idea what that meant when I married him—I was very naive. Our wedding was beautiful—lots of satin and diamonds and magnificent gifts. But afterward . . ." She trailed off, gazing out the window. "We have never lived as man and wife."

I handed the portrait back to her, and she set it in its place on her desk. A word leaped into my head: *unconsummated*, the word in my sister's diary. It must mean "never living together," I thought, and nodded again, and she told me the story.

"Soon after we were married, I was appointed honorary commander-in-chief of a Hussar regiment. Two years later, my brother Misha introduced me to the regiment's acting commander, Colonel Kulikovsky. Almost immediately, Kolya and I fell deeply in love. I asked Petya for a divorce, but he refused. Then I went to your Papa and asked him to grant me a divorce. He told me I had to wait, and I've been waiting ever since. Petya lives at the other end of the palace, and Kolya lives here with me." She saw my astonished expression. "Yes, dear Nastya, we are lovers, and we live in sin, because we are not allowed to marry. And this is a secret. Do you understand? A secret that most people know, but we do not discuss it. I know that you will say nothing."

"I promise," I said, thrilled that Aunt Olga trusted me enough to confide in me, but wondering, *Does Mama know all this?*

Later, we changed into the dresses Mama had sent for us from Tsarskoe Selo with our maids and went down to the palace ballroom, where the other guests were gathered. Uncle Petya stopped by briefly, greeted us, and disappeared. When tea was served, a buxom, florid-faced girl named Katya sat down beside me. Katya was a year or so older than I and very talkative.

"Well," said Katya, starting at the outside of her heaping plate and working her way around it, "I see that Duke Peter Ivanovich has put in his appearance for the afternoon and gone on his way."

"Yes," I said, and took a tiny bite of a *pirozhok*.

"Olga Alexandrovna is such a lovely woman. It's too bad she's stuck with him."

"Um-hmm," I said.

Katya paused for a sip of tea. "They've been married for more than ten years and he still refuses to give her a divorce. Such a pity that she can't marry the colonel."

So Aunt Olga is right! It's a secret that everyone knows! I looked away, studying the design on the honey cake. But Katya was waiting for me to say something, and so I murmured, "How do you know that?"

"Oh, my dear Anastasia Nikolaevna!" she said, staring at me as though I were a simpleton. "Why, everyone knows! It's been the court gossip for the longest time. I'm amazed you haven't heard of it, since she's your aunt." She dropped her voice to a whisper. "They say he's . . . *you* know!"

I was actually relieved when my cousin Nikita, who had once falsely accused me of biting him, challenged me to a game of dominoes. I was even happy when Mama's friend Baroness

Buxhoeveden arrived to escort us back to Tsarskoe Selo. We kissed our aunt and made her promise that she would come with us to Livadia.

"Without fail!" we cried, and she replied, "Yes, yes, of course, my darlings!"

CHAPTER 9

Visitors and Visits

LIVADIA, SPRING 1914

I loved being back at Livadia, where every day was different and so much more amusing. We rode horses up into the pine forests, and my mare behaved docilely. Papa plunged into the chilly water every day, but OTMA unanimously declared that it wasn't yet warm enough for swimming. I had more tennis lessons.

"You must keep your eye on the ball, Anastasia Nikolaevna!" the tutor shouted from across the net, and I shouted back that I *was* keeping my eye on the ball, but that my arm was too short or my racket too long, and that was why I so often failed to hit it.

Visitors came down from St. Petersburg. Uncle Sandro and Aunt Xenia arrived with their six sons and a lot of noise and nuisance. My swinish cousin, Nikita—actually, they were all swine, in my opinion, but Nikita was the worst—lurked around, gleefully bragging that he enjoyed spying on me.

Papa's cousin Grand Duke Georgii Mikhailovich and his wife, Princess Maria, came from their estate nearby with their two daughters, Nina and Xenia. Uncle Georgii was a kind and gentle man, but Mama described his wife as a "difficult woman." Princess Maria was from Greece and never missed a chance to tell us how much she disliked living in Russia.

Normally, I would have enjoyed having girls my age around, but not those two. We weren't often together, which was fortunate, because I detested them both. Nina was two days younger than I, but she was already much taller and slenderer, and she thought that made her superior. Xenia accused me of cheating at a card game, and I called her a liar.

Nina said, "Nobody likes you, Nastya, or your mother! My mother says the empress is a *hypochondriac*, always complaining about being ill, and there's nothing wrong with her except a bad temper. My mother says your mother is pretentious and condescending and she's under the power of that awful Rasputin and she'll ruin the country."

I had no idea what a *hypochondriac* was, but I understood the rest of it, and that's when I slapped her and pulled her hair.

The girls ran to their mother. Nina claimed that I'd also scratched her, but that was another lie, though I wished I had. Princess Maria immediately carried the story to Mama, who asked me what had happened. I cried and said I couldn't tell her. "If you won't tell me, then I shall have to punish you, Nastya."

Still I refused, and I was punished by not being allowed to come to any more meals while they were our guests. The punishment suited me just fine.

"I'm taking my girls to England in June for their health," Princess Maria told us before they finally left. *Good*, I thought. *Maybe you should just stay there.*

But what Nina said about Mama gnawed at me. I hated my cousin for it, but I couldn't help wondering: Was any of it true? That nobody liked my mother? That she was pretentious and condescending? And what was that other word she used— *hypo-something?* Was it like a mistress? That obviously couldn't be possible, but it certainly wasn't good.

Aunt Olga had come to Livadia, as she'd promised, and I decided to ask her the question. "What's a hypo-something, can you please tell me?"

My aunt looked puzzled. "I don't know what you mean. Where did you hear it?"

"I can't say." I tried to remember the word, but I could not go beyond the first two syllables.

Aunt Olga shrugged. "I need more clues," she said. "If you tell me who spoke the word, I may be able to figure it out."

Why not just tell her? "Nina," I said. When I thought of Nina, another syllable came to me. "Hypochon—" I began.

Aunt Olga's eyebrows lifted. "Hypochondriac? Is that the word?"

I nodded.

Aunt Olga hesitated, frowning. "Did it have something to do with your mama?"

I nodded again.

"All right," Aunt Olga said. "I'll tell you what it means. A hypochondriac is someone who imagines she has a serious illness when in fact she doesn't, and she spends all her time worrying about her symptoms and perhaps staying in bed."

That did sound a lot like Mama. Could my mother be imagining that she was ill? But why would she do that? Maybe Nina was right, but I did not regret slapping her or pulling her hair. "Do you think Mama is one?" I asked.

"No, I don't," Aunt Olga said firmly. "But I do think she is a very nervous person who dislikes being out in society and worries a great deal about your brother, and this often makes her feel ill and weak. I also think Nina is a badly spoiled child and should be banished forever, along with her sister and her mother, whom I have never cared for. You needn't mention this to anyone, though. Understood, my darling Nastya? I've heard that you behaved badly to Nina and consequently you are under some sort of punishment. Is that true?"

I admitted that I had and it was.

"Well, I hope you smacked her good and hard, because she surely deserved it. Now come with me, and we'll take a walk together, shall we?"

There was more unpleasantness that spring. Mama, who always seemed so much happier when we were at Livadia, now seemed not to be happy at all, and it had something to do with Anya. Anya was with us—when was Anya *not* with us?—but she and Mama were not getting along. Marie and I tried to guess the reason, but we could not. Tatiana probably knew, because she spent more time with Mama than any of the rest of us did, but Tatiana wasn't talking.

That left Olga's notebook.

Who would ever believe this: Mother has become mortally jealous
and suspicious of Father and Vyrubova! Anya goes for long walks
with him, sits and talks with him, even plays tennis with him,
and although she plays badly, he seems to find that amusing. Anya
told someone, who told someone else, and Tanya heard it, that
Mother is so often ill, and does so much praying and weeping, that
Father is in need of feminine companionship and Anya is happy to
provide it. Mother is lonely and deeply depressed. She and Father
have always treated Anya like a member of the family, and now
Mother feels very bitter toward her for betraying her friendship.
Imagine, being jealous of a fat, frumpy woman like Anya!

I was shocked by what I read and full of questions and
annoyed because I couldn't say anything to anybody without
revealing how I knew.

That was not all I read that day in Olga's notebook. I had
promised myself—several times, in fact—that I wouldn't read it
anymore, that I would give it up forever. But when I realized how
much went on that I would never have known about otherwise,
things kept from me because I was "too young," or subjects that
it didn't seem proper to discuss with a girl who did not yet have
a bosom, then I knew that I could not give it up. Not yet.

I did, though, continually worry about getting caught.
I had had a couple of narrow escapes, usually when Tatiana
appeared unexpectedly and looked at me suspiciously when I
obviously had no good reason to be in their room. Someday
I surely *would* be caught, and I would be in disgrace. But that
wasn't the worst. The worst was that I would no longer know
what was going on.

A few pages on, I read this:

I had no idea when Foreign Minister Sazonov arrived in frock coat and striped trousers three days ago from St. Petersburg that I was the main subject of his visit. He has convinced my parents that Crown Prince Carol of Romania is a good choice of husband for me and a desirable match politically: "The marriage will make Romania a closer friend to Russia." I know it is my duty to help my country, but marriage seems a ridiculous way to do it. Isn't there a more sensible way?

Father was very kind when he asked me to consider it seriously, but of course I wept. I know that I must stop thinking about Pasha. If only I had been allowed to marry the man I loved (still love) so deeply! Nevertheless, I have agreed to visit Romania in June, to spend time with Carol and his parents. His mother is another of Queen Victoria's grandchildren, so that makes it rather cozy for Mother. They were at my sixteenth birthday ball, and I danced twice with Carol but I hardly remember him—I was much too enchanted with Pavel to pay any attention. I do remember thinking that Carol seemed foolish and immature (he's two years older) and not worth my attention.

The trip to Romania next month is "just a diplomatic visit," Father says, but I suspect arrangements are already in progress for an engagement. How I dread it.

From then on, all anyone could talk about was the coming trip to the port city of Constanta and the "diplomatic visit" to Crown Prince Carol and his family. We would travel on the *Standart*, and that made Olga all the more unhappy because it would remind her of Lieutenant Voronov. Olga was so gloomy, it was almost impossible to talk to her. I tried to show her on the schoolroom map that Romania was right next to the Ukraine and that Constanta was on the Black Sea. "You could sail across to visit us in Livadia whenever you choose!"

I thought my suggestion sounded very reasonable, but it just upset Olga even more. "I wouldn't be living in Constanta!" she said. "I'd be in Bucharest, the capital, and that's a long, long way from the coast. Nastya, don't you understand? When I'd come home, I'd be a foreigner in my own country! I'm a Russian, and I mean to remain a Russian! And Father promised not to make me marry anyone I don't want to marry."

"What does Mama say?" I asked.

"Oh, you can just imagine! Mother's upset with me again. She says she wants me to be happy, but she also reminds me that we all have certain duties and obligations as grand duchesses. She says that she was just fortunate that she didn't have to marry some oaf and could marry the best and kindest man in the world. I doubt that I'll be so lucky!"

Olga and the rest of us know well the story of how Mama became the wife of "the best and kindest man in the world." She and Papa met for the first time when she was twelve years old and had come to Russia for the wedding of her sister Ella to Papa's uncle, Grand Duke Sergei. Papa was sixteen. They met again five years later when she came to visit Ella and stayed for several weeks. "Your mother was so beautiful," Papa has told us. "I fell in love with her immediately." It took time, though, for everything to work out. Other handsome young men were courting Mama, and then I suppose Kschessinskaya, the dancer, came into the picture. But there was a much bigger problem: Mama was a devout Lutheran, and she felt she couldn't change her faith to Orthodoxy—even for love. Fortunately for all of us, Papa was persistent, and Mama changed her mind. They became engaged in April 1894 and planned to marry the following January, but our grandfather, Tsar Alexander, died suddenly in November. Papa and Mama felt they had to marry immediately. The wedding was exactly one week after Grandfather's funeral.

I just hoped things would go well for Olga and end happily for everyone, as they did for our parents.

We sailed from Yalta on the *Standart* one evening in the middle of June, and the next morning we arrived at Constanta. A band was playing on the quay, flags were flying, boats shot plumes of water into the air, and the artillery on the hill above the city boomed a salute.

Old King Carol and Queen Elisabeth and the whole Romanian royal family were there to meet us. After the official greetings—they're all pretty much alike everywhere—and a service at the cathedral came the private luncheon in a pavilion by the sea with just the two families. In the afternoon Mama and Papa invited the king and queen, Prince Ferdinand and Princess Marie, and Crown Prince Carol and a slew of brothers and sisters to board the *Standart*.

The white-haired queen, who was even older than our grandmother, made it a point to speak to me. She was a poetess who wrote under the name "Carmen Sylva," and when I said that I liked to read poetry, she promised to give me one of her books. I was watching Olga, who was chatting away with Carol. Olga was always good at being charming in such situations, no matter how she really felt.

"What do you think?" I whispered to Marie.

"She doesn't like him," Marie replied. "You can see that she's just putting on an act."

"I mean, what do you think of *him*?"

"Well, he's not bad looking, I'll say that much."

"But his hair, Mashka! It looks like a mop. I don't think he combs it."

The day wore on. We had to witness a military review. Our photograph was taken with us wearing our big hats. We attended a formal tea. By then Mama was exhausted, and Olga was sick of being gawked at by ministers and aristocrats and ordinary Romanians who were probably wondering if the Russian grand duchess might be their future queen.

At eight o'clock in the evening, we changed clothes *again* (that made it the third time) and went ashore for the gala banquet. Papa sat at the center of a very long table, with Queen Elisabeth on one side and Princess Marie on the other. Mama sat between King Carol and Prince Ferdinand. Olga, of course, had to sit beside Carol. I was far down the table, stuck between a couple of his sisters. I'd sat through countless state dinners before, and this one was just as dull as all the rest. Toasts were made—both Papa and the king spoke French, and so did everybody else. Olga struggled bravely to keep up a conversation with Carol. When the dinner was finally over and everybody had greeted everybody else, we returned to the yacht. The

Standart was leaving that same night to sail to Odessa.

"Farewell, Romania!" Olga cried as a brilliant display of fireworks lit up the night sky and as we got ready to sail. "And I'm never coming back!"

Marie and I looked at each other and laughed. "Guess we know what Olya decided. Poor Carol will be left with a broken heart!"

The next morning we were in Odessa for Papa to review the troops, the day after in Kishinev in Bessarabia for the unveiling of a monument, and three days later we were back in Tsarskoe Selo after a very long, very hot train ride.

What an impossible person! Every time we were together, Crown Prince Carol tried to impress me with jokes that were not in the least funny. He told them in French, but his accent is so awful that I may not have understood them. He would tell his joke and then laugh uproariously while I sat there with a fixed smile. This happened several times. Meanwhile, I searched frantically for something to talk about—a book he'd read, a trip he'd taken, a subject that interested him. Nothing!

I can't imagine spending another evening with him, let alone my whole life, and I've told Mother and Father NO NO NO to Crown Prince Carol. I also told them this: I will never leave my country, even if it means that I do not marry.

She didn't write in the notebook what Mama and Papa had to say, but it was easy to see that she was in a vile mood.

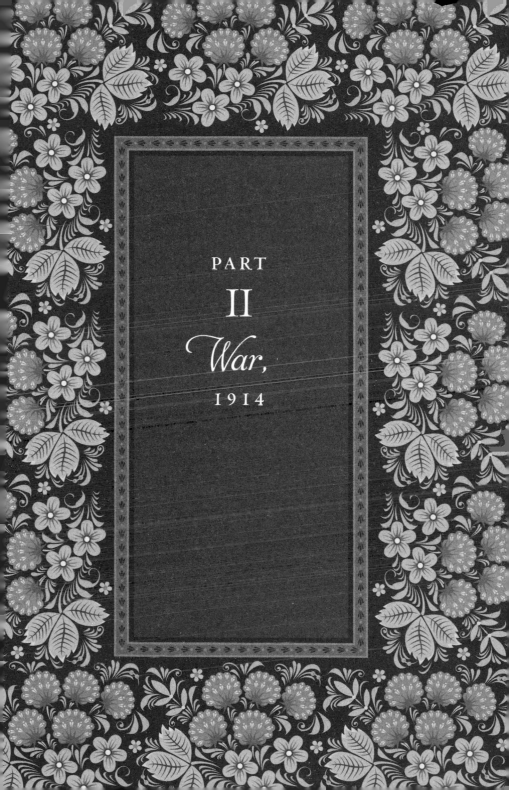

PART

II

War,

1914

CHAPTER 10

Things Go Badly

atiana turned seventeen, Marie had her fifteenth birthday, and I was thirteen at last! This, I decided, was the beginning of my *real life*, although I wasn't sure what that would be, or even what I *wanted* it to be—just as long as it was more exciting than the life I had when I was twelve.

Every summer we spent a week by the edge of the sea in Peterhof, at our dacha. We never stayed in the Great Palace, which Mama said was just too big, but in the Lower Palace, which reminded her of places she used to stay in England. I was born in the Lower Palace.

I loved spending my birthday at Peterhof. Aunt Olga came with us, and Anya, too. Whatever had upset Mama had been patched over. Dr. Botkin brought his children, Gleb and Tatiana. I was happy to see Gleb, who was good-humored and sweet as always and, I believed, truly had forgiven me for joking about his becoming a smelly *starets.*

Before luncheon we all went for a walk on the beach, looking for pretty shells and interesting stones. Gleb found a piece of sea glass, polished smooth by sand and water, and presented it to me with a low bow. "A birthday gift for Your Imperial Highness," he said earnestly, and kissed my hand. I was surprised that he would be so formal and serious, and, without thinking, I kicked sand at him. Poor Gleb—I was always saying or doing the wrong thing and then having to apologize. The sea glass was a deep emerald green, almost the same color as his eyes, and I thanked him and put it away with my other little treasures.

At my birthday luncheon I received a thirteenth diamond for my necklace as well as other gifts, including one I disliked immensely: another porcelain doll, this one with real hair and a French wardrobe, sent by Cousin Willy! I wished somebody would please tell the man that I was now thirteen and practically a woman and had no need for dolls, even beautifully dressed ones. I held two fingers over my upper lip like a mustache and imitated the stiff-legged march of Kaiser Wilhelm's troops. Papa laughed, but Mama pursed her lips and said I should not be disrespectful.

Aunt Olga, who understood me perfectly, gave me an easel and a new set of watercolors. She knew that more than almost anything else, I loved to paint. I decorated the pages of my photograph album with flowers and leaves.

Later that day the two of us set out by the water, wearing

big straw hats to protect us from the sun. "Someday when I'm older, I'm going to become an artist, like you," I confided as we walked along, looking for a scene to paint. "Marie is welcome to have twenty children. I can't imagine that Papa and Mama will allow her to marry a soldier, but maybe by the time it's the third daughter's turn, they won't insist that she marry a prince. I don't care if I marry or not. I want to be an artist, maybe even a famous one."

"Better just to focus on painting, and not on being famous," she advised.

We paused several times and gazed out at the sea toward Kronstadt, where the *Standart* was anchored, until we found a place to have the servants set up our easels and parasols. We arranged our paints and brushes, and Aunt Olga showed me how to make a rectangle with my fingers, framing the scene. We worked for an hour or two, not saying much, and when it was time to pack up and go back to the dacha, Aunt Olga had a lovely picture of a sailing ship, and I had a blotchy mess that had started out as a flowering bush and gone completely wrong, but it didn't matter. It was still a wonderful day.

At the end of June, before we left for our summer cruise on the Baltic, we visited Grandmère Marie at the Cottage Palace, her favorite palace at Peterhof, for one big birthday party that she gave for Tatiana, Marie, and me. Inside a box tied with a huge pink bow, cradled in a nest of tissue paper, was the most beautiful gift imaginable: a silver music box with a ballerina posed *en pointe* in a graceful arabesque. She turned slowly when I wound the mechanism to play "The Waltz of the Flowers" by Tchaikovsky.

"Don't forget, *ma chère*," Grandmère whispered to me as we were leaving. "We'll visit Paris when you're sixteen."

Three more years! *It might as well be a lifetime,* I thought, holding the music box on my lap on the train back to Tsarskoe Selo and entertaining my favorite daydream: *When Grandmère Marie and I come back to Russia from Paris, I'll concentrate on becoming a very, very good painter. Maybe then I'll also become famous.*

We left for our summer cruise from Peterhof, making the short trip to Kronstadt on the *Alexandria,* where Pavel Voronov now served. It must have been hard for Olga to see him. She had not mentioned him, or her meeting with Crown Prince Carol, but a few words in the notebook said it all.

> *I saw him today, thanks be to God! It has been so long, and it still breaks my heart. We didn't speak, only smiled and nodded. I tried not to let it show how much I care.*

> *After that awful meeting in Constanta, I told Mother and Father there was absolutely no possibility of a match with C.P. Carol. "Perhaps you'll reconsider," Father said, "when you're both older and he's more mature."*

Perhaps NEVER, *I thought, but didn't say.*

Four enormous British battle cruisers steamed into Kronstadt to pay us a visit. They dropped anchor and invited us to luncheon on the flagship *Lion.* It was OTMA's unanimous opinion that Admiral Beatty of the British Royal Navy was the handsomest admiral we had ever seen anywhere, and the mid-shipmen who were our escorts on the *Lion* were so charming and funny that even sour old Olga was laughing and smiling. It had been a long time since I'd seen her enjoy herself as we did that day.

Later, as we were going up the gangway to the *Standart* at anchor nearby, Alexei somehow hurt his ankle. He had been doing so well that we'd all hoped he was better, or that he'd learned to be more careful. But boys in general aren't careful, and Mama was upset that Nagorny and Derevenko hadn't seen to it that he made it safely. Alexei was in a lot of pain. Gilliard tried to take his mind off it by reading to him.

Even worse, news arrived that a crazy woman had attacked Father Grigory with a knife while he was visiting his village. He was so badly wounded that it was feared he might die. Anya was nearly hysterical. "Who could wish harm to such a good man?" she wailed. "Who could do such a terrible thing to a man of God?"

Mama, too, was very upset, but she was much quieter about it.

But the most important event that summer, though I didn't realize it immediately, happened far, far away from where we were cruising along the coast of Finland. Archduke Franz Ferdinand, son of Emperor Franz Josef of Austria-Hungary, had been assassinated. The archduke had gone on an official visit to Sarajevo, in Serbia. As he and his wife were being driven in an open motorcar through the crowded streets, a revolution-ary fired a gun at them and killed them both. Papa got the news of the murders over the wireless, and the possibility that this would lead to war was all anyone talked about all evening. Papa ordered our cruise on the *Standart* cut short. The *Alexandria* took us back to Peterhof, giving Olga another glimpse of Voronov that must have been like a knife twisting in her heart. *War, war, war*—it's all we heard.

There were so many agreements and treaties among countries that an incident like this could certainly get everyone involved on one side or the other. Pyotr Petrov tried to explain the alliances to my sisters and me. Russia was on Serbia's side, Austria and Germany were on the other side, and some countries were neutral. It was hard to keep them straight. The Austrians believed the Serbian government was really responsible for the murders, not just some crazed revolutionary, and Emperor Franz Josef sent an ultimatum to Sarajevo. But he didn't wait for a response. Austria declared war on Serbia. Papa sent orders to his generals, ordering Russian troops to help the Serbians if Austria attacked them.

Adding to all the tension, the president of France, Monsieur Poincaré, arrived by ship for an official visit that must have been planned much earlier. For four days Papa and Mama went through the motions of the usual ceremonies, speeches, and dinners for all those gloomy Frenchmen with long faces. Probably all they talked about was which country was going to war against which other country. Except for an appearance at a reception, Marie and I were not involved in any of the events, but Olga and Tatiana were forced to sit through a long, tedious dinner. Mama looked very beautiful in a low brocade gown and a diamond tiara, but Olga told us afterward that she was afraid Mama was going to faint before it ended. When the French delegation finally bid adieu and sailed away, Mama was exhausted and relieved and Papa looked tired and worried, with huge bags under his eyes.

A week later, on a Sunday, the thing that Papa had been most worried about actually happened. After early evening prayers in our chapel, Papa went upstairs to his study to read the telegraph messages that had come for him while we were gone. We waited in the dining room for him to come down. We waited and waited, but still he didn't come. Mama was about to send Tatiana to find out what was delaying him when Papa appeared, his face as white as chalk. "Germany has declared war on us," he said in a hoarse voice.

Mama let out a little cry. "What? Germany, against us? It can't be true!" She laid her head on the table and began to sob.

My sisters and I looked at each other. Had Cousin Willy actually done this? He wasn't joking when he marched around in his dreadful spiked helmet. He and Papa might actually be fighting each other.

Seeing our mother so upset, we began to cry, tears running down our faces and falling onto our napkins. The servants peered in, ready to serve dinner. Papa told them to go ahead. I was the only one with any appetite—no one else seemed able to swallow even a mouthful.

By late that evening, important people had begun arriving by launch and by motorcar from St. Petersburg. I recognized Sergei Sazonov, the minister of foreign affairs who had been so keen to match Olga up with Crown Prince Carol. Next, the

English ambassador stepped out of a sleek limousine. Voices were low, somber. There was no laughing, hardly any smiling.

Mama was calmer now and sent us to bed, promising, "There is nothing to worry about, girlies, all will be well." We desperately wanted to believe that. "But we must be up early tomorrow to go to St. Petersburg with Papa. He will make an announcement to the Russian people that our beloved country is at war."

The door closed and only a nightlight was left burning. Marie and I lay talking quietly as we usually did before we fell asleep. "What do you think it will be like, Nastya, being at war?"

"I don't know. Probably awful. But it does mean there will be a lot of soldiers around. Maybe you'll meet the one you want to marry and have twenty children with," I said brightly, trying to cheer her.

It had the opposite effect. "And then he'll be killed!" she choked between sobs. "That's what happens in war, Nastya. People get killed. Especially soldiers."

I was sorry for saying something to upset her, but Marie was like that. Madame Becker must have been paying her a visit. She was always glum and weepy during that time of the month.

We were silent for a while and I thought Marie was asleep, until she whispered, "Nastya? Are you awake?"

"Umm."

"I've been thinking about Mama," she said. She was sitting straight up in bed. "She must feel terrible. Her mother was English, but her father was German! She was born in Germany!

Her brother, Uncle Ernie, lives in Germany. She might still be there if she hadn't fallen in love with Papa and come to Russia to marry him. She had to learn to speak Russian, and she even gave up her religion for ours. Mama is as Russian as anybody, and she must hate it that Cousin Willy is doing this wicked, awful thing."

I'd been so sad for Papa that I had forgotten how bad Mama must have also been feeling. I crawled out of my bed and went to sit next to Marie, my arm around her, and the two of us cried and cried.

Shura woke us very early, before sunrise. "Your papa wants both of you to go with him for morning prayers. Quick, quick now, my girls!"

Papa looked as though he hadn't slept at all. He took the two of us by the hand, as if we were still small children, and led us to the chapel. "Pray hard, my darlings," he said. "Harder than you ever have in your life." And we did.

My sisters and I were going with Papa and Mama to St. Petersburg. Mama dressed in white and chose white outfits for all of us, and we wore big picture hats to protect our faces from the sun. Papa was wearing a plain khaki uniform and his colonel's insignia. "Because of the solemnity of the occasion," he said.

Alexei had to stay in Peterhof, because he could not walk and our parents didn't want the tsarevich to be seen on this day, of all days, as an invalid. Nagorny and Derevenko promised him all sorts of amusements, but nothing cheered him.

"Be a brave soldier," Papa told him. "We'll be back soon,

and Grandmère Marie is coming in a few days to celebrate your birthday."

Alexei, nodded, weeping, too upset to speak. I ran back and kissed him again. "I'll tell you everything that happens," I promised, and then hurried to board the launch for the trip to the capital.

CHAPTER 11

War Fever

ST. PETERSBURG, SUMMER 1914

Everyone was bursting with pride to be Russian.
Huge crowds had gathered for hours along
the Neva River. Our launch maneuvered through
hordes of boats of every size filled with people
cheering and waving flags. We stepped off the launch onto
the quay and into our carriages and inched toward the Winter
Palace while police guards struggled to hold back the throngs.

"*Batiushka!*" they cried. "Little Father, lead us to victory!"

The feverish enthusiasm, more intense than at the tercentennial celebration, did not die down. I'd been to many celebrations, attended many ceremonies, and the attention paid to my
father was to be expected. But this was different. The fervor of
the people sent a shiver of excitement down my spine. I could
tell by my sisters' faces that they, too, felt it.

We worked our way slowly through the crowd inside the

palace. People fell to their knees, tears streaming down their faces, and reached out to kiss Papa's hand, and Mama's, too. An altar had been set up in the huge hall. Papa signed a paper declaring Russia's war on Germany and Austria, and after a choir sang the *Te Deum* he recited an oath, swearing in a firm voice never to make peace so long as a single enemy remained on Russian soil.

Thousands of people in the great hall were weeping and smiling at the same time. Suddenly they began to sing "Save us, O Lord." I carried a linen handkerchief in my left hand—we had been taught by our governesses to do this whenever we were out in public—and I was glad I had mine when the tears began.

"The people want another chance to see their *Batiushka* and *Matushka*," Papa said, and led Mama out on the balcony to greet the enormous crowds that packed the square. We were told to stay behind, but we crept close to the doors to watch and listen. A sea of people roared when my parents stepped out, and the roaring didn't stop even when Papa raised his hand and tried to speak. Then the whole enormous crowd began to sing the imperial anthem:

God save the tsar!

Mighty and powerful,

Let him reign for our glory. . . .

"You see?" said Olga, close beside me. "You see why I will never leave Russia?"

I nodded. I did see. I understood.

The Cossack guards pushed back the crowd to let our carriages through, but the people were in such a jubilant mood that they didn't seem to mind. Not everyone was jubilant, though—we heard later that an angry mob had rushed to the German Embassy and attacked it, pulling down two huge bronze horses from the roof and rampaging through the inside. The Germans were now Enemy Number One.

"Everyone hates Cousin Willy," I said.

Tatiana told me to hush, because Mama was worried about Uncle Ernie back in Germany. As if I didn't remember.

Alexei was waiting in Peterhof to hear about everything that had happened. Dr. Botkin and Gleb and his sister had been with us, and Gleb was pleased to provide the details. His usually pale cheeks were flushed with excitement and his green eyes glowed. "The Germans don't know how to fight!" Gleb assured my brother. "They only know how to make sausages! All we have to do to win is to throw our caps at them."

Alexei laughed and applauded. But he was still upset that he had missed such a thrilling event. "Don't worry," I assured him. "There will certainly be more."

I hoped Gleb was right, though, that victory would be easy—and quick, too.

We'd been waiting anxiously for Grandmère Marie to arrive at Peterhof from a visit to England, and when she finally did, she was exhausted and in a fury. Her train had been stopped in Berlin and a howling mob had attacked it, smashing the windows, ripping down the blinds in her car, and screaming profanities at her.

"I have never been so terrified in my life," she told us. "That cursing and shrieking pack of rabble tried to grab me! Thank God the police arrived in time to save me. And that barbarian, Willy, wouldn't allow me to cross Germany! Can you imagine the effrontery? What a vulgar and detestable man! He ordered my train diverted to the Danish frontier. A horde of madmen threw stones as we left the station. The damage to the train is considerable—you can see it for yourself. Willy didn't dare keep me, but he did detain Felix and Irina. Xenia is beside herself, as you can imagine, and I don't know where they are now. Oh, this is just too, too horrid! I have hated Germany for fifty years, and now I hate it more than ever."

Felix and Irina were still on their honeymoon when "that barbarian" refused to let them go, until Felix's father arranged for them to return to Russia through Finland.

Alexei had been promised a tenth birthday celebration when Grandmère Marie came, and he was not disappointed. She had arranged for a Shetland pony and a pony cart to be sent by ship from England. Alexei was delighted and became totally absorbed in thinking of a name for the little pony. "He'll be a friend for Vanka," Alexei said, Vanka being the donkey Papa had gotten Alexei when he was five. There was also a cake and ice cream and a serenade by the balalaika orchestra, but a constant parade of generals coming out from St. Petersburg occupied Papa's attention.

"Some are saying the war will be over by Christmas," Papa told us.

"All we have to do is throw our caps at them," I said.

Papa sighed. "If only that were true," he said, and for just a moment I wondered if Gleb and the generals might be wrong.

A week later the whole family—including Alexei—traveled to Moscow, the old capital of Russia before Tsar Peter the Great built St. Petersburg. It was an ancient tradition for the tsars to go to the Kremlin in Moscow to ask God's blessing on any war they were about to enter. Before we left Peterhof, we attended services in the white-and-gold chapel where all five of us children had been christened. Then we boarded the imperial train. It rolled quietly through the night and arrived in Moscow the next morning.

It seemed as though everyone in the entire city had come out to greet us, thousands and thousands of Russians hanging out of windows and over the edges of balconies, balancing on the limbs of trees—anywhere they could find—to cheer and wave banners. Church bells rang like mad, and at every church we passed, a priest came out to bless Papa.

We entered the walls of the Kremlin the way tsars always entered the fortified center of the city, through the Iberian gate, and our carriages delivered us to the Grand Palace, with its fireplaces carved out of alabaster, desks and tables inlaid with jade and topaz, porcelain clocks from France, and gold everywhere.

We were hardly settled in the imperial apartments when Alexei began to complain that his leg hurt so badly he was afraid he wouldn't be able to walk to the cathedral the next day. "I must walk tomorrow!" he cried, gritting his teeth, his face twisted with pain. "I must!"

My parents were still determined that Alexei's future sub-jects not be allowed to believe that he was an invalid, but when we awoke the next morning, it was obvious that walking was impossible. Mama was in despair, and Alexei was sobbing.

"Never mind," Papa told Alexei. "You will be present at the ceremony. Our biggest, strongest, handsomest Cossack guard will carry you, and you'll see everything."

At eleven o'clock we left the imperial apartment and climbed the fifty-eight steps of the Red Staircase to St. George Hall. "Lucky you," I told Alexei, in the arms of the Cossack. "You get to be carried."

Mama's sister Ella joined us, dressed in her pale gray nun's habit. "She looks so elegant in that robe, and she doesn't even have to wear a corset with it," I whispered to Marie. "Or bother deciding which jewels to wear. It's almost enough to make me consider becoming a nun myself."

Marie giggled, and Tatiana hissed, "Hush!"

Standing in the center of the great hall, Papa read out a proclamation in a strong voice: "From this place, the very heart of Russia, I send my soul's greeting to my valiant troops and my noble allies. God is with us!" It was a solemn occasion, the most solemn in the world, but somehow I couldn't stop grinning—proud to be not only Russian but the daughter of the tsar.

A bridge connected the palace to the cathedral on the opposite side of the Palace Square, filled with more cheering crowds—the people would surely be hoarse by the end of the day—and after lots of prayers and hymns, incense and candles, we could finally go back to the palace for luncheon. A good thing, because I was starving.

The next day Alexei and Gilliard went out for a drive in a motorcar to a scenic spot above the city. On the way back through narrow streets jammed with peasants, someone recognized Alexei and began to shout, "The heir! The heir!" Suddenly the crowds surrounded them, blocking their way, pressing closer, all determined to see the tsarevich. The eager peasants climbed up on the steps of the car, scrambling to reach my brother. Alexei had never had anything like this happen to him, and it frightened him.

"Neither the driver nor I knew what to do," Gilliard reported, still trembling. "The *moujiks* meant no harm, but we were trapped. Then two huge policemen ran up, shouting and waving, and the crowd fell back and slowly drifted away."

"They wanted to touch me, as though I was a religious icon, something holy!" Alexei said. "It was embarrassing. I didn't like it."

We went home to Tsarskoe Selo. Everyone seemed excited about going to war. It was all people talked about now. The trips to St. Petersburg and Moscow had been thrilling, but my sisters and I felt anxious. It was terribly confusing.

In our schoolroom, Pyotr Petrov tapped on the map of the world with his pointer. "The Germans and the Austrians are our enemies," he said, though we needed no reminding, "and so are the Turks. The French and the English are our closest allies—the Serbians, too, of course—and so far the other countries such as Romania are neutral." The neutral countries included Switzerland, where Gilliard was from. "Monsieur Gilliard had thought to go home," Petrov said, "but it is nearly impossible to get there, for all communications have been cut, and if he did manage to get home, he would have no chance of getting back here before the end of the war."

"But Pyotr Vasilyevich," I reminded him, "everyone says the war will be over by Christmas! That would not be such a long time to be away." I liked Gilliard very much, and would miss him if he left, but I would not miss a few months of French lessons.

Petrov hung his pointer on its hook. "I pray that those who are so optimistic are also correct," he said quietly.

Papa appointed Grand Duke Nikolai Nikolaevich—Papa's distant cousin, but we called him Uncle Nikolasha—to be commander-in-chief of the army. But this was just temporary. "Until I can get to Stavka and take command," Papa said. Stavka was the army headquarters, near Bialowieza, site of our hunting lodge in Poland.

Marie and I lay on our beds, whispering in the dark. "What do you think will happen now?" Marie asked, and I could tell that she was close to tears. She was always very emotional.

"I don't know," I said.

I did not want to tell her what I had read in Olga's notebook. I still glanced at it now and then, though not as often as I had when she was madly in love with Voronov, because her entries after he married someone else weren't as interesting. But this was upsetting:

I'm so worried about this war. Mother and Father received a letter from Fr. G, who is in his village in Siberia and recovering from the awful attack by that crazy woman. The letter made Father so angry he wanted to tear it up, but Mother wouldn't let him.

She showed it to Tanya and me, and I'm writing here what I can remember:

"A terrible storm cloud lies over Russia. Disaster, grief, murky darkness and no light. A whole ocean of tears, there is no counting them, and so much bloodshed. I can find no words to describe the horror. Russia is drowning in blood. Disaster is great, the misery infinite."

What if Fr. G is right? I can't bear to think of it.

Marie was still asking questions in a worried whisper. "Papa's going to be leaving soon for Poland," she said. "How long do you think he'll be gone?"

"I don't know, Mashka," I said, rolling away so that my back was to her. I was thinking about what I'd read in the notebook. *Russia is drowning in blood.*

"Mama says we must say our prayers and trust in God," Marie said with a little catch in her voice. She was close to tears again. "Do you think God will help us?"

"Of course He will," I said. *Disaster is great, the misery infinite.* "Now, let's go to sleep. Aunt Olga is coming tomorrow."

Soon Marie's breathing deepened, but I lay staring into the darkness, my thoughts churning. *Maybe Father Grigory is wrong and it isn't going to be a disaster. Russia will triumph. Father Grigory doesn't know everything.*

Our aunt's Saturday visit wasn't like any of her earlier visits. She was flushed with excitement. Papa had changed the name of St. Petersburg, which was a German name, to Petrograd. "Much more patriotic," he'd said, and Aunt Olga agreed.

"Talk about patriotism!" she remarked. "I've witnessed the most extraordinary sights over the past week: the thrilling sight of men going to war. Every day from early morning until after sunset, hundreds and hundreds of men marching down Nevsky Prospect to the Warsaw Station to board a train for the front. People walk beside them, cheering them on. They're fighting for Holy Russia and for the tsar, Nicky!"

Papa nodded. "Yes, it's such a stirring sight. I would have done anything in my power to avoid this war, but I am deeply moved by the dedication of the men."

While they talked, I was sitting on the floor with my brother, playing with his toy soldiers, shoving them back and forth as he issued commands. But I was also listening to what the adults were saying.

"My Hussars have been called up," said Aunt Olga. "The regiment is being sent to the front in the southwest. Kolya is going with them, of course." She said it very matter-of-factly, but my ears perked up when I heard her mention Kolya, and I turned slightly in order to hear better. Alexei noticed—he always noticed if you weren't focusing completely on him—and started to protest, but I shushed him.

"Of course," Papa said. "It's his duty."

Her voice rose slightly. "Before he left, Colonel Kulikovsky told me that the junior officers were asking if they shouldn't pack their dress uniforms for the victory parades. He told them the proper uniforms would be sent along later."

I thought of what Gleb Botkin had said—*The Germans don't*

know how to fight! They only know how to make sausages! Yesterday he'd told us that his two older brothers, Dmitri and Yuri, were on their way to the front. Gleb was very proud of them and deeply disappointed that he was too young to fight.

Dmitri Pavlovich arrived for tea, proudly wearing the Cross of St. George, a military honor, pinned to his chest. I hadn't seen him for a long while, and I'm afraid I did grin too much when he was around, because later Tatiana remarked in her stern governess voice, "You make it so obvious that you have a crush on Dmitri."

He had been at Stavka with Nikolai Nikolaevich, the commander-in-chief. "What a giant of a man!" Dmitri said enthusiastically. "He's nearly seven feet tall. And such a commanding presence!"

"Appropriate for a commander," Mama said sourly. She didn't much like Uncle Nikolasha, and made no secret of it. Father Grigory didn't trust him, she said.

Dmitri and Papa talked for a long while after the tea things had been cleared away—I don't know about what—and I think he would have stayed longer had we not been expecting a visit from Father Grigory, the first he'd come since the crazy woman attacked him. Dmitri was one of the people who didn't like Father Grigory, and he didn't even try to hide his dislike. Naturally that offended Mama, who couldn't bear to hear the slightest criticism of a man she believed could work miracles.

Father Grigory was very late arriving, and Mama began to fret. Papa, too. I wanted to see him and wished I could stay to overhear the conversation, but our parents decided that we should go to our rooms since the visit was going to be so late.

"Nobody ever keeps the tsar waiting!" Shura said as she brushed my hair for the night. "It's the height of ill manners." Shura was one more who didn't like the *starets*, but she was careful not to say anything that would anger Mama.

We didn't see Father Grigory that night, and so we have no idea if he tried to convince Papa that Russia was going to drown in blood. Whatever was said did not change Papa's mind, and in the days that followed, he went calmly about his preparations to leave for Stavka. On the morning he was driven off in his motorcar, we all cried because our dear papa was going away. Mama cried most of all.

Then Anya moved from her little yellow cottage into rooms in our palace, to keep Mama's spirits up while Papa was away.

CHAPTER 12

Changed Lives

TSARSKOE SELO, AUTUMN 1914

Almost overnight our lives changed completely.

Mama announced that it was her duty to provide care for the wounded. She developed a plan for turning the Catherine Palace, which she had never liked anyway, into a hospital. The Winter Palace in what was now called Petrograd and a couple of imperial palaces in Moscow became medical units to care for the wounded, with space set aside for the soldiers' wives and mothers to stay when they came to visit. Mama sent our Dr. Botkin to Yalta to open hospitals on the estates of wealthy families. She also created smaller medical facilities called lazarets. Feodorovsky Gorodok, the village that Papa had built in Tsarskoe Selo to remind him of "old Russia," became one of the lazarets. Then she organized special trains to bring the wounded men to the hospitals from the front.

I was amazed at whatever had come over Mama. Our mother, who had always spent most of the day reclining in her mauve boudoir, announced that she and Olga and Tatiana were going to become nurses and actually work in those hospitals. They would undergo two months of training by the Red Cross, with classes in the morning and actual duties in the wards in the afternoon. They would then become qualified as "sisters of mercy."

"And what about Mashka and me?" I asked. "Can't we become nurses, too?" I could not bear to be left out of what seemed such a great adventure.

"You girlies are too young to be full-fledged sisters of mercy," Mama said firmly. "But that doesn't mean you can't both serve proudly and usefully. You will be patronesses at the lazaret at Feodorovsky Gorodok. That will give you plenty to do, and I'm sure you will accomplish a great deal of good."

Once they were qualified, Mama and our older sisters put on long gray uniforms and white aprons with a big red cross on the chest and white wimples that covered the head and neck. You could hardly recognize them when they were in uniform, as they now were every day.

"In uniform, everybody is the same," Tatiana said. "We're not there as the empress and the grand duchesses. We're there as Russian nurses."

Mama was up and dressed at seven o'clock and on her way to the hospital at the Catherine Palace every morning at nine. She and Olga and Tatiana came home exhausted at the end of the day. They did really hard, awful work—cleaning bedsores and changing bandages and helping with the surgeries.

Sometimes Mama assisted at as many as three surgeries, one right after the other, each lasting a couple hours.

"Sometimes the doctors have to cut off an arm or a leg without enough anesthetic," Olga said, her face etched with sadness at the sights she had witnessed. "The doctors are so tired they can hardly stay on their feet. And yet every hour more trains arrive from the field hospitals at the front, more filthy, moaning men are carried in, and we clean them up for the nurses to examine and the doctors to operate on. It's unbearable! Mama is so brave—she holds the cone over their noses and drips ether onto it to put them to sleep, but sometimes there isn't enough ether and they scream in agony. And then she helps to carry away the mangled flesh or the amputated hand or arm—" My sister shuddered. "And the smell! You can't imagine the smell, all those infected wounds."

"I think I'd throw up," I whispered.

Olga forced a wan smile. "At first I did," she admitted. "I threw up more than once. But you get used to it after a while."

"Some of them are screaming and praying to die," Tatiana said. She had kicked off her shoes and was rolling down her stockings. They were spattered with something dark. "Then we sit with them while they're dying. It's the most awful thing you can imagine." She shook her head, as though ridding herself of the terrible sights and sounds. "Oh, I do hope it will be over soon. But I'm afraid it won't."

Marie and I went daily to the lazaret. We didn't have uniforms, and that was a disappointment—we were almost the only people in the whole imperial compound wearing ordinary clothes. I was glad that we didn't have to witness grisly wounds and horrible surgeries. The wounded men in the lazarets had already been treated, and while they might have been suffering and in pain, most were able to talk and were glad for the company. When Alexei was able, we took him with us. The wounded soldiers seemed happy to see us and overjoyed to see the tsarevich. We helped the men write letters to their families—often Marie wrote the letters for them, because many were simple peasants who had never been taught to read or write. I especially liked reading to the men—they said I read very well, that I was a good actress and it was almost like being at a play. That was nice to hear, and I began to think that maybe, when the war was over, I would consider becoming an actress as well as an artist.

But there was a bad side to my work: Every day I visited wounded soldiers who in the morning were murmuring their thanks for my reading them letters they had received, letters full of love and longing, and who in the afternoon were dead, a white sheet pulled over their faces, and I'd had no chance to say good-bye. It was enough to break one's heart, over and over. Suffering and death were all around me, and I never did get used to it.

It was easy now to have a chance to read Olga's notebook without the risk of getting caught. Sometimes she even forgot to put it away. But there were times when I wished I hadn't read it.

One must pity Mother. She works so hard at the hospital, spares herself nothing, no duty is beneath her. Some of her patients can't believe the empress herself is actually there, sleeves rolled up. Most

adore her, call for her, kiss her hand if they can. But there are
many who despise her and make no secret of it, because she was
born a German. Mother is Russian to the very depths of her
soul, but they don't know that, or don't want to know it. And
I'm afraid it's not just a few ignorant soldiers who feel this way.
Mother is a quiet person, and she has not won the hearts of the
Russian people the way our grandmother has. The people truly
adore Father, but they are suspicious of Mother and even dislike
her. She has done nothing to deserve that.

Poor Mama! She never hurt anyone, never meant to do anything but good. Reading it made me feel sorry for every naughty thing I ever *thought* of saying to my poor darling mother, and I cried.

Papa came home often from Stavka, but he never stayed long, especially when Alexei seemed to be doing well. We missed him awfully and took turns writing to him every evening, trying to find amusing things to tell him that would cheer him up. Sad and discouraging as life was during this time, some surprising things did happen. Tatiana may have actually fallen in love! The object of her affections was an officer named Dmitri Malama. He was seriously wounded, and she met him when he came under her care in the hospital. They began by talking about dogs. Tatiana told the lieutenant that she thought French bulldogs were irresistibly adorable, and the next thing we knew, a French bulldog puppy arrived at Alexander Palace. Tatiana named him Ortino. Mama's dog, Eira, took great exception to this new rival, growling and barking. Olga's cat, Vaska, chased the newcomer around the palace, the two of them knocking things over and getting into all sorts of mischief.

Tatiana doted on that little dog, but he was not well trained and my sister kept a little shovel handy to clean up his messes. I enjoyed writing to Papa about Ortino, but I thought it was better not to say anything about Tatiana possibly being in love.

Everyone was so busy helping with the war effort that we almost neglected to celebrate Olga's nineteenth birthday. Chef Kharitonov reminded us that he was preparing an excellent dinner for her with all her favorite dishes—he kept records for all of us—but there was no music, no dancing, no invited guests. Then she rushed off to a meeting. Besides their nursing duties, both Olga and Tatiana had organized committees to help the wounded soldiers, and they often had meetings to attend.

Meanwhile, Anya was being particularly annoying. She always did expect a lot of attention, and she acted offended if Mama didn't spend a couple of hours with her every day, as she used to. Anya wanted to be pitied and fussed over, and I got sick of it. Only good-hearted Marie seemed willing.

War news was not often good. We saw proof that the Germans knew how to do much more than make sausages— they knew how to fight. Wounded soldiers poured into the hospitals where Mama and Olga and Tatiana worked every day alongside many other volunteers, including Tatiana Botkina, who had also trained as a nurse. They came in huge numbers to the smaller lazarets, where Marie and I did what we could to make the suffering men feel a little less alone.

The men sometimes talked about those who hadn't been

so lucky, the ones who had been killed. "Mowed down like wheat," one soldier muttered, turning his face toward the wall. "Our officers are brave," he said. "And also foolish. They order us to crawl forward, always forward, bellies on the ground, while our leaders stand up and walk straight into enemy fire. They say it would be cowardly for them to take cover. And the Germans shoot them down like ducks in a shooting gallery."

One of those brave officers was Dr. Botkin's eldest son, Dmitri, a lieutenant in the Cossack regiment serving on the eastern front. We learned to our great sorrow that he was among the dead.

So many officers had been killed that Papa ordered fifteen thousand university students to take special training to become lieutenants. On one of his visits home Papa said, "I told my young lieutenants that I had not the slightest doubt of their bravery and courage, but I needed their lives—they are of no use to Russia if they are dead—and for them to take care for themselves. Then I reminded them of the value of prayer before going into battle. 'With prayer you can do anything,' I said, and I believe they took it to heart."

No one talked about it, but obviously the war had not ended by Christmas.

The officials of the church had announced a ban on Christmas trees, because they were a German custom. We were disappointed—lighting the trees had always been a part of our family celebration—and Mama was furious. "I'm going to find out the truth of who gave that order and make a row about it," she said. "Why take away the pleasure of a beautiful tree from the wounded and children because the tradition comes from Germany? The narrow-mindedness is too colossal!"

I was not at all sure Mama could actually make a row, as she called it. To most people she was *Matushka*, "Little Mother," but many called her *Nemka*, "German woman," and said she was a traitor because she'd been born in Germany.

Aunt Olga told us about her French-speaking friends who'd been hissed at in shops by people who didn't recognize any language but Russian and thought they were speaking German.

What stupid people!

When Papa came home for Christmas, we had a small tree just for ourselves, but Papa said it was wiser not to have any large public tree. Our celebration on Christmas Eve was just as it had always been—bowls of traditional *kutya*, almond soup, and roast carp—and we attended Mass at midnight in the chapel, as we always had. On Christmas Day we exchanged small gifts and had a visit from Irina and Felix Yussoupov. But we didn't go out on the balcony to greet the people, who used to gather to wish us a joyous Christmas. Too many Russians were upset about the war, angry at our family. It seemed better not to make public appearances until the mood improved.

And Olga wrote this in her notebook:

All the good feelings we had last summer when a million people in Petrograd and Moscow cheered until they were hoarse—all that has vanished. Irina says that in Petrograd some of the noble families with German-sounding names are being told to find documents proving that they're descended from Catherine the

Great. Orchestras in Petrograd are not allowed to play music by Bach, Brahms, or Beethoven. Felix says he witnessed the windows of German bakeries being smashed.

So the war was not over by Christmas. Surely by *next* Christmas it will be only a bad memory.

CHAPTER 13

A Year of War

I n January, the train on which Anya Vyrubova was traveling from Petrograd to Tsarskoe Selo was wrecked. She was nearly dead when she was dragged from under the demolished carriage and taken to the hospital in the Catherine Palace. Her legs were crushed and her head and back were badly injured. Mama and Papa rushed to her bedside—Papa had not yet returned to Stavka after Christmas—and the doctors told them, "Do not disturb her. She's dying."

Mama immediately sent for Father Grigory. We were in her hospital room, kneeling by her beside and praying, when he arrived. Anya moaned and muttered, calling for him. He nodded to Papa and Mama and went to Anya's bedside, took her hand, and spoke to her. "Annushka! Annushka, rise!"

At first nothing happened. Sweat bathed his face. None of us dared to breathe. Then, the miracle: The third time Father

Grigory called her name, Anya opened her eyes. When he ordered her to get up, she actually tried to do it, and when he commanded her to speak to him, she murmured something I couldn't hear. It was the most amazing thing I'd ever seen.

Mama was weeping, tears pouring down her cheeks. "Grishka, I beg you to tell me! Will she live?"

Father Grigory nodded wearily. "God will give her back to you if she is needed by you and the country. If her influence is harmful, He will take her away. But she will be a cripple for the rest of her days. Now you must excuse me," he said. He staggered away, exhausted by the effort he'd made, and Mama collapsed into Papa's arms.

Soon after that dramatic scene, Papa left again for Stavka. We hated to see him go, and it took days to become accustomed to his absence. The only good thing about Papa being away was that we had unlimited use of his huge swimming bath. Alexei loved it, too. And Tatiana's silly dog, Ortino, was a witness to our cavorting, barking his head off.

It was a dreadfully sad day when one of Mama's patients died, a young officer named Grobov. Mama was extremely upset by this. Although she was confronted daily with death in the course of her work at the hospital, she had become quite attached to him, and now he was gone.

Anya was eventually well enough to leave her hospital room and move back to her quarters in Alexander Palace. Now Mama had Anya to look after as well as her work with the wounded soldiers. She demanded so much of Mama's time and energy, always complaining that she wasn't getting any attention, no one came to visit her, she needed to have her wheelchair pushed here and there. And if she didn't get her way, she pretended to faint!

Father Grigory came to see her nearly every day. Afterward he spent an hour or so with Mama, discussing what should be done about Anya. They talked about the war and what Papa should be doing, and about who should be in charge of what. Mama missed Papa terribly, and in the evenings she wrote him long, long letters, passing along to him the advice Father Grigory had given her.

I wrote him long letters, too, telling him what we were learning from our tutors—not much, in my case. Mr. Gibbes, our English tutor, said I was "lacking motivation and self-discipline," which translated as "lazy," while the other tutors continued to torment Marie and me with math, French, and geography.

The huge map that Pyotr Petrov had hung on the wall of our schoolroom became the center of a daily examination of the progress of the war. We focused on the part of Russia that lay west of the Ural Mountains, as well as Hungary, Austria, and Poland, where the fighting was taking place. We had little boxes of pins—white for the Russian army, black for the Germans, yellow for the Austrians—and as news reports came in about the progress of the war, we moved the pins. It was awful to see the black pins advancing and the white ones retreating, but in March there was some good news. Fresh recruits had arrived at the front, and Uncle Nikolasha led the army to a brilliant victory, capturing lots of prisoners and big guns at a fortress in Galicia, a small kingdom west of the Ukraine that belonged to Austria. Papa was so pleased that he presented him with a beautiful gold sword decorated with diamonds.

There were no more gay weekend parties with Aunt Olga—she was now a nurse, too—and no more formal luncheons with Grandmère Marie, who had left St. Petersburg and moved far away to Kiev in the Ukraine. Olga and Tatiana were at the hospital most of the time, but Mama had not been feeling well lately and often had to stay in bed. Visitors were rare, but Mama's friend Lili Dehn sometimes came out from Petrograd with her little boy, nicknamed Titi. Titi was four years younger than Alexei and worshipped my brother, following him around like a slave.

The winter was long, cold, and gray. During those cheerless months, we learned that the *Standart* and Grandmère Marie's *Polar Star* had been taken to Helsinki—the admiral believed the yachts would be safer in the Finnish harbor from German attack—and their crews had been reassigned. Lili Dehn's husband was now the captain of a Russian destroyer, and Olga wrote in her notebook that Lieutenant Voronov was serving on a ship in the Baltic to lay mines underwater to blow up German ships.

There would be no visit to Livadia at Easter and, unless there was a miracle before summer, no cruises on the *Standart*.

That year the gorgeous Fabergé egg that Papa commissioned as a gift for Mama was designed to honor the ladies in Papa's family who had become Red Cross nurses. Inside the white enameled egg were five tiny portraits on ivory of Mama, my two older sisters, our cousin Dmitri's sister Maria Pavlovna, and Aunt Olga, who was working at the hospital she'd established near her villa in southwestern Russia. In their portraits, all were wearing white nurses' wimples. It was the plainest egg

Papa had ever ordered, and Mama pronounced it "beautiful in its simplicity, and absolutely appropriate to the times."

Spring wore on, and again news about the war turned abysmal. Any victories were won at huge cost of lives and didn't last. We were suffering one defeat after another, and the black pins of the enemy on our map moved closer to Russia. "I don't want to do this with the pins anymore," I told Petrov. "It's too depressing."

No one spoke to Marie and me about the losses, but we had ears to hear, and what we heard was that more than a million men had been killed, wounded, or taken prisoner. Mama seemed either consumed by her nursing duties at the hospital, writing page after page to Papa, or involved in deep conversation with Father Grigory. He and Mama blamed Uncle Nikolasha for what was happening to the Russian army.

Tatiana Botkina endured the horrible experience of seeing her brother Yuri's mangled body brought to the hospital where she worked with Mama and my sisters. He survived only a few days, and she was with him when he died. We observed a deep change come over Dr. Botkin after the loss of his two older sons. And Gleb, always soulful, became even more serious, and the stories he made up were less fanciful and much darker.

Aunt Ella sometimes left her convent and fled Moscow for the peace and quiet of Tsarskoe Selo and a short visit with us. "The mobs are running wild in Moscow," she said. Her hand shook when she reached for her cup of tea. "They hate everything German, and burn down houses and shops belonging to people with German names. They rushed the gates of the convent and accused me of hiding German spies. They said I was hiding our brother."

"But Ernie's not even in Russia!" Mama said. "He's an officer in the kaiser's army!"

"So I informed them, but they wouldn't believe me—even
when I invited them to come into the convent and have a look
around so they could see for themselves." Her face was drawn,
and she had dark circles beneath her eyes. "Several shouted,
'Get the German woman! Take her away!' Then someone threw
a stone. It didn't strike me, but I was afraid the next one would.
Still, I refused to back down. A company of our soldiers arrived
just in time and broke up the crowd."

We were silent, too shocked to say anything. Marie crept
closer to Aunt Ella and reached for the pale hand that lay trembling in her lap.

"They shout insults wherever I go," she continued. "They
call for Rasputin to be hanged. They shout for Nicky to be
deposed and Nikolasha to be made Tsar Nicholas the Third."

Mama, white-lipped, could barely speak. "And me?" she
managed to say. "What do they say about me?"

"That you should be shut up in a convent," Aunt Ella
whispered.

What about my sisters and me? And Lyosha? I wondered, but I
couldn't bear to ask.

Summer came. Three of us had birthdays—Tatiana had her
eighteenth, a week later I was fourteen, and the week after
that Marie turned sixteen. I can't say that we "celebrated" the
birthdays—*observed* is a better word—but we did have nice little
family dinners with Aunt Olga and Grandmère there for each
of us. Marie received her special necklace of sixteen diamonds

and sixteen pearls. Chef Kharitonov produced delicious meals in spite of the shortages of food that were beginning to appear, and Alexei serenaded us with his balalaika. I made the stupid mistake of talking about the wonderful party we'd had at Livadia for Olga's sixteenth birthday four years earlier. I hadn't meant to make everyone sad, especially Olga, who was probably thinking of Pavel Voronov when she suddenly burst into tears and rushed away from the table. I believe she was still in love with him—hopeless, of course, since he was now married to Olga Kleinmichel, but I suppose it's not possible simply to decide *not* to be in love with someone.

At the beginning of July Papa came home. Mama got very excited whenever we expected Papa's return, almost the way Olga used to be when she thought she'd be seeing Lieutenant Voronov. Papa stayed through most of August, and for a little while things seemed almost normal for our family. In fact, one very funny thing did happen.

Prince Carol of Romania came to visit. He was no longer just a crown prince but a full-fledged prince, because his grandfather had died and his father had succeeded as King Ferdinand of Romania.

A year earlier, when Carol had been considered a possible husband for Olga, she'd flatly rejected the idea. Now, when she heard that he was coming, she suddenly had a full schedule of meetings involving her various war projects. "I will have absolutely no free time to spend with him," Olga announced. "I'm terribly sorry, Father," she added.

"You don't sound the least bit sorry, Olya," I said.

"But it's true that I'll be too busy."

"The visit is purely diplomatic," Papa assured her. "One part of Romania shares a border with Russia and another part borders Austria-Hungary, and Romania therefore has remained neutral in the war. I believe King Ferdinand is sending Prince Carol to discuss Romania joining Russia to fight against Germany. It might help if you were here."

"I sincerely wish I could be," she lied. "But I simply cannot."

I found it all very amusing. Carol arrived, accompanied by a huge suite of courtiers, mostly old men and ladies and nobody young and interesting. I found him just as irritating as when we met with him at Constanta, and I expected the whole visit to be hugely boring. As it turned out, though, the visit was *not* purely diplomatic.

Toward the end of the prince's visit, Marie came shrieking into our bedroom with the news. "Carol asked Papa if he would consent to let him marry me!"

"Prince Carol wants to marry *you*, Mashka?" My mouth was probably hanging open.

"You needn't act so surprised that someone would want to," she huffed. "Anyway, Papa just laughed and reminded him that I'm still just a schoolgirl and not in any way ready to marry or even to consider an engagement."

"Well, congratulations, dear sister. You've had your first proposal."

She grinned mischievously. "He still has that mop of uncombed hair," she said. "But if you're lucky, Nastya, he'll be back again in two years to ask for *your* hand."

I rolled my eyes.

When they'd gone, Papa said that Romania had decided to remain neutral.

One warm August afternoon as we were having tea with Anya on Mama's balcony, Papa appeared suddenly, looking pale as a ghost, a telegram in his trembling hand.

"Nicky, what's wrong?" Mama cried.

"Warsaw has fallen," he said hoarsely. He sank down onto a chair, tears in his eyes, and buried his face in his hands. "It cannot go on like this," he said. "It simply cannot."

Within hours Papa had made up his mind that his place was with the army. From then on, he would spend all of his time at Stavka. We must prepare to see much less of him.

At the end of August he kissed us all good-bye and left Tsarskoe Selo with the guard saluting, flags waving, and church bells ringing. Headquarters had been moved from Poland, where the advancing German army had taken over the area, to Mogilev, a Russian town on the banks of the Dnieper River. At the old Stavka, Papa had lived aboard his imperial train. His new quarters were in a mansion on a hilltop overlooking the river.

Barely a month later Papa made another big change: he ordered Grand Duke Nikolai Nikolaevich to the Caucasian front to lead the fight against the Turks, who were on the side of Germany and Austria. Papa was taking over as commander-in-chief of the army.

Mama was pleased. She had never liked Uncle Nikolasha, mostly because he plainly despised Father Grigory.

Olga wrote about the situation:

*It's quite amazing. Some people hate Fr. G and think he has too
much influence on Mother, who then has too much influence on
Father, none of it good. Fr. G did everything possible to win over
Uncle Nikolasha's favor, even offering to go to the front to bless
icons for the soldiers, but, according to gossip, Uncle Nikolasha
told him, "Good! Come here, and I will hang you." Could he
really have said that?*

*Whether it's true or not, the story got back to Mother, and no
doubt that's why she urged Father to dismiss Uncle Nikolasha
and take command himself. Mother, of course, depends upon Fr.
G entirely and thinks he is a saint who gives only the best advice.
Anya worships him, and I understand why—he did seem to
perform a miracle when she was so badly injured.*

*Aunt Olga disapproves of Papa's decision, and so does Grandmère
Marie, and probably our other relatives as well. They believe Papa
is needed here, as sovereign of the people, and not at the front,
because they say he's not really a military man. But none of this
means a thing to Mother, who agrees with everything Fr. G says.*

*I continue to hear stories from the servants that Fr. G has
improper relations with many of the great ladies of Petrograd and
Moscow and who knows where else. His behavior toward me and
my sisters is always correct, but I do sometimes get the uneasy
feeling that he is undressing us with his eyes.*

That last part bothered me: *undressing us with his eyes.* Why
would he want to do that?

• • •

After Papa moved his headquarters and took command of the army, he and Mama began to talk about allowing Alexei to join Papa in Mogilev. They discussed it for days. Papa thought it would be good for Alexei to see more of the country he would some day rule as tsar, to be exposed to masculine influence instead of being surrounded by females who treated him like a china doll. Mama was deeply afraid that something awful might happen to Alexei while he was at Mogilev, that he would seriously injure himself again, but she also believed the presence of the eleven-year-old tsarevich would do tremendous good for the morale of the troops, and also for Papa.

So it was decided. Papa and Alexei left for Mogilev in October, with Alexei's two doctors, his two sailor-attendants, and Monsieur Gilliard as his tutor, because Mama insisted that he not fall behind in his studies.

Marie and I were still spending long hours at the lazaret, reading to the wounded men, writing letters for them, even teaching some of them to read, and simply keeping them company. How lonely those soldiers must have felt! Then we passed exciting evenings at Alexander Palace knitting woolen socks and sewing shirts for the soldiers. I didn't dare complain about the dullness—I'd risk a ferocious frown and a barrage of sharp words from Tatiana, all about "duty" and "sacrifice." But I did wish I could have gone with Alexei and Papa. I envied my brother.

I was thrilled when Mama announced that we were going to visit them. Anya traveled with us. I found this annoying, but Olga felt even more strongly about it:

I'm not sure why Mother has insisted on including Anya in this excursion. Since her accident Anya is plumper than ever, wears the most dreadful clothes and hats, needs a crutch to get around, and—this is what is so embarrassing—behaves like a schoolgirl with a crush whenever she is around Father. I suppose the best thing about Anya, from Mother's point of view, is that she shares her devotion to Fr. G. He can do no wrong! And not all of Mother's friends share that opinion. Aunt Ella has deep reservations about him, as does Grandmère Marie, but Anya is on her side, and that must be why Mother puts up with her.

We traveled to Mogilev on the imperial train, a day's journey, and the train was our home once we'd reached our destination, because the mansion where Papa and Alexei stayed was too crowded to allow for visitors. Alexei could not wait to show us his quarters: He shared Papa's bedroom, sleeping on an army cot next to Papa's and closest to the stove. There was a small table by the window where they played dominoes in the evening. "I usually win," Alexei boasted.

Papa was busy during the mornings of our visit, meeting with the officers, reviewing troops, and so on. Mama seemed content to sit and gaze out over the river. Sometimes she asked to be driven around the town of Mogilev and out into the countryside, taking two of us with her, and stopping now and then to chat with the peasants.

Just before one o'clock each day, several motorcars arrived at the railroad siding and drove us to the mansion for luncheon with the officers. I enjoyed those luncheons, because Papa seemed so calm, so relaxed, almost his old self, now that he was among the officers and men who were fighting for Russia. In the afternoons we were taken on tours of the area and had a chance to speak with the soldiers. At the end of the day, another fleet of cars was sent to our train to fetch our maids and the dresses and jewels Mama wanted us to wear for dinner with the officers.

"Nothing too bright or elaborate," she said. "This is wartime and we aren't attending a ball, but a feminine presence is surely good for the men's morale."

When the weather was mild, the officers organized hikes and picnics for us, and one day we boarded a launch and took a long, leisurely cruise on the Dnieper. "I'm sure they need time to relax more than we do," Mama declared. "We're doing them a favor coming here."

During this visit, Marie met a lieutenant who was serving as officer of the day at headquarters. His name was Nikolai Dmitrievich Demenkov, and the next thing I knew, my sister was showing serious symptoms of being in love. Somehow she managed to arrange opportunities to meet him "accidentally." "Kolya" became part of our regular conversation, as in "Kolya says" this, and "Kolya did" such and such. I missed no opportunity to tease her about him.

At the end of ten days we kissed Papa and Alexei goodbye and boarded our train again for the trip back to Tsarskoe Selo. Papa made plans to take Alexei on a long tour of the battlefront, from end to end. Alexei, who had been marching around at Mogilev in the uniform of an army private with leather boots up to his knees, was beside himself with joy at the prospect. It was hard for Mama to leave Alexei behind, although she must have been pleased to see how happy he was with his life there—the life of a man. She also had a hard time leaving Papa, because she was always lonely without him. And Marie was downcast as well, for an obvious reason: Kolya.

We were welcomed back by our pets—Mama's dog, Eira, Olga's cat, Vaska, Alexei's dog, Joy, and my spaniel, Jimmy—but learned the sad news that Tatiana's French bulldog, Ortino, had sickened and died. Tatiana had so loved that misbehaving little dog! But her friend Dmitri Malama had already been informed of the death, and before Tatiana had even dried her tears, a replacement bulldog arrived at the palace. She named the new puppy Ortino the Second.

I asked her, "Do you love Dimka as much as you love the puppies he's given you?"

Tatiana glared at me and answered in her stern Governess voice, "What a ridiculous question, Nastya! Loving a dog is not the same as loving a person." Then she softened a little, picked up the new Ortino, and nuzzled him. "This is not a good time for falling in love," she said. "Dimka is going to the front, and who knows when I'll see him again."

I knew what she meant: "*If* I'll see him again." Our men were dying by the thousands. Tatiana was right: It was not a good time for falling in love.

A few weeks after our visit to Mogilev, Mama got an urgent telegram from Papa. Alexei had a nosebleed—the result of a terrific sneezing fit while they were traveling to Galicia, where Uncle Nikolasha had had his brilliant victory, to inspect regiments of the Imperial Guard. The bleeding wouldn't stop, and Papa was bringing him home.

We were with Mama at the station to meet the train when it arrived close to midnight. Alexei's bandages were soaked with blood, and he was so pale he looked as though he might be dead, except that his eyes were huge with fright. The doctors did everything they could think of, cauterizing the tiny blood vessel in his nose, but nothing seemed to help. The bleeding went on and on. We thought certainly that this was the end and that Alexei was going to die. In a panic, Mama sent for Father Grigory.

We were kneeling around Alexei's bed, praying with all our hearts, when Father Grigory quietly entered the room. Mama uttered a low moan, but Father Grigory laid a hand on her shoulder, and with the other hand he made the sign of the cross as he gazed down at my brother. "Don't be alarmed," he said gently. "Nothing will happen."

Without another word he walked out of the room and left the palace. Within minutes Alexei was sleeping peacefully. The bleeding had stopped. The crisis was past.

Perhaps Father Grigory, known as Rasputin and hated by so many people, actually was a miracle worker. Or maybe it had just taken a while for the doctors' efforts to succeed. I didn't know. All I knew for certain was that Alexei was alive and he was getting better.

CHAPTER 14

A World Turned Upside Down

TSARSKOE SELO, 1916

n New Year's Day, at Mama's urging, Alexei started keeping a diary, "just like Papa does." He had a curious habit of writing about things he'd done *before* he actually did them, like describing what he'd eaten for dinner before he even sat down at the table. He claimed that he didn't always have time later, and anyway, what difference did it make?

"Writing in a diary every single day is boring," he said. "My *life* is boring," he complained, adding wistfully, "unless I'm at the front with Papa, and then it's not."

The important thing, Papa told him, was to be diligent with his diary. "Someday," he said, "your future subjects will want to know what your life was like before you became their tsar."

I saw Olga and Tatiana exchange quick glances, and I could guess what they were thinking: *Will Alexei live long enough to become tsar?*

Papa returned to Mogilev. Alexei did not go back with him, and that made both of them sad. It took Alexei a long time to recover from those awful setbacks. Who could imagine that a person could almost die from a sneeze!

We resumed writing to Papa every day. Marie asked him to give her regards to Kolya. She even signed her letters "Mrs. Demenkov," which I thought was terribly silly. When Demenkov was reassigned to the palace guards and could often be seen from Mama's balcony, Marie found constant excuses to stand there, waiting for a chance to wave and grin at him and even shout down at him. She persuaded Anya to invite him to tea, and we were all present to observe her flirting. There was nothing subtle about it. And she was overjoyed when she spotted him in church and got to talk to him when we came out. He was not the handsomest boy I'd ever set eyes on, being somewhat chubby, but he did seem pleasant and sweet.

Marie, only sixteen, was still too young to be concerned about a future marriage, but Tatiana would be nineteen in a few months, and Olga was twenty, certainly old enough. If it had been a challenge before the war for our parents to come up with approved suitors, it was now practically impossible.

Then, apparently out of nowhere, Olga got a marriage proposal from Grand Duke Boris Romanov, a son of Papa's oldest uncle. I hardly knew him, because he wasn't included in any of our family gatherings. He was thirty-eight and going bald. It was well known that although he was a military man and supposedly in charge of a Cossack regiment, Boris had so far avoided doing any actual fighting. He had a son my age, but he hadn't married the boy's mother. Mama said Boris had a reputation for flirting with married women and doing things that shocked and appalled her.

"All Boris cares about is taking his pleasure wherever he can find it," Mama sniffed. "Many a woman has shared Boris's life!"

Mama and Boris's mother could not stand each other. They were exact opposites. His mother, Grand Duchess Marie Pavlovna, ranked third in the Empire, after Mama and Grandmère Marie, and she loved to entertain at great parties in her grand palace on the Neva. She had sent the marriage proposal jointly with her son.

"That woman is always looking for ways to raise the standing of her profligate son," Mama said bitterly. "But she will not do it through any daughter of mine."

And that was the end of that.

Mama and Olga and Tatiana put in long days at the hospital, and Marie and I spent mornings with one or another of our tutors. Every day Pyotr Petrov brought us the latest war news that had come in on the telegraph, and we resumed moving the pins on the big map. When we got good news and the pins moved in the right direction, we were buoyed and cheerful—we were winning the war! But the good news didn't last, and everything began to go wrong again. Workers went on strike, there were shortages of food, revolutionaries stirred up trouble, and everyone seemed unhappy with everyone else.

Marie longed for a glimpse of her Kolya. She had begun having conversations with him on the telephone, forbidding me to come anywhere near while she murmured and giggled into the receiver. "This is *private*, Nastya!"

The day came when Kolya received his orders to go to the front. Marie decided to make him a shirt, and every evening for a couple of weeks she concentrated on her sewing. When she'd finished the shirt, she wrapped it with one of her handkerchiefs dabbed with a few drops of her lilac-scented perfume, to remember her by. She arranged to spend a few minutes alone with him, and I suspect that they kissed and made promises to write. After their last time together she looked so sad and puffy-eyed that I couldn't even tease her that Lieutenant Demenkov would go into battle smelling like a flower.

We didn't see much of our cousin Dmitri Pavlovich, which I thought was a shame, because he was always so amusing, so charming—even Mama said so. She was quite fond of him, but she complained about him, too. She thought he was spending too much time in Petrograd, drinking and carousing with Irina's husband, Felix, and she advised Papa to order Dmitri back to his regiment.

Olga had a very low opinion of Felix. "He's nothing but an idler," she said. He had gotten out of joining the military through a law that exempted only-sons, although he did enter the Cadet Corps and even went through officers' training and liked to parade around in his brown uniform—but he avoided joining a regiment. Olga visited Irina at their main palace on the Moika River and noted that Felix had converted one wing into a hospital for wounded soldiers. "Probably Mama shamed him into doing even that much," Olga said.

In March we had a visit from another Dmitri, Dmitri

Malama, who had given Tatiana her first Ortino, now dead. Dmitri sat beside Tatiana in the mauve boudoir with the new Ortino he'd given her romping around, three sisters listening to every word, and Mama observing every move.

Mama called him "my little Malama." "What an adorable boy he is still," she told Lili Dehn, "even though he's become a man. He would have made a perfect son-in-law. Why are foreign princes not as nice as he is?" It's hard to say what Tatiana was thinking. She was the last to let anyone know.

Easter was disappointing. We'd expected to have Papa with us, but he could not leave Mogilev. He felt he had to spend all his time now with his troops. The Fabergé egg that year was terribly ugly, made of steel and mounted on four bulletlike legs. Papa called it a Military Egg. I hoped he didn't have such an awful-looking thing sent to Grandmère Marie. She'd have hated it.

In May Mama was finally persuaded to let Alexei join Papa at Stavka. Alexei was overjoyed—not only to be back with Papa and the men, but also to be promoted from private to corporal and have a second stripe sewn on his sleeve.

Father Grigory was spending more and more time with Mama, and Mama insisted she didn't know what she'd do without his advice. "Your papa relies on me to keep things going as smoothly here as possible," she said. "He has so much to do as commander-in-chief of the army—someone at home has to attend to the behavior of some of those awful men in the Duma. They do everything possible to thwart him at every turn. And just as Papa relies on me, I rely on Father Grigory to suggest which ministers can be most helpful and which ministers are a hindrance and must simply be sent on their way."

We listened and nodded, not saying anything. But Olga had serious worries:

> *I hope the advice Fr. G gives Mother is good, because she does just what he says. She writes long, long letters to Father every day, so I have to believe he knows what is happening.*

> *Mother seems blind to everything going on around her and deaf to what so many are saying. At the hospital, many of the soldiers, even those to whom she has been kind, speak about her disrespectfully. Even the doctors are unkind! She works so hard, and to hear them refer to her as Nemka is painful. They laugh behind her back, forgetting that I'm there or maybe not caring if I overhear them, suggesting that she and Rasputin—Fr. G—do the most disgusting things together. I don't mean just discussing the war and the Duma!*

> *Tanya and I considered trying to warn her about what people are saying, but my sister believes it would do no good and will only anger her. I suggested speaking to Father when he comes home next, but Tanya thinks he already knows what lies people are repeating and is powerless to stop the lies and to stop Mother's reliance on Fr. G.*

I read that passage and cried, forgetting that I might be discovered with Olga's notebook. But maybe it didn't matter if I was caught. Maybe my older sisters would realize that I was no longer an infant and should be included in conversations about matters that at my age—I was now fifteen—I was certainly old enough to understand. Marie was a different story. She still believed absolutely in the goodness of Father Grigory—*starets*, man of God, and worker of miracles.

As I put Olga's notebook away, I wondered if she already knew I was a regular reader. Maybe this was her way of letting me know what was going on without actually *talking* about it. Or maybe I was just making excuses for prying into her private world.

There was one bright spot in the midst of the gloomy war news. Aunt Olga finally persuaded Papa to allow her to divorce Uncle Petya and marry Nikolai Kulikovsky, the cavalry officer she's been in love with for years and years. In November they were married in the Church of St. Nicholas in Kiev. Unlike her elaborate wedding to Uncle Petya—I suppose he is no longer our uncle—this was a simple ceremony. Grandmère Marie, who was now living in her palace in Kiev, Aunt Xenia, Uncle Sandro, and the officers of Aunt Olga's Akhtyrsky Regiment, as well as nurses from the hospital she had founded, were the only guests. Aunt Olga sent us a photograph. She's wearing a plain white wool dress with a little white embroidery, a wreath of flowers on her head, and a short veil. Kolya is dressed in his uniform.

I so wished we had been allowed to go to that wedding, but Mama wouldn't hear of it.

"Had she chosen to marry in Petrograd—better yet, here in Tsarskoe Selo—it might be a different story," she'd said, but

I wondered if that was true. I could tell by the tight line of Mama's mouth that she didn't approve of the marriage. "Olga Alexandrovna has not been discreet about her affair with Kulikovsky. They've been carrying on quite openly for years."

After the war, I hoped, Mama would get over her disapproval, and we'd meet Uncle Kolya. Maybe Aunt Olga would be invited to bring her new husband to Alexander Palace, or to Livadia, or on the next cruise of the *Standart*. I was sure we'd love him, if Aunt Olga did.

We saw so few people that we were all pleased when Mama's sister Ella came again from her convent in Moscow to spend several days in Tsarskoe Selo. Mama arranged to take time away from her hospital duties—Olga and Tatiana, too—and ordered Chef Kharitonov to prepare a special luncheon. Mama just picked at her food, as she always did, but I ate my share and would have eaten hers as well if she had not frowned at me so disapprovingly. Lately she had become concerned that I was getting fat—"round as a barrel," according to Olga and Tatiana, who were both tall and slender. I was short and *not* slender, though describing me as a barrel was going too far.

The talk during the meal was mostly about the war, the shortages in Moscow, the dark mood of the people, the anti-German insults that were often aimed at Aunt Ella.

Coffee—another scarcity—had just been served, a special treat for Aunt Ella, who for some reason preferred it to tea, when she brought up the subject of Father Grigory, suddenly blurting out, "I beg you, Alix, to consider not just your own devotion to Grigory Efimovich, to you a holy man, a man of God—"

"There is nothing to consider," Mama interrupted sharply. "He is all that you have said I believe he is. I have no doubt of his miraculous ability to heal. You know what he has done for Baby and for Anya Vyrubova as well."

Aunt Ella leaned forward and attempted to say something, but Mama held up her hand and continued. "In addition, he offers me excellent advice whenever I ask for it. As you know, while Nicky is at the front, I have tried to help him by taking over some of his responsibilities here at home, replacing ineffectual ministers with those Father Grigory agrees with me are more appropriate. Since Nicky cannot be two places at once, this is a great help to him and to Russia."

"Of course he cannot be two places at once, but Nicky should be in Petrograd, leading the entire country, not at the front with the army. He's not a military man, Alix. He's a tsar. I wonder if he's forgotten that."

Mama, who'd greeted Aunt Ella so warmly when she stepped out of the carriage that morning, had turned cold as ice. "You spout absurdities! Nicky knows exactly where his duties lie, and I support him in that. And Father Grigory supports me." She said this in a tone that we, her daughters, understood meant *This conversation is over.*

I glanced uneasily at my sisters: Olga and Tatiana sat stiffly, their faces masks of calm, but Marie had tears rolling down her cheeks. She was always the one to show her feelings.

"And that is what is particularly alarming," Aunt Ella continued, ignoring Mama's harsh tone. "Rasputin is thoroughly despised by almost everyone. He is not seen as a man of God but as a ruffian who consorts with prostitutes, drinks, and carouses." Aunt Ella glanced at us, but she didn't stop. "He is suspected of being a German spy. You and I know that none of this has even a grain of truth in it, but I don't believe you realize, Alix, how your association with this man is damaging the reputation of the tsar almost beyond repair. Rasputin is taking the Romanov dynasty to ruin, and you are doing nothing to stop it."

"Enough!" Mama cried, slamming her fists on the table so hard that the silverware rattled—and I jumped. "Not one more word, Ella! Everything you have said about Father Grigory is slander and completely baseless. You and I have no more to say on this subject."

"I will not be silenced," said Aunt Ella calmly. "You must hear the truth, and I believe there is no one better suited than I, your own sister, to speak it."

"It is not the truth, not a word of it, and since you will not respect my wishes to speak no more on this subject, I must ask you to leave."

Aunt Ella slumped in her chair. "Perhaps it would have been better if I hadn't come," she said sadly.

"Yes," Mama replied. She called a servant, instructed him to summon a carriage to take Aunt Ella to the train, and stalked out of the dining room.

We four sisters stared miserably at our aunt and at Mama's empty place at the table. No one dared say a word. Marie was sobbing quietly. When Aunt Ella reached out to take her hand, Marie shrank away. Aunt Ella sighed, rose from her chair, and walked slowly around the table, laying a hand on each of our heads and whispering a blessing. Then she left without another word. Marie's sobbing grew louder, Olga buried her head in her hands, and Tatiana pulled out a cigarette and lit it, a habit she had recently acquired. I waited for somebody to say *something*, but no one did. Eventually we left the table, and my older sisters went to change into their uniforms and return to the hospital.

"Mashka, are you coming to the lazaret?" I asked.

She shook her head. "Maybe later," she said miserably. "It's all too sad."

It was snowing hard when I left Alexander Palace for Feodorovsky Gorodok. We did not speak again of Aunt Ella's visit.

Just before Papa and Alexei were due to arrive home for Christmas, something terrible happened that shattered Mama's world: Father Grigory disappeared.

Anya came late one evening with a strange story. She had gone to Father Grigory's apartment in Petrograd to deliver a gift from Mama. He mentioned that he'd been invited to the Yussoupovs' Moika Palace to meet Princess Irina, and Felix was sending a car for him at midnight. Mama knew that Father Grigory often spent time with Felix, but Anya's story puzzled her.

"None of this makes sense," Mama said. "Midnight seems an odd time to visit anyone. And Irina isn't in Petrograd! Xenia told me that she's gone to Crimea."

The next morning while we were having breakfast in her boudoir, Mama left to receive a telephone call. When she returned a little later, her always pale features had turned deadly white. She looked as though she was going to collapse. Tatiana leaped up to help her to her daybed.

"That was the minister of the interior," she said, gasping. "He called to report that gunshots were heard last night at the Yussoupov palace, and one of Felix's friends, quite drunk, bragged to a policeman that he'd killed Rasputin."

Too shocked to know what to say, we gathered close to her.

"Perhaps it's a mistake," she said. "I ordered the minister to investigate. And now I must send a telegram to your father and beg him to come home immediately."

Olga ran to fetch Anya. "He's dead!" Anya wailed when she heard the news. "Murdered! I'm sure of it!"

We sat with Mama and Anya throughout the day, weeping and praying that a miracle would happen and we would have word from Father Grigory, but none came. Rumors flew. Not only was Felix involved—he was even heard boasting about it, saying that he had done it for the good of Russia—but so, too, was Dmitri Pavlovich. Our cousin Dmitri, who'd spent so much time with us, who'd danced the Boston with me—a murderer? Papa had even thought of him as a possible husband for Olga. Impossible!

The minister of the interior reported to Mama that Dmitri's father had asked Dmitri to swear on a holy icon and a picture of his dead mother that he had not murdered Rasputin. He had sworn it, but Mama did not believe him— she'd warned Papa that he was on the wrong path. She ordered Dmitri and Felix to be held under house arrest.

Father Grigory's body was found under the ice of the Neva River. He had been dead for three days. The authorities claimed he had been poisoned and then shot, tied up, and shoved through a hole in the ice. Somehow, they said, he'd survived all that and died by drowning.

Papa and Alexei arrived home to a desolate, grieving family where no one wished to eat, and sleep brought the only relief from our sadness. Papa ordered Dmitri to leave Petrograd immediately and to join the Russian troops fighting in Persia, not even allowing him a chance to say good-bye to his father and receive his blessing. Felix and Irina were banished in disgrace to one of the fifty-seven Yussoupov palaces.

On a bright winter morning, dressed in black mourning clothes, we were driven to the unfinished chapel that Anya was having built in an imperial park at some distance from Tsarskoe Selo. A grave had been dug in a corner of the park, an open wound in the sparkling white snow. The *starets's* body in a plain wooden coffin arrived in a police motor van. Anya was already there, and Lili Dehn joined the seven of us—not because she loved him, but because she truly loved Mama. Before the coffin was sealed, Mama placed on the dead man's breast an icon that we had all signed and a letter she'd written to Father Grigory. She'd brought some white flowers and gave some to each of us to scatter on the coffin after it had been lowered into the grave.

And that was the end of Grigory Efimovich Rasputin, our Father Grigory.

CHAPTER 15

After the Murder

The murder of Father Grigory shook all of us, but Mama most deeply. She no longer had the adviser she depended on while Papa was away at the front, and she did not have the comfort of knowing that Father Grigory could do for Alexei what none of his doctors seemed able to do. Father Grigory had often told her, "If I die or you desert me, you will lose your son and your crown within six months." She believed that.

Papa didn't return to Stavka in January but spent long days shut up in his study, poring over his maps, planning the army's next moves. Our "Ethiopian," the American Negro Jim Hercules, stood guard at his door, hour after hour. Jim knew us well, but he would not let us in to see Papa, even for a minute. It had never been that way in the past. "Strict orders from His Imperial Majesty," Jim told us stiffly. Then his face relaxed in a grin. "Papa says no."

When Papa did leave his study, he looked tired. He had always been thin, but he seemed to have lost even more weight. He smoked constantly. This was not the Papa I knew. Both of my parents were different people. So much had changed since we were all in Mogilev.

During his stay in Tsarskoe Selo, Papa had visits from Uncle Sandro, Irina's father, who made the long journey from his home in Kiev. Uncle Sandro, Papa, and the five of us had luncheon together, but Mama stayed in her boudoir. We made the greatest effort to be cheerful. Uncle Sandro must have felt terrible that Felix, his son-in-law, had done such an awful, horrible, unforgivable thing to Father Grigory. But that was not even mentioned, at least in the presence of me and my sisters and brother. Instead, leaving his food barely touched, our uncle talked about the Russian railways and how they were not able to transport goods.

"The problem has reached a crisis point," he said. "It's necessary to discuss this, Nicky. We're on the verge of a catastrophe, there is no more coal being shipped, food shortages are growing, we are living from day to day, everything is in complete disarray—"

Papa smiled, a wan, unhappy smile, and held up his hand. "Not now, Sandro," he said. "This is neither the time nor the place for such a discussion. My son and certainly my daughters have no need to be involved in such unpleasant conversations. You've told me that you want to talk to Alix about some of the problems facing our beloved country, and she has agreed to do that. But for now, out of consideration for my children, I suggest that we enjoy our meal and put aside such matters until a later time."

I glanced at my sisters. Olga was frowning, a thin line deepening between her eyebrows. Tatiana's face was a perfectly expressionless mask. Marie reached for another sweet. Alexei leaped into the conversation. "Uncle Sandro, you should come to Stavka with Papa and me. We're going back next week, aren't we, Papa? And it's so much fun, being with all the soldiers!"

It was hard to believe, but Uncle Sandro ignored Papa's wish to stop talking about "unpleasant matters." He barely acknowledged what Alexei had just said and pressed on. "It's not just a few extremist revolutionaries and troublemakers who are dissatisfied, Nicky," he insisted. "You must listen to the ministers, the members of the Duma, the Russian people!"

Papa rose slowly to his feet. "That's quite enough, Sandro. I believe the empress is ready to receive us." He forced another humorless smile. "Excuse us, please, my darlings," he said, and steered our uncle out of the dining room.

Alexei was incensed. "He's rude!" he grumbled.

"Perhaps he's also right," Olga said softly—so softly I may have been the only one to hear.

I was curious to see what she would write in her notebook about Sandro's visit. It was even worse than I expected.

What a terrible day! Uncle Sandro came and asked to meet with Mother. Father was with them. After a tense luncheon, I stood outside the door to her boudoir and tried to listen. Sandro began to argue, his voice growing louder until he was almost shouting. "You must stop interfering, Alix! I say this as your friend of many years, but you refuse to listen. You are doing great harm to your

*husband and to Russia. Everyone opposes what you are doing. You
must stop at once and allow Nicky to share his powers with
the Duma."*

*I couldn't make out Mother's reply, but I could guess what she
was saying, because I have heard her say it many times: "The
tsar is the autocrat, the absolute ruler by divine right. All power
is vested in him, as it should be, and he answers only to God!
Certainly not to the Duma!"*

*Tanya happened to come along and demanded to know why I
was eavesdropping. I hushed her and signaled her to listen. Sandro
was roaring, "I have been silent for thirty months, while you
and Rasputin took over the government. You and Nicky may
be willing to die, to let the monarchy die, but what about your
family? You are dragging all of us down with you."*

*Neither Tanya nor I waited to hear any more. Uncle Sandro's
visit was a lot like Aunt Ella's visit—very upsetting but
accomplishing nothing.*

I replaced the notebook and sat shaking on my bed. My
dog, Jimmy, jumped up beside me and licked my hand. I
stroked his silky ears and tried to think. What was happening
to us, to our family? To Russia?

And what was going to happen next?

PART

III

Revolution,

1917

CHAPTER 16

Abdication

aybe Uncle Sandro was right. Certain basic foods had become scarce. Butter Week almost didn't happen, not the way it once did. Kharitonov managed to get enough butter and cheese for our blini, but when Count Benckendorff brought Mama the day's menus, he told her that it was a good thing the Great Fast was beginning.

"The chefs will do their best, Your Majesty, but for the next seven weeks we shall all be eating very simply, even sparingly."

Since our parents ate simply and sparingly anyway, this news didn't seem to bother them as much as it did me.

"By Easter things will certainly be better," Papa said, trying to cheer me up. "We'll celebrate *Pascha* with a grand feast."

Harder to endure than our dreary diet was Papa's decision

late in February to go back to Mogilev—without Alexei. It was a bitterly cold day when we watched him drive off. The guards saluted smartly, frost glistening on their mustaches, and church bells rang out as they always did to mark the tsar's departure. I thought their clamor sounded mournful, and Alexei was weeping with disappointment.

Within hours after Papa had gone, Olga and Alexei began complaining of headaches. When Dr. Botkin came for his daily visit, he took their temperatures, peered into their throats, and announced his diagnosis: measles. Mama remembered that a week earlier some boys from the military school had come to play with Alexei. One of the cadets was coughing and looked flushed.

"I should have sent him away," Mama said. "The boy was coming down with measles but we didn't know it. Alexei caught it, and now Olga, too, is ill. It's only a matter of time until the rest have it."

Tatiana and Anya were the next victims. Marie and I did what we could to help, bringing tea for Mama to give to the patients, fetching hot water bottles one minute and ice bags the next. We weren't allowed in the sickrooms, which were kept dark because light hurt the eyes of the sick ones.

Mama called Lili Dehn and asked her to take the train from Petrograd to spend the day. Whenever Lili came for a visit, she usually brought delightful pastries for our afternoon tea from a shop near her mansion, but this time there were no pastries—only disturbing news.

"People broke into the bakeries, shouting that there was no bread and grabbing whatever they could get their hands on," she told us. "The Cossacks drove them off, but only after they'd done a lot of damage. The Cossacks weren't using their whips—the Duma had ordered them not to interfere. Now the strikes are spreading, and nobody is doing anything to stop them."

Mama shrugged it off. "They're just a lot of hooligans trying to make trouble, Lili."

Lili waited until the servants had poured tea from the samovar and left the boudoir. "Better not to talk about it in front of the servants. You don't know what they may have heard or what they're thinking."

"Good heavens, Lili!" Mama said. "Our servants are completely loyal and trustworthy! They would never cause problems."

"I'm just suggesting that it's better to be cautious. You're awfully isolated here," she said. "I don't think you understand how bad it is in the city. It's been so cold and the snow is so deep that the trains haven't been able to bring coal and flour into Petrograd. Some say it's the troublemakers and not just the snow that halted the trains. People are hungry, and they're angry. They've taken to the streets and brought Petrograd to a standstill. I had trouble just getting to the train station."

"Nicky knows about it. He's ordered troops from the garrison here in Tsarskoe Selo to settle things. We have nothing to worry about."

Mama sounded completely confident. Maybe Uncle Sandro was wrong. Papa would solve the problem. I told myself to stop worrying.

But as the day went on, the news kept getting worse: The

soldiers garrisoned at Tsarskoe Selo had defected. Many other units were going over to the revolutionaries, and the railway workers would not let any new troops arrive.

So maybe Uncle Sandro was right! I started worrying again.

Lili's son, Titi, was at home in Petrograd with his governess. "I'm sure they'll be fine," she said. Lili was like Mama, trying to put the best light on the situation, but I could see the anxiety in her eyes.

She decided not to try to get back to Petrograd that day but to stay the night with us. To keep us both occupied, we worked on a jigsaw puzzle, the pieces spread out around us on the carpet. Mama went out to talk privately to the grand marshal. "Count Benckendorff will know exactly what to do."

Most of the puzzle seemed to be either sky or ocean, some shade of blue or gray. I tried a piece here, a piece there. Progress was slow. Mama came back, dropped into a chair nearby, and watched us. She looked exhausted. She was caring not only for three sick children, but also for Anya, and Anya seemed to require more of her attention than the others did.

"How are you feeling, Nastya?" she asked. I assured her that I felt fine. "No headache or sore throat or fever?"

"I'm fine, Mama, truly."

"I want you to get plenty of rest," she said. "Be a good girlie and go to bed now, please."

I started to protest. I wanted to stay and listen to the conversation, but Lili shook her head, raising one reproving eyebrow, and I dragged myself away. Mama was probably going to tell Lili something—something important—that she didn't want me to hear.

I went looking for Shura. My governess spent a lot of time with Monsieur Gilliard—I suspected they were in love—and our tutor would no doubt have learned something. He always did. When I found her warming my nightgown by the stove, her eyes were puffy from crying. She helped me undress and put on the cozy nightgown. I sat down at my dressing table, and she began to brush my hair. "Please, Shura," I begged, "tell me what you know."

More long, slow strokes of the brush. "Well, I can tell you this much: Your papa ordered a train to take all of you away, but your mama wouldn't even consider leaving, because so many of you are sick." Shura paused, brush in midair. "She says she will wait for your papa to come home. She's sure he'll be here soon."

"It's serious, isn't it?" I asked her reflection in the mirror.

"Yes, dear child, it's serious."

I spun around and faced her. "Shura, why do so many people hate us?"

She stepped behind me and continued brushing to avoid meeting my eyes. "It's true, many people are angry. But many others are devoted to the emperor and the empress, and they— we—will remain loyal, no matter what." Suddenly the brush fell from her hand. "I beg your pardon, Anastasia Nikolaevna," she sobbed, and rushed out of the room.

I picked up the brush and considered what to do. Marie's bed, opposite mine, was still empty. Where was she?

I wished I could talk to Olga—she seemed to understand so much more than I did—but Mama had given instructions that I must not go into her room. I'd had no chance to look at the notebook since she'd fallen ill. Probably, I thought, she'd been feeling too bad to write in it. It was possible that she didn't even know what was going on—about the angry crowds in Petrograd, about Papa wanting us to leave on a train and Mama refusing. But maybe I was wrong and she'd managed to scribble a few lines.

Disobeying Mama's orders, I pulled a robe over my night-gown and crept from my room to Olga and Tatiana's room and quietly opened the door. A small lamp with a scarf thrown over the shade glowed in the corner. I stepped closer to Olga's bed.

"Olya?" I whispered. "Olya, are you awake?"

No answer, and no sound from Tatiana either, except for their ragged breathing.

When my eyes had adjusted to the dim light, I could make out the row of books on the shelf next to Olga's bed. I counted four from the left, its usual position on the shelf, and slid out the notebook with the leather cover that she had once again disguised as a book of devotions. Concealing it beneath my robe, I hurried back to my own bedroom. In the minute or two I'd been gone, Marie had come into our room. She was sitting at her desk, writing a letter—probably to her Kolya, who was now at the front.

"Where have you been, Nastya?"

"Oh, just walking around." It sounded so stupid, even to me, she would have been foolish to believe it, but she nodded and went back to her letter.

I shoved the notebook under my pillow. I was pretty sure Marie hadn't noticed, but now I'd have to wait to read it until she'd fallen asleep or gone to the lavatory.

Fortunately, I didn't have to wait long. Unfortunately, though, I had taken the wrong book—it actually *was* a book of devotions! If I'd been sensible, I would have spent the rest of the evening reading the prayers. Instead, I lay in bed, maddeningly frustrated and trying to imagine what Olga had done with her secret notebook. Had she hidden it in a different place because she suspected I'd been reading it?

Papa's telegram had arrived late the previous evening, after I'd been sent to bed. He was on his way home. But now—it was the next morning—Mama had been trying to reach him and could not. The telegrams she'd sent, one after another, were all returned, undeliverable.

"There's no way for him to communicate with us from the train," Mama said fretfully. "If only I had some way to find out where he is!"

The hours ticked by. Count Benckendorff reported that the railway lines around Petrograd had been seized by revolutionaries. Nervous servants reluctantly passed along rumors that a horde of drunken soldiers was coming to seize "the German woman" and "the heir." In every new rumor the size of the mob grew bigger. Was it just a few dozen drunken soldiers or a mob of hundreds or even thousands? No one knew for sure.

I was really frightened, but Mama seemed unruffled. "We must not be afraid," she told everyone, trying to calm them. "We are in God's hands, and when the emperor arrives, he will know exactly what to do and all will be well."

Count Benckendorff called for fifteen hundred men from

the Marine Guard to defend Alexander Palace. Hour after hour we waited anxiously for the revolutionary mob to attack, but when the sun set at around four o'clock that afternoon, nothing had happened. Papa had still not arrived and there had been no word from him. The bitter cold deepened. The guards built fires to warm themselves, and a kitchen was set up outdoors to feed them hot food. This homely scene was reassuring—these were men who had been our guards on the *Standart*.

Marie and I watched from the window, breathing clearings on the frosted panes. She looked at me carefully. "Are you getting sick?" she asked.

"Of course not," I lied. In fact, I did have a little a headache, a scratchy-feeling throat, maybe a slight fever. "I'm perfectly fine. What about you?"

"Oh, I'm fine, too," Marie said. Maybe she was also lying.

Then Mama asked Marie to go out with her to speak with the guards. "To encourage them," Mama explained. "To thank them for their loyalty."

Marie went for her coat and warm boots. "I'll stay here," I said.

My head started to throb. I wanted to curl up in my bed under a warm blanket, but I made myself stay at the window as Mama and Marie, swathed in thick furs, woolen scarves, and gloves, stepped out into the palace courtyard. Count Benckendorff, a stiff old soldier, went with them. Some of the guards were kneeling in the snow with their rifles raised, and more guards stood behind them, also ready to fire. Mama and Marie walked up and down between the rows of soldiers, stopping often to talk to them.

When my mother and my sister came back inside, stamping their feet and blowing on their numb fingers, Mama looked almost *happy*. "They're our friends!" she exulted. "I've told the officers to allow the men into the palace to warm themselves with hot tea."

That night I slept fitfully. I kept hearing gunshots, and when I crawled out of bed the next morning, I discovered that a huge gun had been set up in the courtyard. What a surprise that would be for Papa! Mama kept assuring us that he would certainly arrive that morning. Everything would be better once he was here.

But still he didn't come, and everything was getting steadily worse. The soldiers who had been protecting us began to desert, going over to the other side. The electricity and water had been cut off. Without electricity, the elevator didn't operate, and Mama, whose rooms were on the first floor, had to be half-carried up the stairs to our bedrooms on the second floor, where Olga and Tatiana and Alexei lay ill. We lit candles in our rooms, but the halls were dark as a moonless night. Servants broke the ice on the pond and melted it for cooking and drinking.

I willed myself *not* to get sick, but I knew that I was. Marie, too, looked feverish.

Some of our servants who had gone into Petrograd before the trains were stopped managed to make their way back to Tsarskoe Selo. A few borrowed horses; others walked, arriving cold and exhausted with blisters on their feet. They came to Mama's room to show her the printed leaflets they said were being handed out all over Petrograd.

"I do not believe it!" Mama cried, and shredded a leaf-let into pieces. "I will *not* believe it! It's nothing but a vicious rumor."

Marie picked up a leaflet and read it. Weeping, she handed it to me.

Angry red headlines announced that Tsar Nikolai Alexandrovich had abdicated, Grand Duke Mikhail Alexandrovich had renounced his claim to the throne, and a Provisional Government had been established.

My mind was fuzzy. Perhaps it was the fever. I couldn't think properly. *Abdicated?* What did it mean, exactly? What had Uncle Misha to do with it? What was a Provisional Government? *Papa* was the government, wasn't he? Papa was the tsar!

Except that now, if what was in the leaflets was true, he wasn't the tsar anymore. How could that be?

In a voice thick with tears, Lili tried to explain. "If it's true, it means that your father has given up his throne, relinquished his power. He is no longer the emperor, the tsar."

"But what about Lyosha? Isn't he the tsarevich? Isn't he supposed to be the next tsar, after Papa?"

"Yes, we all hoped and prayed that he would be. I don't know exactly what happened, but perhaps your papa under-stood that Lyosha is too young to be tsar, and he is often ill, and perhaps your papa then decided that it would be better to pass the crown to his younger brother, who is next in line after Lyosha. Then, for whatever reason—perhaps he was forced to do so—Mikhail Alexandrovich also gave up his claim. And now some sort of government is taking over."

"But maybe it isn't even true!" I insisted. "You've only read a leaflet, a meaningless piece of paper! That doesn't make it true, does it?"

Lili shook her head, dabbing at her eyes. "I wish I could agree with you," she said.

Oh, if only Papa would come and make it right!

That evening Uncle Pavel, father of my cousin Dmitri, who had helped murder Father Grigory, came to see Mama. Lili and I were in the next room, keeping our hands busy with knitting. We'd abandoned the jigsaw puzzle, but by then I was feeling too poorly to keep my mind on my needles, and I kept dropping stitches. In the next room voices rose and fell. After a while, silence—Uncle Pavel must have gone.

The silence continued, and Lili murmured that perhaps she should go check on Mama, make sure she was all right.

Then the door opened, and Mama just stood there. I cannot describe the look of agony on her face. Lili jumped up and ran to catch her before she could collapse.

"Abdicated!" Mama cried. "It's true! He has abdicated!"

Abdicated. I understood now what it meant. Papa was no longer the Tsar of All the Russias.

I guessed what Mama was thinking. *If I die or you desert me, you will lose your son and your crown within six months,* Father Grigory had often told her. She believed that. Now at least part of his prediction seemed to be coming true.

"Nicky telephoned," Mama said brokenly. "Just now. We spoke a little."

Lili helped Mama to a chair and knelt beside her. Mama was making a great effort to pull herself together. "It's God's will," she said in a faint and trembling voice. "God brings this to us in order to save Russia, and that's all that matters." She swallowed hard. "And my poor darling Nicky! He's back at Mogilev. The train was stopped at Pskov, and that's where he . . . where he signed the papers. And I'm not there with him, to help him, to console him."

She waved us away. Her hand was shaking. "I need to be alone for a little," she said. How pale she looked! Then she added, "And Lili . . . Nastya . . . say nothing to the other children just now, will you? They're so sick, they shouldn't be disturbed."

Lili nodded, I did, too, and we quietly left the room. Before the door closed, I heard my mother's wrenching sobs.

My head was pounding, and I felt weak with fever. I could scarcely think, but it was slowly beginning to sink in—if Papa was no longer tsar, then Mama was not the tsaritsa, and Alexei was not the tsarevich. I supposed that now my sisters and I were not grand duchesses, but simply girls like any others. Overnight we had become an ordinary family. An extraordinary ordinary family.

"What's going to happen now, Lili?" I asked.

"I don't know," she whispered. "I simply don't know."

And then we, too, clutching each other's hands, began to cry, and I cried until someone—maybe it was Shura—carried me off to bed.

CHAPTER 17

A "Normal Routine"

A man in uniform with rows of medals parading across his chest arrived at the palace and introduced himself: General Kornilov, commander of the military in Petrograd. The general spoke politely to Mama. He was there to inform her that she was under house arrest. Papa had already been arrested at Mogilev.

"The former tsar will arrive tomorrow," Kornilov said. "He, of course, will also be under house arrest. I shall see to it that everything is done to keep you as safe and comfortable as possible." A British cruiser was already on its way to Murmansk, he said, to pick up our entire family and take us to England, as soon as we children had recovered from the measles and were well enough to travel.

There was more from the general: Mama's ladies-in-waiting and Papa's gentlemen were permitted to stay—and also be under house arrest—or they could leave, but if they chose to go, they could not return. Most of the members of Papa's and Mama's suite quickly left. Many of the servants fled, too.

Anya stayed, of course, as well as Baroness Buxhoeveden, Count Benckendorff and his wife, and Monsieur Gilliard. Dr. Botkin sent Gleb and Tatiana to live with the grandmother of close friends and promised to remain with us. So did Lili Dehn.

"But what about Titi?" Mama asked.

"He's with Anna, my maid," Lili said. "She'll do anything for him. And I have asked my father to come from Crimea to look after them until I return."

It was very late when the general and his aides had gone. All the doors to Alexander Palace were locked, except for the main entrance and another entrance near the kitchen. Guards stood at both doors. We were prisoners, but we didn't feel it yet, because now all of us were sick. I, too, had come down with measles. Marie had developed pneumonia in addition to measles. Tatiana and I both had painful ear infections, and Tatiana seemed quite deaf.

When a motorcar arrived from the train station early the next morning, no church bells rang to greet the tsar who was no longer tsar. Mama met Papa alone—we were too sick to go down—and a little while later he came to our rooms to see us. When he leaned down and kissed me, his mustache bristling against my cheek, I threw my arms around his neck and hugged him with all my strength. My dearest papa was home at last.

The soldiers who'd been assigned to guard us were scandalous. They weren't like the soldiers Marie was so fond of—not at all like her Kolya, who had not been heard from in months. These men didn't bother to shave or comb their hair, their boots were filthy, they went about with their jackets unbuttoned. Worse, they roamed through the palace, peering into our rooms and handling our things without permission or any sense of decency. When Dr. Botkin came to check on his patients, to listen to our hearts and look into our throats and our ears, the soldiers walked right into our bedrooms to watch. Dr. Botkin shooed them out, but they stood in the doorway, gawking at us and making rude comments.

The soldiers were not the only ones to behave disgracefully. Since Alexei had been a tiny boy, he had depended on two loyal sailor-attendants, Nagorny and Derevenko, assigned to keep him as safe as possible. For years those sailors, who were once part of the crew of the *Standart*, had done everything for my brother, patiently distracting him, amusing him—anything to prevent him from getting hurt. Now one of the sailors, Derevenko, turned viciously against him. Anya saw Derevenko slouching in a chair and shouting orders at Alexei: "Bring me this!" "Do that, and be quick about it!" "Who do you think you are?"

Alexei must have thought it was some sort of stupid game, and he hustled around, trying to do what he'd been told. Anya told Papa what she'd witnessed, and when Papa confronted Derevenko, the disgruntled sailor stormed out. None of us could understand it. Had Derevenko been seething with resentment all this time, and no one knew it? How many others were there like him? Nagorny was furious at Derevenko's boorish behavior and gave his word that he would stay.

Papa was amazed by the behavior of the soldiers. "I'm shocked. I know of General Kornilov—he was a prisoner of the Austrians until he escaped last summer and returned to duty. He's been twice awarded the Order of St. George and several other medals. Not the sort of man I would have expected to allow his men to exhibit such complete lack of discipline. I shall certainly speak to him the next time he comes here."

But we did not see General Kornilov again.

Mama and Papa concluded that maintaining a normal routine was the best way to cope with our new situation. Once we'd recovered from our illnesses, we rose at the same hour, made our own beds as we always had, ate breakfast at the same time, and dressed in the outfits Mama had chosen for us. Then Alexei, Marie and I—Olga and Tatiana were exempt—went off to the schoolroom. The adults divided up the tutoring chores: Papa taught history and geography, and Mama was in charge of religious studies. Monsieur Gilliard still tried to pound French into our heads. Baroness Buxhoeveden instructed us in English and piano. Mademoiselle Schneider—dear Trina, who had long abandoned her efforts to teach us German—was in charge of mathematics, hoping to convince us of the joy of algebra, geometry, and trigonometry. Mama's friend Countess Hendrikova volunteered to give art lessons. Even Dr. Botkin was recruited as a tutor in Russian, replacing Pyotr Petrov, who had gone away and not come back.

The other person missing from our prison school was Mr. Gibbes.

"Where is Sydney Ivanovich?" Alexei asked.

"He was in Petrograd when the new government took over," Papa explained. "I'm told that he came back to Tsarskoe Selo, but he wasn't allowed to enter Alexander Palace, or to see us or talk to us."

"Why?"

"I have no idea. Maybe they think he would help us escape."

This amused my brother. None of us could imagine the Englishman doing anything of the sort. "The men who are making us prisoners must be very stupid," Alexei said.

"Possibly," Papa agreed with a little smile.

"What about Pyotr Petrov?" I asked, but no one knew. He was simply not there. Only his maps remained.

I enjoyed the art lessons and could have done without the rest of the instruction, except from Papa, who was always so kind and gentle that I wanted to please him, and sometimes Mama, who was stern and kept us focused on our lessons.

Olga was glad not to be a student. She wanted only to be left alone to read. I suspected that she had resumed writing in her notebook, but I couldn't find it. I made several quick visits to her room to search, always risking being found out. Finally I discovered it—a new notebook, hiding inside the cover of a book titled *Advanced Mathematics*.

Have my parents lost their minds? The situation is ridiculous. Father is no longer the tsar, he is "Citizen Romanov," and he seems not to mind too much, although Mother minds a great deal and looks angry most of the time. He sits and smokes and says that when the weather is warmer we will have a garden. Mother seems to think we are all still "children."

When she talks about us, it is always "the children." I am twenty-one, an adult by anyone's definition. In a few months Tanya will be twenty, and Mashka will be eighteen. Our mother was only a year older than I am when she and Father married, but she still chooses what we are to wear each day, while the world falls apart around us. Tanya weeps secretly for Dimka—"our little Malama," as Mother calls him, as though he, too, were nothing but a child. We have had no word of him for months. Mashka mopes and writes letters to her Kolya but receives no reply. Both are no doubt dead, but I don't say that, and my sisters keep hoping for news.

Nastya is going on sixteen and smokes—she thinks no one knows, but I've seen her with a cigarette. I was sixteen when I fell in love with Pavel, and I wonder when our Nastya will have a chance to fall in love. I do pity any man she marries—she'll make joke after joke and tease him until he begs for mercy.

So—Olga believed I would drive any man crazy, forcing the poor fellow to beg for mercy! I had to swallow my annoyance, at least for the present. As for smoking, it was true; I'd tried it a few times. Papa smoked steadily, and Mama said that smoking calmed her. Probably my sisters smoked, too.

There would be no Easter in Livadia; that was obvious. There was no point in even talking about it, because talking just made us more unhappy. We had been told that we had to stay inside and were not allowed to go out—not even to the cathedral for services. Mama's sitting room was made into a private chapel, and we brought the holy icons from our rooms. Four soloists from the imperial choir sang beautiful hymns, while outside the palace soldiers paraded up and down and a band played the "Marseillaise." Mama prayed, tears pouring unchecked down her cheeks. Papa prayed, his thin face like the face of a martyred saint in an old icon.

On Saturday, before the Easter Eve service, a priest came from the cathedral to hear our confessions. I was supposed to contemplate my sins while I waited my turn. Should I confess that I had made a habit of reading my sister's secret notebook—not just once, but as often as possible? Was that really a sin? Olga would probably say that it was, but what about God? Would He think it was a sin, and if so, why? The priest was likely to agree with Olga. I decided not to mention it.

When I knelt beside the screen that had been set up to conceal the confessor, I rattled off a list of minor sins—speaking unkindly to Mashka or to Shura, complaining about my lessons, sneaking a forbidden sweet during the Great Fast. But suddenly I burst out passionately, "My gravest sin is hatred. I *hate* Uncle Willy for starting this ugly war! I *hate* the Germans who kill our Russian soldiers! More than anything, I *hate* the revolutionaries who forced Papa to abdicate!"

I was talking loudly instead of murmuring quietly, and the priest hustled out from behind his screen to calm me. He gave me my penance, instructing me to pray for those I hated and to pray for God to enter my heart and cleanse it of all anger.

Not much chance of that, I thought.

At midnight we stood behind a glass screen for the Easter Eve service, which lasted a couple of hours. I wondered how

Mama was able to stand for such a long time, when she usually spent so much of her day on her daybed or in her wheelchair, but her fervent love of God must have given her the strength.

We were forbidden to have a procession, but at the end of the service, when the priest turned to us and cried, "Christ is risen!" we did manage to shout, "He is risen indeed!" Then we all returned to the library.

Food shortages were still serious, but in spite of that Kharitonov and the kitchen staff had laid out a traditional Easter feast of *paskha* and loaves of sweet *kulich*. Besides the servants who still remained with us, and our tutors and maids, Papa had invited the officers of the men ordered to guard us.

"But they're not protecting us," Olga remarked. "They're here to keep us from escaping."

"They are Russians, and they are Christians," Papa explained in his quiet, patient way. "We embrace them on this holy day as fellow human beings."

I did not understand how Papa could do this. All I could think about was how much I hated the people who had put us in this terrible situation, despite the priest's orders that I must cleanse my heart. I thought Mama agreed with me more than she did with Papa.

Papa had ordered jeweled Fabergé eggs for Mama and Grandmère Marie, as he always did, but only my grandmother's gift had been delivered. Mama's egg had not been finished by Easter. Monsieur Fabergé apologized to Papa, closed his shop, and fled from Petrograd.

This year's egg was made of a special kind of birchwood with scarcely any trimming on the outside, very austere, but

inside was a tiny mechanical elephant studded with diamonds. The problem was how to get it to Grandmère Marie. Papa was deeply worried about her. She had traveled on her train from Kiev to Mogilev to spend a few days with Papa before he came home. She'd returned to Kiev, but now Papa had no way of communicating with her. He decided to send the egg to Uncle Misha at his palace in Gatchina, and asked him to find a way to deliver it to their mother.

"Things will be different next year, Alix," Papa promised Mama. "And you shall have your egg."

We all pretended to believe him. Only Marie actually did.

We had mostly recovered from the measles and the infections, and we were feeling better, but we looked genuinely awful. The medicines Dr. Botkin prescribed made our hair fall out in clumps, and Mama decided it would be best to shave it all off and let it grow back naturally. The court hairdresser came to our rooms with an assistant, and, one by one, we each became as bald as eggs—chicken eggs, not the gilded Fabergé kind. When I looked in the mirror, I didn't know whether to laugh or cry.

I made a stupid joke about when we were going to hatch, and we found scarves and hats and sometimes wigs to cover our naked skulls. We were wearing straw hats when Monsieur Gilliard lined us up for a photograph one bright and sunny day, and by prearranged signal we swept off our hats and grinned for the camera just as he was about to snap the picture. That photo is one of my favorites. Naturally, Mama wasn't pleased.

We mugged for the camera, but in private we struggled

with our confusion and our fears. Marie was determinedly optimistic: "Everything will work out! A British ship will take us to England, where we'll be safe until we can come back. We must have faith, we must not waver, and we must do everything we can to keep Mama's spirits up, and Papa's, too."

Tatiana steadfastly reinforced everything Mama said and emphasized that we must stay together. "We are OTMA. We must always remember that what one of us says or does must support the others. We are a team, a single unit, no matter what. It's the best way to get through this trying time."

I was the *shvibzik*, the one who crossed her eyes, stuck out her tongue, mimicked the court ladies with their imperious ways, laughed at Dr. Botkin's French perfume that signaled his arrival and Count Benckendorff's monocle that dropped out of his eye when he was excited. But I had difficulty sleeping, my dreams were troubled, and I woke up crying out.

I clowned, Marie cheered, Tatiana exhorted, but Olga said little. She seemed very far away. For long periods she didn't even write in her notebook. Then I found this:

From my earliest memories our lives have been orderly and predictable. We were told which hours we would spend with our tutors. We had luncheon with guests at one o'clock, a meal that lasted exactly fifty minutes. Dinners with the family, Sunday lunches with Grandmère Marie, and afternoon parties at Aunt Olga's. In summer we cruised on the Standart *or stayed at Peterhof, traveled by train to Livadia in fall and spring, endured the hunting lodges for Papa's sake. It was a calm, well-ordered life. I could imagine no other.*

And yet I was not satisfied. I yearned to escape that predictable life, to find something different. The only way out was through marriage, but not if it meant leaving Russia. I was clear about that. And certainly not if it meant spending my life with an oafish character like Prince Carol! Mother and Father were understanding, to a point. I would not be forced to marry someone I did not love, but that didn't mean I could marry someone I did love.

Now everything has changed, and it will never again be the same. My calm, orderly, predictable life is over, and no one knows what will come next. Mama and Papa no longer speak of the British cruiser supposedly waiting for us in Murmansk. It was all a lie.

But still we did not talk about how we felt—about being prisoners, about the future. As if talking about what we feared most would somehow make it happen.

CHAPTER 18

$\mathscr{H}$ouse $\mathscr{A}$RRest

I n the weeks after Papa came home from Mogilev, we struggled to adjust to our situation. The first time Papa tried to go out into our park for a walk, a half dozen soldiers surrounded him. They pushed and prodded him with their rifle butts and ordered him around, telling him, "You can't go there, Mister Colonel," or "You're not permitted to walk in that direction, Mister Colonel."

Anya was watching from a window. "Your poor papa said nothing at all to those coarse brutes. He simply turned around and came back to the palace. The tsarevich was with him, and he was in tears, seeing how they treated your father. The total lack of respect was appalling. Baby held his head high and was silent, but anyone could see that he was deeply wounded."

After that, Monsieur Gilliard and several others joined Papa and his friend Prince Dolgorukov for morning and afternoon walks. First, they had to wait in the semicircular hall for the officer in charge to unlock the gates to the park. Guards surrounded the little group for the short distance they were allowed to walk—not even as far as the pond, which we could see from Mama's balcony—and they all had to return together.

It bothered Papa to have his walk cut so short. He always took a lot of exercise. Besides the swimming bath in his bathroom, he had an exercise bar—there was even one on our train—and he loved long hikes. I remembered one such hike when I was eight or nine: I insisted on accompanying him on a walk around our special island on the Finnish coast. Papa warned me that it would be a very long walk, but I was stubbornly determined. It turned into a twelve-mile march, and I wept through most of it.

To the soldiers, Papa was a prisoner deserving no respect, but to people like Count Benckendorff, Papa was still the tsar. Others weren't quite sure how to address him.

One day Papa's favorite Delaunay-Belleville limousine with Papa's chauffeur behind the wheel drove up to the entrance to the palace. Out stepped an official of the new government. Count Benckendorff went to greet him.

"I am Alexander Fyodorovich Kerensky, minister of justice in the service of the Provisional Government," said the man. "I have come to inspect the palace and see how you live, and to speak with Nikolai Alexandrovich."

We were at luncheon when this happened and knew nothing about it until the old count told us later that he had taken the minister of justice on a tour of the palace while we ate. Kerensky had ordered his men to go through each room of our quarters, searching drawers and cupboards, even peering under the beds.

One of our maids, still trembling from the experience, described what she had seen. "They went into the room where Madame Dehn was having lunch with Madame Vyrubova. The ladies were terrified! Madame Vyrubova was still feeling very weak, and when she heard them coming, she crawled into bed and tried to hide under the covers. I stood very still and prayed that he would not notice me! Kerensky pulled back the blanket and shouted at her, 'I am the minister of justice. Dress and go at once to Petrograd!'"

Poor Anya had been too frightened to answer, and the minister summoned Dr. Botkin and asked him if she was well enough to leave. The doctor said that she was, and that made Anya furious. She never forgave him.

The minister of justice now wished to see us. Papa decided we would meet with him in our schoolroom. Suddenly this familiar place felt strange and threatening. Anya and Lili were there, waiting to be taken away. Lili was worried about her little son, Titi—he'd been ill when Lili came to help us, and she'd had no word about him for days because the palace telephone line had been disconnected.

Mama told them sadly, "This good-bye matters little. We shall meet in another world."

"But surely we'll see them again soon!" Marie cried.

Olga stared at the floor and shook her head once, very slightly. Tatiana ran to her room and brought two little portraits of Mama and Papa for Lili to take with her. I hugged Lili again and again until the soldiers came. We watched them being led down the staircase, Anya hobbling on her crutches. Mama surely believed that was the last time we would ever see them.

We were all crying when Minister Kerensky entered the schoolroom. I didn't know what to expect—a monster, possibly, but Kerensky did not look like a monster. His hair was cut very short, and he had neither a beard nor a mustache. He was not a tall man, but Papa is not a tall man either, and they looked at each other eye to eye. Neither of them seemed to know what to do next. Then Papa put out his hand, and so did Kerensky, and they shook hands and actually smiled at each other.

Mama was *not* smiling, even when the minister of justice—he kept reminding us of his title—tried to reassure us. "You must not be frightened, madame," he said. "Please have complete confidence that all will go well for you."

For almost a week nothing happened. I began to feel that maybe we really could trust the minister of justice and that all would go well. But when Mama asked to have some fresh flowers brought from her greenhouse—flowers always cheered her—she was told that flowers were a luxury to which she was not entitled.

Then Kerensky separated our parents in order to question them, and kept them separated for eighteen days. We worried, not knowing what was happening.

"Kerensky is not a bad sort," Papa told us when it was over. "He's a good fellow. One can talk to him. We began to get along and developed a kind of mutual respect. I wish I had met him long ago. He would have had a position in the government."

Mama agreed—I had not expected that! "He told me that the king and queen of England have been asking for news of us."

That cheered us immensely. Maybe Olga was wrong—it wasn't a lie. We told each other excitedly that it surely meant arrangements were being made for us to leave for England. A cruiser could still pick us up at Murmansk. We waited for more information.

"We must be patient," Papa said. "Kerensky is our friend. I'm sure of it."

I had been prepared to hate Kerensky, but I began to feel hopeful again.

Spring is coming, according to the calendar, but it's still awfully cold and damp—inside the palace as well as outside, because Benckendorff says there is now a shortage of firewood.

I try not to think of Livadia, where flowers are blooming and the air at this time of year is soft and warm. I also try not to think about Pavel, about any of the life I wanted—or even of those brave young men I met at the hospital. That's over.

What surprises me most is Father. I was shocked when he came home from Mogilev. He has aged so much, his face is so deeply lined, he is thinner than ever. And his eyes are so sad! Mother's beautiful hair has gone completely gray. She never smiles, but why would she? There is really nothing to smile about, and I wonder if there ever will be again. Tanya says I must not be so gloomy, that my low mood affects everyone, and to demonstrate her joy in life she walks around with a fixed smile. Mashka is lucky—she lives in her own dream world, loving everybody, grinning at Kerensky as though he was her best friend. I trust him not at all—not because he is a bad man, but because I believe he is powerless, almost as powerless as we are.

Then there's Nastya, clowning around and pulling silly faces, a true shvibzik. *But sometimes I catch her watching me, as though she knows what I'm thinking. I pray that she does not, because I see nothing good ahead for any of us. The youngest OTMA may be the only one in the family I could talk to honestly, but*

That's where Olga stopped writing. Someone must have come in and interrupted her, and she slapped the *Advanced Mathematics* book shut, smearing the last word, before she shoved the notebook back on the shelf. "But" *what*? What was she thinking? I wondered if I would ever find out.

Our life as spring slowly unfolded was very strange. We could spend more time outdoors, but waiting for an officer to meet us with a key to our own park was annoying. The soldiers jeered at us and shouted stupid insults. One soldier poked his bayonet in the wheel of Papa's bicycle and made him fall off. If I had been Papa, I would have been furious, but if he was angry, he didn't show it. I wanted to stick out my tongue and cross my eyes and make fun of those idiotic soldiers, especially the young ones with pimples on their faces and teeth that they hardly ever brushed.

"What girl would ever want to kiss you!" I shouted at them, but I shouted in English so there was no chance they'd

226 · C A R O L Y N   M E Y E R

understand. I felt better when I'd done it, but soon after that a
new rule was imposed: We were not allowed to speak English
or French, even to each other—only Russian.

Every day crowds of ordinary people jammed against the
fence surrounding the park and gawked at us, as though we
were animals in a zoo. Some whistled and yelled insults, most
of them directed at Papa. This drove Alexei crazy. He couldn't
stand seeing Papa treated so disrespectfully. "They used to kiss
Papa's shadow when he passed by," Alexei raged. "And now
they call him names and spit at him."

Papa seemed less concerned about all of this than he was
about the progress of the war, which he followed in the newspapers he was still allowed to read. Soldiers were deserting
by the hundreds, maybe thousands, and the army seemed to
be melting away. "I worry that the Provisional Government
isn't strong enough to pull itself together to win the war," he
told Mama. "It would be a disaster for Russia if England and
France make peace with Germany."

Whenever they talked about the war, I thought of Olga's
Pavel and Tatiana's "little Malama" and Marie's Kolya and
all those brave wounded soldiers Mama and my sisters and
I had cared for in the hospital. Were any of them still alive?
Sometimes I could not bear to think of it anymore.

In May a new officer, Colonel Kobylinsky, was put in charge of
the soldiers at Tsarskoe Selo. On the whole, the officers were
not a bad lot. Many of them were actually quite decent men,
and it wouldn't have surprised me if Marie had taken it into her
head to fall in love with one of them. Colonel Kobylinsky was

one of the best—he seemed to like us, and we liked him, too. He had been a member of the Imperial Guard and had fought at the front, until he was wounded. But the regular soldiers were mostly boorish louts, shooting off their guns at all hours, killing the tame deer in the park and even the beautiful swans floating regally in the pond. The least thing put the soldiers in an uproar. One day they found Alexei playing with a toy gun and demanded that he surrender it. Colonel Kobylinsky got it back and smuggled it to my brother, piece by piece, but he sternly ordered Alexei not to march with it outside.

When the last of the snow had finally disappeared and the ground was thawed, Papa announced that we would plant a kitchen garden in the park. We set to work, digging up the grass and carrying it away. Our tutors and most of the servants helped with the huge effort of preparing the soil. Even some of the soldiers pitched in. Mama watched from her wheelchair, a blanket over her knees and a needlepoint project in her lap.

Papa supervised the layout, deciding which vegetables should be planted where. We sowed seeds, putting in row after row of carrots, five hundred cabbages, and every kind of vegetable. We hauled water from the kitchen in barrels on wheels. We'd never worked so hard in our lives, but Papa insisted that physical exercise was far better than sitting and brooding, and no doubt he was right. It was certainly better than being cooped up all day in our schoolroom, memorizing French parts of speech. Even Monsieur Gilliard grudgingly admitted that.

The days passed with the endless cycle of watering and weeding. The garden thrived during the long hours of daylight, and the cabbages were growing huge. When I teased Papa that he would be eating cabbage three meals a day, he replied, "And for tea as well."

He moved on to cutting down dead trees in the park. He and Monsieur Gilliard chopped the trees into firewood, and we stacked it in piles.

"Think how warm this will keep us next winter!" Papa said cheerfully, and I saw Olga look at him and guessed what she was thinking: *If we're still here next winter.*

In the evenings we were weary to the bone, but it was a *good* kind of weariness. We did needlework in Mama's mauve boudoir while Papa read to us from the Russian classics. I loved Gogol's short stories. My favorite was "The Nose."

We observed another round of birthdays. I was now sixteen.

Grandmère Marie once promised that we would celebrate my sixteenth birthday in Paris. I had always imagined that we'd go there by imperial train. But was there such a thing now as an imperial train? Or was it called something else? It seemed better not to say anything about it. I could imagine Olga's dour look if I did. But no one could stop me from dreaming.

My best present was a birthday greeting from Gleb Botkin. He was sometimes allowed to visit his father in the guardhouse, and he'd made a little card that folded like a fan, small enough to fit in Dr. Botkin's boot. On the title page he had printed: *The Adventures of Anastasia Mouse,* followed by a series of drawings in colored pencil. In the first the mouse wore a court dress, her tiny paws peeking out of the open sleeves and a *kokoshnik* perched above her pink ears. In the background were the onion-shaped domes of St. Basil's Cathedral by the Kremlin in

Moscow. In the next drawing Anastasia Mouse peered out of the window of the imperial train, next she was on a yacht with *Standart* lettered on the bow, and finally she stood by the Eiffel Tower. The mouse had made her way to Paris!

On the last page he'd written, *To Anastasia Nikolaevna on the occasion of her 16th birthday. With kind regards from your friend, Gleb Evgenievich.*

In low voices we discussed what might happen next. Minister of Justice Kerensky had spoken again of a ship to take us to England. Papa's cousin King George V would see to it that we were allowed to stay there. Their mothers were sisters, and in old photographs King George and Papa looked so much alike it was hard to tell them apart. There had been disagreements between them; King George believed in the English parliamentary system with a cabinet and a prime minister, and Papa believed a tsar was destined by God to rule as an autocrat. Nevertheless, Papa started sorting through his books and papers, deciding what he would take with him.

But everything remained unsettled. Kerensky was sympathetic to Papa and our family, and he held an important position in the Provisional Government—he had been promoted to prime minister—but a militant group, the Bolsheviks, opposed that government. The Bolsheviks were not sympathetic to us—they hated us!—and they controlled the rail lines. Kerensky said now that he feared we'd never get through to Murmansk. He told Papa he thought we'd be safer somewhere else in Russia.

"I suggested Crimea," Papa reported to us with a rare smile.

230 • Carolyn Meyer

"And Kerensky says it might be possible. In any case, he told me we should start packing."

Livadia! How splendid that would be! Grandmère Marie had left Kiev for Crimea, and so had Aunt Olga and her new husband and the baby we'd learned she was expecting, and Uncle Sandro and Aunt Xenia were there with loads of cousins—who were probably still barbarians, but it didn't matter. Mama was sure the Tatars who lived in the mountains around Yalta were our friends. We were so excited that we could talk of little else— until Count Benckendorff warned us that this constant talk of Livadia was unwise.

"You may be unaware of it," he said, "but there are spies in every corner of the palace, listening to every word you say and passing it along to their superiors."

We became very careful then, wondering which of our servants might be eavesdropping. Who could be trusted and who could not? We spoke in whispers, never sure there wasn't someone crouching on the other side of the door with an ear to the keyhole or taking note of our chatter over the cabbage soup at dinner.

The day before Alexei's thirteenth birthday, Kerensky came to the palace and spoke privately to Papa for a long time. After he'd gone, Papa gathered us together to tell us the news: We would leave Tsarskoe Selo very soon—possibly within two days.

"To Livadia?" Mama asked hopefully, but anyone looking at Papa's face could see that we were not to get what we had wished for.

"Kerensky would say only this: 'Pack your furs and plenty of warm clothes.'"

I sighed. "Could it be Murmansk after all?" Tatiana suggested. "And then on to England?"

But Olga said doubtfully, "It doesn't get that cold in England."

Papa shook his head resignedly. "Probably Siberia."

Mama groaned. "Oh no! Perhaps if you spoke to him again, Nicky?"

"If this is what he says we must do, then we have no choice. We have to trust him."

For the next two days it was a mad scramble to get ready, with only a pause long enough to observe Alexei's birthday. Mama asked for a certain holy icon to be brought from the church. A flock of solemn, black-robed priests with beards down to their waists accompanied the icon, and we followed them into the chapel. The realization of what was about to happen was finally dawning on all of us, and everybody was in tears—even a few of the soldiers who were guarding us. The priests called for prayers for a safe journey, to wherever it was we were going.

My brother, however, had just one birthday wish: "Please do not call me Baby anymore," he said. "I'm thirteen. I wish to be called Alexei, or Lyosha. No more Baby."

I personally felt that it was about time to call Alexei by a grown-up name, but Mama wept and said she'd try but could make no promises.

CHAPTER 19

Good-bye to Tsarskoe Selo

ur parents asked our closest, most loyal friends— people who had refused to leave Alexander Palace when they had the chance—to go with us, even though we didn't yet know where we were asking them to go.

Count Benckendorff told us sorrowfully that he could not come. His wife was ill, and he must stay behind with her.

Papa clapped the count on the shoulder. "Then I must ask you, my old friend, to perform one last service for me."

"Whatever you wish, Your Majesty," he said. His monocle popped out, and he wiped away tears with an enormous handkerchief.

"Please see to it that all those carrots and cabbages and so on in the garden are distributed fairly among the servants who helped us with their labor."

"Of course, Your Majesty," snuffled the old count. "The firewood as well."

"Yes, yes, I'll see to it!" By then the count was sobbing.

Papa's good friend, Prince Dolgorukov, agreed to accompany him as his gentleman-in-waiting. General Tatischev, his aide-de-camp, would replace the count as grand marshal of the court—what court he would be grand marshal of, no one could say.

Trina Schneider told Mama, "I have been with you since you were a young bride, Your Imperial Majesty, and I will be with you now."

Countess Hendrikova, one of Mama's closest friends, had had no news of her sister, ill with tuberculosis, for months, but she declared she would leave it in God's hands and come anyway. Baroness Buxhoeveden had to have an operation for appendicitis, but she promised to join us as soon as she was able.

There was no question that Dr. Botkin and Dr. Derevenko would go wherever we were sent. Dr. Derevenko's wife and their son, Kolya, who was just Alexei's age, would accompany him. I was afraid that Gleb and Tatiana would be left with the friend's grandmother who had been looking after them, but Dr. Botkin arranged for them to come, too, and that pleased me.

Monsieur Gilliard said, "Madame, you've been trying to send me home to Switzerland for months, but my home is with your family." I had no worries that Shura, my governess, might choose not to come. By then it was obvious to everybody that she and Gilliard were in love, and if he was coming, so would she.

We didn't know about Mr. Gibbes. Our English tutor had been in Petrograd when we were put under house arrest, and he had not been allowed to see us when he returned to Tsarskoe Selo. No one knew where he was or what he might decide to do.

Some of our servants chose to stay behind—many had families in Tsarskoe Selo or in Petrograd—but others would come: Nagorny, Alexei's one still faithful sailor-attendant; Mama's maid, Anna Demidova; and Kharitonov the chef and Lenka Sednev the kitchen boy; as well as Papa's barber, Mama's hairdresser, and a number of cooks, valets, chambermaids, and a footman—about thirty in all.

We had learned that Lili and Anya had been taken to the Palace of Justice in Petrograd, and that eventually Lili convinced Kerensky to let her go home to Titi and be placed under house arrest. At least we knew she was safe. Anya had then been sent off to the Fortress of Peter and Paul, and as far as anyone knew, was still being held prisoner there. She had often driven us all to distraction, even Mama, with her constant need for attention, but I wished for Mama's sake that she could go with us.

"They're punishing her because she was so close to our dear Father Grigory," Mama said. "It is so unfair."

Papa, always trying to raise Mama's spirits, said, "Perhaps she'll be released soon and come with the baroness."

Kerensky had not given us any instructions about how much we could take with us, but it looked as though we were planning to take just about everything.

Alexei insisted that all of his toys and his balalaikas go with him. Mama was organizing her holy icons and family pictures, while her maids carefully packed her jewels in special chests. Papa favored books, but he was also taking his exercise bar.

I nearly filled one large wooden chest with things I loved: an embroidered scarf given to me by an old woman at our Polish hunting lodge, several of Aunt Olga's drawings, a box of watercolors and brushes, some pretty stones I'd picked up along the beach at Peterhof, the piece of green sea glass Gleb had found years ago—had I really saved it all this time?—and *The Adventures of Anastasia Mouse* that he'd made for me on my last birthday. I was about to throw away some of my old exercise books when I found a couple of funny little drawings Gleb had done of bears and rabbits in traditional Russian shirts and trousers, and I stuck them inside the photograph albums I was packing.

The thing I most wanted to take with me wherever we were going was the silver music box Grandmère Marie had given me for my thirteenth birthday. I remembered my grandmother whispering as we were leaving the Cottage Palace after my birthday luncheon: *Don't forget, ma chère. You and I will visit Paris together when you're sixteen.* At the time—three years earlier—that seemed impossibly far in the future. Now it was just impossible.

I wound up the music box and listened again to Tchaikovsky's "Waltz of the Flowers," watching the little ballerina on top turn and turn, slower and slower, until the music stopped and so did she. I did this again, two or three times, before I wrapped it in a woolen scarf Alexei had knit for me at Christmas—it was yards long—and buried it among the clothes I'd stuffed helter-skelter in a trunk.

Tired of the sorting and deciding, I drifted down the corridor to Olga and Tatiana's room and casually checked the shelf by Olga's bed where she usually kept the notebook, fourth book from the left. *Advanced Mathematics* was still there. Mama and Papa were burning all their private papers, and I hoped Olga hadn't decided to destroy her notebook.

Tatiana saw me lingering and frowned. "Have you finished packing, Nastya?"

"Almost," I replied, untruthfully. When I went back to my room, Shura had taken everything out of my trunk and was repacking it carefully.

The trunks and chests and boxes were piled up in every room, waiting for servants to carry them down to the semicircular hall beneath the huge dome. We wandered through the palace, taking one last look at everything and saying good-bye to the servants who wouldn't be leaving with us. Tatiana was very brisk about her good-byes. Olga looked glum and murmured farewells as though she was at a funeral. Marie hugged everybody tearfully and made them promise to write. I tried to make jokes, but they all fell flat.

The farewells were hard for everyone, perhaps hardest of all for Alexei. Colonel Kobylinsky kindly arranged for him to go to the stables to say good-bye to his donkey, Vanka, and to the little Shetland pony Grandmère Marie had given him for his tenth birthday. But when he begged to go to our zoo for a last visit with the elephant, Kobylinsky stalled. The elephant was no more. A week or two earlier we had been horrified to learn that the poor beast had been shot dead by one of the revolutionary sailors. That it might have been one of our sailors from the *Standart* was so awful to contemplate that Papa decided simply to tell Alexei the elephant had died of old age and warned my sisters and me not to say any more.

In the midst of this emotional turmoil, Uncle Misha arrived and immediately went to speak to Papa. We saw him come, and a little while later we saw him go—head down, wiping his eyes—but none of us had a chance to speak with him. He rushed past us without even a glance.

"I wanted to talk to him!" Alexei complained. "Why won't they let me?"

"Maybe it's better if you didn't, Lyosha," Tatiana said, trying to soothe him.

I dreaded leaving, but I also hated waiting for the time to come. I just wanted to get it over with. We were tired, all of us, even the dogs. Of course we were taking Alexei's Joy, my Jimmy, and Tatiana's Ortino. Mama's Eira would come later with Baroness Buxhoeveden. At the last minute Count Benckendorff agreed to adopt Olga's cat. The count looked so funny holding Vaska, who rubbed against the count's whiskers and purred.

Kerensky sent word that we were to be ready at midnight. Soldiers were ordered to carry our trunks from the palace to the train station, which they did, grumbling and complaining, even after the count paid them each three rubles.

"What time is the train coming?" I asked for maybe the third time.

"It's supposed to be here at one o'clock," Papa said patiently. "That's all I know."

We sat in the hall, waiting. The hours passed. The night was hot, and we were exhausted. We weren't used to staying up so late. Mama went to her room to lie down, fully dressed. But we were restless. Alexei's dog, Joy, bounced around on his leash, pulling Alexei first one way and then another.

Colonel Kobylinsky, who we were pleased was to accompany us, kept checking his watch. He was restless, too.

Finally, as dawn was breaking, several motorcars arrived to drive us to the station. It was time. The train was ready. The baggage had been loaded. Mama, in an agony of weeping, had to be carried to the motorcar. All of us were crying, except Olga, who was always so reserved. She may have shed her tears in private, like the words in her notebook.

The train waiting on the tracks was not the dark blue imperial train with the golden Romanov crest emblazoned on the cars. This was an ordinary train marked RED CROSS MISSION and flying Japanese flags. How strange that seemed! Another train stood behind it, but it wasn't a decoy like the one that always went ahead of the imperial train or behind it to deceive any revolutionary plotting to blow up the tsar's train. This second train carried three hundred soldiers who would guard us when we arrived at our destination.

"We're traveling in disguise," explained Kobylinsky. "It's better if the people in the little towns along the way don't know who's on board." He laughed nervously, showing lots of crooked teeth. "When we are passing through villages, I must ask you to close the blinds of the car in which you are riding."

He looked at me, shut one eye, and wagged his finger. "No peeking, Anastasia Nikolaevna!"

We climbed aboard. Clouds of steam hissed from the locomotive, and the train lurched forward. The sun was just coming up, bathing the world in a golden glow. We were on our way to Siberia, leaving behind everything beautiful, everything we loved.

The journey was hot, dusty, and monotonous. All we wanted to do that first day was sleep. When I awoke around noon in the sweltering heat, I was told that luncheon would be served at one o'clock. And it was! Then I had another long nap until teatime. After tea, the train halted somewhere out in the countryside, and we were allowed to get out to walk the dogs along the tracks. Mama stayed on the train, sitting by an open window and fanning herself. The sun was still high in the sky, and the heat shimmered on the steel rails. We climbed aboard again, and I peeled off my sweaty clothes and ran cold water on my wrists to cool off. Choking dust settled everywhere, on everything, and gritted between my teeth.

The two trains chugged steadily eastward. Each time we approached a town or station, we obediently pulled the curtains across the windows, but I ignored the colonel's "no peeking" order and peered through a small gap. On the third day there was a change; we were crossing the Urals, where it was much cooler. Papa took this opportunity to lecture us on the mineral wealth of the mountain range, everything from diamonds and emeralds to coal. The Asian steppes stretched on to the horizon and, after thousands of miles, to the Pacific Ocean.

"Wouldn't it be wonderful," Papa suggested quietly, "if Kerensky has arranged for the train to keep going, all the way across Siberia to Japan."

"So that must be why we're flying the Japanese flag!" I said excitedly.

Everyone told me to hush.

On the fourth day, very late at night after we'd all gone to sleep, the train came to a halt. I woke up and looked out. It was mostly dark, but I could see that we had stopped at a station near a river. There was a low murmur of voices, and figures were carrying our trunks and boxes and crates from the baggage car and loading them into small boats that were then rowed out into the river. This went on throughout the night. I watched until I could not stay awake any longer.

Long before sunrise we were roused by a knock on our compartment door and told to dress quickly. The train would take us no farther. Our possessions had been ferried across the river to a steamer tied up at the dock. A curtain of fog shrouded the opposite bank.

We huddled silently in a launch that puttered across the river in the darkness, before the residents of the town—it was called Tyumen—noticed the presence of strangers surrounded by dozens and dozens of soldiers and started asking questions. Mama clung to Papa's arm as we climbed the gangplank onto the steamer. Tatiana said wistfully, "Do you remember when we took the steamer on the Volga River, on our way to the village where Mikhail Romanov was born?"

That was four years earlier during the tricentennial celebration, the people shouting "God save the tsar!" and wading into the ice-cold river, just to get a look at the tsarevich. It made me sad to think of it.

Once we were aboard, Kobylinsky revealed our destination: Tobolsk, a small river town two hundred miles north known chiefly for trading in fish and furs. "The governor's mansion is being prepared for you. The people will be friendly to you," he promised. "No revolutionary sentiment has taken root there."

Now we knew where we were going to live. It wasn't Crimea or England or Japan but some remote town none of us had heard of.

PART

IV

Exile,

1917

CHAPTER 20

The Governor's Mansion

efore daybreak the steamer, *Rus*, had slipped away from the dock and nosed out into the Tura River, smoke billowing from the stacks, paddle wheels churning. My sisters yawned and went immediately to our quarters. I was too restless to lie down and climbed to the upper deck as the fog was lifting and the sun edged above the horizon. I found Gleb already there, making drawings in a sketchpad as we steamed past a field on the outskirts of Tyumen. Peasants were cutting hay. I went to stand at the rail next to Gleb.

"It's like a dream, isn't it, Anastasia Nikolaevna?" he asked. His pencil glided swiftly over the smooth paper, and an image of a peasant swinging his scythe emerged.

"You draw so much faster than I do," I said. We were standing so close that my hand brushed the sleeve of his jacket. With a few strokes of his pencil, a woman carrying a basket appeared.

Gleb glanced at me. "It just takes practice, Anastasia Nikolaevna. You have the talent, I know you do. I've seen some of your paintings—"

"They're not really paintings," I protested, pleased but a little embarrassed. The air was cool, but my face was hot. "They're nothing, just something I do."

"You don't take your painting seriously enough. You should, you know."

"I once told my aunt Olga Alexandrovna that I wanted to be a famous artist someday," I confessed. "And she said I must concentrate on painting, and not on being famous."

"That was good advice."

I stayed quiet for several minutes. The sun climbed higher and the light changed. I glanced sideways at Gleb's profile. The gawky boy who'd once been convinced that all the Russians had to do to defeat the Germans was to throw their caps at them had turned into a handsome young man. When had that happened?

Then I blurted boldly, "We were at Peterhof for my thirteenth birthday when my aunt said that. You found a piece of green sea glass and gave it to me." As soon as I'd said it, I wished I hadn't. It sounded foolish.

"You remember that, Anastasia Nikolaevna?"

"I still have it," I said, adding, a bit too abruptly, "and I wish you wouldn't address me formally. If you can draw me as a mouse, surely you can call me by my familiar name."

Gleb looked at me with a puzzled smile. "You would prefer that I address you as Anastasia Mouse?"

Blood rushed into my head, and I felt dizzy. "No—just as Nastya. And I don't believe I've thanked you properly for that birthday greeting. It's very clever, you know, very—"

Gleb, still smiling, laid his pencil and sketchpad on a bench and placed his hands on the rail next to mine. I stopped gazing at his face and studied his long fingers instead. I couldn't think what I wanted to say, my words were tumbling out all muddled, but I wanted this conversation to continue. I willed his hand to touch mine, and it did. It moved closer until our hands were not only touching, but our little fingers were linked.

If Dr. Botkin had appeared with his medical bag, as he did every day, and checked my temperature and listened to my heart, he would surely have diagnosed a mild fever, my heart banging against my rib cage, and irregular breathing—all symptoms caused by those two linked fingers.

A familiar voice startled us. The fingers separated.

"Good morning, Gleb Evgenievich!" Papa called out cheerily. "And there you are, Nastya! Your mother has been asking for you. Please go down to her, will you?"

"Yes, yes, of course, Papa," I said, shoving both hands deep into the pockets of my skirt. Without another word to Gleb, or even a look at him, I turned and fled.

I was grinning madly. Everything between us had changed.

Later that morning, when I felt calmer and less likely to do or say something silly or stupid, I climbed back to the upper deck. I hoped to find Gleb, but I was also afraid he might be there. How could I have both feelings at once? And there he was, sketching!

But Papa was there as well, dressed in his army uniform as usual, staring moodily off into the distance.

I settled onto a wooden bench with a book I'd brought along, close enough to watch Gleb but far enough away that it wouldn't draw attention. I tried to read, but I could hardly concentrate, turning the pages without remembering a single word. My sisters and Gleb's sister came and went, as did others. As much as I was dying to talk to Gleb, I didn't want to attract Papa's notice or, worse, the attention of Olga or Tatiana, who would certainly have a lot to say about it to me, and possibly to Mama.

It was enough just to have him nearby, even if we didn't exchange a word.

So I was surprised when Gleb approached the bench where I was sitting. "May I join you, Anastasia Nikolaevna?" he asked with a little bow. He was speaking formally, I understood, for Papa's benefit.

"Of course, Gleb Evgenievich."

"Beautiful day, isn't it?" He sat down—close, but not too close.

"Indeed it is." When I was sure my voice wouldn't shake, I said, "Will you show me some of your drawings?"

Side by side, we turned the pages slowly, going backward through time. There was the guardhouse at Tsarskoe Selo where he'd visited his father every week while we were under house arrest. His sister, Tatiana, dressed as a nursing sister early in the war. The *Standart* sailing off on a Baltic cruise before the war began. In a sleeve at the back of the sketchpad were a few worn photographs: his brothers, Yuri and Dmitri, now dead, when they were cadets, and a photo of a pretty young woman with an uncertain smile.

"My mother," he said. "Before their divorce. My father doesn't know I have it. It's been years since I've seen her." He gazed at the photograph.

"Where is she?"

"In Germany, if she's still alive. She left Father for our German tutor. She said my father was devoted to the tsar, and not to her."

I studied his profile—the elegant nose, sensuous lips, well-shaped chin. I thought I saw a strong resemblance to the photograph. "It must have been very painful," I said, because I could not think what else to say.

"It was." He slid the photograph back into the sleeve with the others. "I try not to think about her. I hardly ever look at the photo. I wanted you to see her."

Impulsively, I reached out and took his hand. It seemed like the most natural thing to do, and I held it just for a moment before I let it go.

As the hours passed and the steamer moved steadily with the current, everyone seemed calmer, more relaxed, as if all the usual rules had been suspended. If I was observed spending more time than usual talking with Gleb, no one seemed concerned.

On the afternoon of the second day on the river, our family had gathered on the upper deck. The boat was steaming close to the shore by Pokrovskoe, the village where Father Grigory had been born.

"That must be Grishka's home," Mama said, pointing to a handsome two-story house with a riot of flowers blooming in window boxes and a little front garden. "He caught fish in this river and brought them to Tsarskoe Selo. He predicted that one day we would pass by here." She turned to us, her eyes shining. "I believe he has sent us a sign," she said as the village receded behind us. "Our friend is with us, I'm sure of it."

Later that day we had our first glimpse of the Tobolsk fortress, looming in the distance, then the church towers came into view, and soon after sunset the *Rus* eased next to a dock. My sisters and I were eager to go ashore to see our new home. We tried to imagine what the governor's mansion would be like.

"Maybe it will be something like Peterhof," I suggested.

"Probably it will be more like Spala," Olga predicted glumly. "Damp rooms that smell like mold, so dark you have to keep the electric lights burning all the time." The hunting lodge in Poland was the least favorite of all our palaces and lodges.

But I was excited for another reason, one I couldn't mention. Now there would be more chances for conversations with Gleb, talks about art and painting, maybe even talks about our dreams for the time when our imprisonment would be over and we'd be free again. But I could not say anything about this to my sisters—not even to Marie, who would certainly have loved to hear it.

Colonel Kobylinsky went on ahead to inspect the governor's mansion, while we waited anxiously. Hours later he returned with a grim expression. "My apologies, Nikolai Alexandrovich, but you and your family must spend another night or two on the steamer," he informed us. "There is work that must be done before you can move in."

When Mama asked if she might be permitted to tour our new home the next morning, Kobylinsky put her off. "To be truthful, madame, the house is in some disrepair, and several pieces of furniture must be supplied. I beg your patience."

A *lot* of work, as it turned out, and the governor's house was as empty as a barn, with not a stick of furniture to be found in it. Papa found the situation amusing. "The inability even to arrange for lodgings is astonishing," he said. "We might as well retire early with the hope that our new home will be ready for us tomorrow, or the next day, or the next." Or perhaps the day after that.

To keep us from expiring of boredom while a small army of plasterers, plumbers, carpenters, electricians, and painters was hired to fix the house, Kobylinsky arranged for the *Rus* to take us on excursions on the river. He said we could stop and get off to go for walks along the way.

I didn't mind at all. Gleb was always nearby, and we even had several chances to talk—sometimes on the *Rus*, sometimes while we walked along the riverbank, past fields where peasants stopped swinging their scythes through the golden wheat to stare at us—although never alone and never close enough to touch. No linked fingers, even for a moment. My sisters and Gleb's sister were always part of the group, and Alexei, too. My brother adored Gleb.

"I'm working on a surprise for the tsarevich," Gleb confided as we returned from one of our river trips. "I think your whole family will enjoy it."

"What is it?"

"I told you, Nastya—it's a surprise. You'll see."

On the morning of our eighth day of waiting, the colonel announced that the governor's mansion was now ready. We left the *Rus*, Mama and Tatiana riding in a carriage while Papa and the rest of us walked along a road ankle-deep in dust. Soldiers armed with rifles and bayonets lined both sides of the road, not allowing us to forget for a moment that we were prisoners, and in their minds very dangerous ones.

Tobolsk did not look like much of a town. Most of the houses were built of logs or rough-hewn lumber, and it was easy to pick out the house where we would live—a two-story white stone building with a balcony on each end of the second floor.

"I would not call that a mansion," Olga muttered under her breath.

Kobylinsky, like a host anxious to please his guests, led us on a tour, glancing at Mama to see if she approved of the colors he had chosen for the walls and the furniture he had bought from townspeople who were willing to sell. There was a large table for dining, for instance, but none of the chairs matched. Our camp beds had not yet arrived; we would sleep on the floor. "But only for a night or two," Kobylinsky promised.

The so-called mansion was barely big enough for our family and a few members of our household. The rest, including the three Botkins and most of our servants, would stay on the opposite side of the street in a house commandeered from a rich fish merchant.

I felt a little sorry for the colonel, because I could guess what Mama was thinking. She said nothing until the tour had ended and Kobylinsky, nervously twisting a button on his jacket, asked, "Is there anything else you wish to have, Alexandra Fyodorovna?"

Mama smiled stiffly. "Yes, Colonel, if you please—a spring mattress for Nikolai Alexandrovich and myself, and a grand piano for my daughters."

Kobylinsky blinked a couple of times and bowed. "Of course, madame."

That same day both were delivered. The mattress gained approval, but the piano was horribly out of tune. A piano tuner was promised.

It was decided that OTMA should have the large corner room next to our parents' bedroom. Both rooms faced the main street, which used to be called Tsarskaia, "Street of the Tsar," but the signs had been changed to read: FREEDOM STREET. Alexei's room was across from ours, Nagorny's next to it. Monsieur Gilliard; Mama's maid, Anna Demidova; and Papa's valet, Trupp, were given rooms downstairs near the dining room and pantry. The kitchen was a small, separate building behind the house.

Grumbling soldiers unloaded our luggage and crates and boxes from the steamer and carted them to the mansion. Mama, seated in her wheelchair, directed where each item should go. Tatiana took charge of organizing our room. We arranged and rearranged the furniture, hanging favorite pictures and icons on the walls, stopping now and then to visit our brother and our parents to see how they were progressing. That night we fell, exhausted, onto a pile of fur coats and blankets on the floor and slept.

After breakfast the next morning we crossed Freedom Street—no one had said that wasn't permitted—to see how the rest of our household had settled in at the fish merchant's house. It turned out that the fish merchant had not lived there for some time, and the house had been used as a courthouse. Kobylinsky had ordered the courtroom on the main floor to be divided into cubicles. Dr. Botkin, Gleb, and Tatiana were assigned rooms on the ground floor, but Trina Schneider, Countess Hendrikova, and Papa's two gentlemen, General Tatischev and Prince Dolgorukov, were crowded into the tiny cubicles upstairs.

Immediately the soldiers shouted objections that the prisoners weren't staying in their prison but were roaming around freely. "You are prisoners of the state, not privileged guests! You will obey rules!" snarled the loutish lieutenant in charge of the guards, and we were herded back to the mansion.

This was the rule: *Prisoners are forbidden to leave the Governor's Mansion except to attend a private Mass early Sunday mornings at the nearby church.*

Although we weren't allowed to leave our enclosure, our friends in the fish merchant's house across the street were at first permitted to cross the street to visit us. I was excited when Gleb and his sister came with their father, even though our conversation was limited to "Lovely weather, isn't it, Gleb Evgenievich?" and "Indeed it is, Anastasia Nikolaevna, although it does seem quite warm."

But even that one-sided liberty didn't last. A new rule was imposed: *Only approved people may enter the Governor's Mansion.* Dr.

Botkin would continue to make daily visits to ensure the health of the prisoners—but those approved did not include Gleb and Tatiana Botkin or Dr. Derevenko's son, who would have been a fine companion for Alexei.

There was no use complaining to Colonel Kobylinsky. He could do nothing. Someone else was giving the orders—who, I didn't know. When I learned about the new restriction, it was one of the worst days since our captivity had begun six months earlier. I tried—and completely failed—to hide my disappointment.

"Perhaps it will change," Papa suggested, but I knew it would not.

Citizens of Tobolsk began to gather outside, curious to see the tsar and his family. Within days Kobylinsky had a tall wooden fence erected around the mansion, to be certain that the citizens had no contact with the prisoners. Dr. Botkin convinced Kobylinsky that the prisoners needed a place to exercise for at least an hour a day, and the colonel ordered a small yard near the kitchen enclosed for us. However, there would be no sitting out on the small second-floor balconies. We were forbidden to open even a single window as a relief from the suffocating August heat, until Dr. Botkin again insisted that it was a matter of ensuring the health of the prisoners. One by one, even the smallest freedoms were taken away.

I had hoped our guards would be different from the soldiers who had taken such pleasure in tormenting us at Tsarskoe Selo, but most were not. Many of the soldiers were sullen and disrespectful, demanding that prisoners be treated like criminals who should get what they deserved.

Luckily for us, there were some who didn't share those feelings. Several soldiers grew fond of Alexei and invited him and Papa to the guardhouse to play checkers. One was a young soldier named Anton Ivanovich, a homely boy with an eye that turned inward and a nose that dripped constantly. Anton was assigned to the guardhouse with various duties. Sometimes he delivered mail or brought messages, and sometimes he was the one to unlock the service door to let us out to the yard for exercise and to lock the door again when our time was up and we'd been ordered back inside.

If anybody could make friends with these lonely men and boys who were far from home, it was Marie. She learned their names and the names of their mothers and wives and children. They told her about their lives before the fighting began. Anton Ivanovich confided that he struggled to send money to his widowed mother and crippled sister. Marie soon got in the habit of giving him little gifts now and then.

"Naturally he's in love with you, Mashka," I teased. "And maybe you're in love with him as well."

"Don't be silly, Nastya," Marie scolded. "I try to help him because he's kind to Alexei. But promise me you'll say nothing to Tanya, because she'll try to make me stop."

I promised.

The townspeople themselves were hospitable folk. Local farmers, merchants, and housewives sent fresh butter, eggs, sausages, and sugar, and nuns brought vegetables from the convent garden—a delicious change from the shortages everyone was suffering in Petrograd and Tsarskoe Selo. Whatever came to us, Kharitonov and his kitchen helpers managed to transform into a good meal. I watched from our upstairs window as men and women passed below, occasionally glancing up and removing their caps as a sign of respect, some even making the sign of the cross. If they noticed Mama sitting by her window, they bowed to her. To the people of Tobolsk, Papa was still the tsar, Mama was the tsaritsa, and Alexei the tsarevich. I suppose that meant my sisters and I were still grand duchesses, but I didn't much care about that anymore.

"We must have patience," Papa urged almost daily. "Thanks be to God that we are alive and together."

He believed that our friends and Romanov relatives were secretly making plans to rescue us. Alexei was convinced that one of these nights we'd be awakened by loyal Russians who had come to save us—maybe not to go home to Tsarskoe Selo or to Livadia, but to a place where we would be welcome. In time the Russian people would understand that Papa was still their *Batiushka*, and they would rise up and demand that he be recognized again as the Tsar of All the Russias.

"It might not be exactly as it was before, but it will be *very good*," Alexei said firmly. "I am absolutely sure of it."

"Absolutely positively?" I teased.

"Absolutely positively and no doubt whatsoever!" he insisted passionately.

It was not easy, OTMA living in such close quarters, four of us and our camp beds and clothes and pictures and books all in one room. I thought I knew exactly where Olga's *Advanced Mathematics* notebook was hidden—in a box under her bed, although possibly wearing a new disguise. But Olga had no privacy for writing, and I had almost no chance to see what she'd written, if she had written anything.

Then one day when everyone else had gone out into the small fenced yard to play at an improvised croquet set and I had volunteered to run back to Mama's room to fetch her shawl, I seized the chance to look for the notebook, and I found it.

How do they do it? I practice on a piano that is laughably out of tune and try to lose myself in the music, in order not to think. Meanwhile, Mashka charms the soldiers with her questions about their families, Tanya plagues us constantly to keep our room neat, Papa and Lyosha play checkers with the soldiers, and Mama writes letter after letter to Anya, to Sophie Buxhoeveden, to Countess Benckendorff, to Lili. And poor Nastya! She appears to be suffering from lovesickness, but at least she has stopped making her usual annoying jokes.

I ignored the "annoying jokes" part, but "suffering from lovesickness"? Had she noticed what I had tried so hard to conceal?

Olga had written more, but there was no time to read it. They were calling to me from the yard, and I stuffed the notebook back in the box under her bed and ran downstairs. Then I remembered that I had forgotten to fetch Mama's shawl.

CHAPTER 21

Making the Best of Things

he single best thing that happened last summer was Gleb's promised surprise. He was writing a story about a twelve-year-old bear named Mishka Toptiginsky who was trying to free the imprisoned tsar of Mishkoslavia and restore him to his throne. Gleb illustrated the tale with watercolor paintings. All the characters were animals: The guards were monkeys, but there were also dogs, cats, pigs—all perfectly pictured in uniform—and a cigar-smoking rabbit-mayor of the city.

Since Dr. Botkin's medical bag was routinely searched, he smuggled Gleb's story to Alexei, page by page, in his boot. The arrival of the latest pages became the highlight of our day, and we read and reread the latest installment and examined every detail of the exquisite watercolors. Alexei adored it, of course, because it was especially for him. I loved it because it was my only contact with Gleb.

The hot, dusty summer ended, and the September weather was actually quite pleasant. Alexei had not been sick for some time. The mansion was crowded but fairly comfortable. Kharitonov and the other servants made sure that we followed the same schedule we always had. We were making the best of things, as Papa said we must.

And the single best thing that happened this autumn was the unexpected arrival of Mr. Gibbes. After we'd left for Siberia, he was finally permitted to collect his things from the palace, and he set out on the long journey by train and boat for Tobolsk. Now here he was, sitting with us in the governor's mansion, drinking tea and eating little sugar cakes sent by the convent nuns, telling us only the amusing stories of all that had happened since we'd last seen him. The other stories—the not-so-amusing ones—could wait until later, he said.

We talked until dinnertime, chatting in English because Gibbes's Russian was still shaky. With our two tutors here, Dr. Botkin and Mama's and Papa's friends, for short periods our life was a little like it once was.

"The next time Colonel Kobylinsky inquires if we need something," Tatiana suggested, "Nastya should ask if he could provide a stuffed aurochs, one of those long-horned wild oxen that used to scare us in Bialowieza. Maybe one for each of us, and we could pretend that we're in the Polish hunting lodge we used to complain about, instead of a prison in Siberia."

We were laughing so much—even Olga!—that two of the guards stomped into our sitting room, demanded to know what we were laughing at, and ordered us to speak Russian.

As long as Colonel Kobylinsky was in charge, we felt reasonably safe, but at the end of September that changed. Two civilian commissars, Pankratov and Nikolsky, arrived. These government officials had authority over us, and over the colonel, too. Pankratov was politely formal and seemed, if not to like us, at least not to despise us. Nikolsky was just the opposite—bad-tempered and ill-mannered. Whenever there was a chance to be insulting or mean, he seized it.

Papa was starved for news of what was happening in Petrograd and Moscow and the rest of the world outside Russia, and he asked several times if he might receive newspapers. Pankratov promised to see that newspapers would be brought, but none were, except the local paper, which had hardly anything in it except items about events in Tobolsk. Papa couldn't even find any news of what was happening in the war with Germany. He clutched at stray wisps of rumor. Was Russia winning or losing? He didn't know.

Nikolsky took pleasure in telling Papa that Prime Minister Kerensky, whom Papa had admired and trusted, had been forced out by the Bolsheviks, the militant group that had opposed the Provisional Government and hated our family. The Bolsheviks had taken over and were running everything. Kerensky had left Petrograd and gone into hiding. We wished we knew where he had gone, and if he was somehow plotting to return. There was no point in asking Pankratov or Nikolsky, and Colonel Kobylinsky didn't seem to know any more than Papa did.

We heard that a man named Lenin had enormous sway over events, but Papa dismissed that as baseless rumor—he thought that Lenin, and another man, Leon Trotsky, were simply German agents sent to disrupt the army. When Nikolsky told Papa that those two were now in power and running the government, he refused to believe it.

My father was deeply distressed. Our beloved country was clearly going from bad to worse. He regretted that he'd abdicated. "I believed I was doing what was best for Russia," he said sadly. "And in fact I have done her an ill turn."

Mama tried to soothe him, assuring him he had done all he could, but he could not be comforted. He was weeping, and I had hardly ever in my life seen my father cry.

We had classes every morning with our tutors, just as if we were living in Tsarskoe Selo. Every afternoon we walked back and forth, back and forth, in our little enclosure for an hour, although for Papa that was not nearly enough physical activity. After dinner a priest came from the nearby church we were no longer allowed to attend and said our evening prayers with us. We sewed and knitted and listened as Papa read aloud. The days grew shorter and the weather colder. Petrograd felt like a million miles away and Tsarskoe Selo existed only in a dream.

When Olga had her twenty-second birthday, the cooks baked a cake for her, and I stole a look at her notebook and wished I hadn't.

Twenty-two today. A prisoner for more than half a year. Every day is like the one before it. Sometimes I am appalled at Father's patience. How does he do it? The one good thing is that my hair

has grown back, and I no longer hate looking in the mirror. Tanya,
Mashka, and I are very thin—too thin. Mother, too.

But not Nastya: She's still round as a dumpling, like a pirozhok
on legs. Strange as it seems, I do believe that something was going
on between her and Gleb. I saw the looks that passed between them
during the journey here last summer when they thought no one
would notice. Of course this romance, if it can be called that, can
go nowhere. The poor boy is not even permitted to cross the street.
If we ever leave this place—and I doubt that we will, although
I say nothing, keep that entirely to myself—Mother would never
allow a match between a grand duchess and the son of an admired
doctor, even though the youngest of four has not much value on the
marriage market. Gleb used to say he intended to become a priest.
Even if he changed his mind, Mother wouldn't change hers. Poor
little Nastya! How sad she looks that he is not allowed to visit here.

I quickly got over her insulting remark—a dumpling on
legs!—and read over again what she had to say about Gleb. *Oh,*
Olya, dear Olya, you're right about me and about Gleb, too, but I hope you're
wrong about everything else.

The Siberian winter closed in with an iron grip. I had never
been so cold in my life. We called our bedroom "the ice house."
The skin that formed on the water in our basins had to be
cracked every morning. We wore our coats and felt boots all
day and piled the coats on top of blankets when we crept into
our freezing beds at night. Mama's fingers were so stiff that she
could hardly hold knitting needles.

We did whatever we could think of to stave off boredom. Papa was upset at not getting enough exercise; his exercise bar had disappeared. Kobylinsky tried to help. He had trunks of trees brought in and provided saws and axes, and Papa and Monsieur Gilliard began cutting up the trees into firewood. They'd gotten quite good at that while we were still at Tsarskoe Selo. Olga, too—she handled an ax as easily as if she'd been raised as a woodcutter's daughter. After each heavy snowfall Papa climbed up on the roof with a shovel to clear it off, although that may have been an excuse for him to have a lookout over the fence. In the evenings Papa read to us, while we mended our ragged clothes and knit fingerless gloves. He's fond of Arthur Conan Doyle, the Scottish novelist who wrote the books about Sherlock Holmes. I often played cards with Alexei. Alexei was mad about bezique.

Gilliard and Gibbes were more ambitious; they adapted scenes from plays and coaxed us to act them out. Chekhov was their favorite. Alexei loved to stomp around with a fake mustache and hold forth in a deep voice, and he tried to convince Dr. Botkin to take the part of a country doctor.

Dr. Botkin refused. "Someone must be your audience, Alexei Nikolaevich," he said.

But Alexei was insistent. "You're the only one who can bring authenticity to the role," he pleaded, and that eventually persuaded the doctor, leaving Mama, Chef Kharitonov, Trupp the valet, and a few others as our audience.

One day I scraped the frost off part of a pane of glass and looked out, hoping to catch a glimpse of Gleb passing by with his father or sister. I was disappointed, as usual, but I did see a woman gazing up at our windows and recognized Baroness Buxhoeveden. "Mashka, come look!" I shouted. "It's Sophie!"

Marie rushed to the window, we cleared another pane, and the two of us jumped up and down like wild things. Baroness Buxhoeveden smiled and waved back, but in an instant the guards were pointing their bayonets at her, probably thinking she was sending us a coded signal. Thank God, Kobylinsky arrived just in time, and we watched him escort her into the fish merchant's house across the street.

"She'll be coming over here to see us soon," I said. "Mama will be so pleased!"

We felt sure that after her long journey from Petrograd the baroness would be allowed to visit us, but when Mama inquired, Commissar Pankratov told her that her request had to be referred to "the soldiers' soviet"—whatever *that* was— for discussion. A few days later, Mama asked again. This time the commissar said that the soviet was "afraid of excesses." It seemed that the more the soldiers saw how much Mama wanted to see her friend, the more determined they were that she should not be granted permission, just to punish her.

"Maybe at Christmastime they'll allow us a brief visit," Mama said. "Just a few minutes. Surely that's not an excess."

We labored for weeks making simple gifts for each of the loyal servants who'd bravely and unselfishly chosen to share our fate. And we had a Christmas tree, a small one cut for us by Anton Ivanovich, the soldier who, I thought, must have succumbed to "Marie's saucers." We spent hours devising decorations for it made from bits of colorful wool and Mama's tiny paintings of holly and berries.

"It's possibly the handsomest tree we've ever had," I declared, and my sisters were kind enough not to call that an outright lie.

On Christmas Eve, surrounded by guards, we crunched through the most recent snowfall to the little nearby church for Mass. We were hopeful that Baroness Buxhoeveden might be there, too, and we would be able to see her and perhaps even to exchange a Christmas kiss. I wished desperately that Dr. Botkin and his son and daughter would be allowed to attend the same Mass. But none of the people we longed to see were there— just the usual sullen soldiers with their rifles and bayonets.

Our situation worsened when the priest made the mistake of praying for the tsar and his family. That prayer had always been the custom, but it had been eliminated since Papa's abdication. When the soldiers heard it, they were furious. After that, we weren't allowed to go back to the church at all, at any time.

One more thing to break poor Mama's heart.

CHAPTER 22

Prisoners

A s the bleak winter wore on, we decided to build a snow mountain like the one our servants had once helped us make at Tsarskoe Selo. We set to work shoveling snow into a great heap in the exercise yard, stopping occasionally to fling snowballs and to chase each other around our little mountain as it grew higher. With everybody helping—even a few soldiers—it took almost two weeks to build our mountain and then to carry water from the tap in the kitchen, some thirty buckets of it, to pour over it. Sometimes the water froze before we could pour it over the piled-up snow, but eventually we managed to create a toboggan run. Chef Kharitonov supplied roasting pans and metal trays, and we immensely enjoyed sliding down on our improvised toboggans.

We learned that the regiment of older soldiers—the ones

we got along with best—was being sent away. Some of them came secretly to say good-bye. On the day the regiment left, Papa and Alexei climbed to the top of the ice mountain, from which they could look out over the fence and watch as the men marched off. Guards immediately spotted them. Within an hour a detachment of soldiers stormed in with shovels and picks and tore down our lovely little mountain, while we watched helplessly.

New soldiers, young recruits, arrived. Most were revolutionaries who made it plain that they hated us. Guards were now posted inside the house as well as outside. They drew disgusting pictures on the wooden fence that we couldn't help seeing. Even "Marie's saucers" and her engaging ways didn't make things any better, and she stopped even wanting to try.

Some of these hostile new soldiers demanded that Papa remove the epaulets from the shoulders of the army uniform he wore every day. These were the insignia of a colonel, the only rank he'd held, even when he was in command of the Russian army. Papa, who was usually very agreeable in order not to upset anyone, stubbornly refused to take them off. His father, Tsar Alexander, had awarded him those epaulets, and he was going to wear them, no matter what. When Prince Dolgorukov told him that it would be better for everybody if he obeyed the order, Papa finally gave in—sort of. He wore a cape concealing them whenever he went out into the exercise yard.

Mama sent a message to Baroness Buxhoeveden through Dr. Botkin that she would stand at her window every day at one o'clock and asked Sophie to stand at hers. Day after day, that is what they did, bundled in their warmest coats and wrapped in scarves, the windows open for a few minutes. I heard Mama speaking, and I could just make out that Sophie was also speaking, but I couldn't make out a word either one said.

"I have no idea what she's saying," Mama said. "The sentries will not allow us to have an actual conversation, and so we simply pretend we do."

Each week brought us new worries and new hardships.

Colonel Kobylinsky, looking ten years older than he had only a few months before, told Papa that he wanted to resign. He explained that he didn't have control over the soldiers anymore and felt he could no longer help us.

"A transfer to Murmansk?" Papa whispered to him. "Is that no longer a possibility?"

Kobylinsky shook his head.

Papa pleaded with him not to leave. Finally the colonel agreed to stay on, at least for a while. Soon after, the two civilian commissars, Pankratov and Nikolsky, were dismissed. We had no idea what to make of that.

Someone had decided that it was costing the new government too much money to feed us. We had to let go at least half of our servants, and that was sad because many of them had families here and would now have no way to support them. Most of the kitchen staff was dismissed. Only Kharitonov and the kitchen boy, Lenka, would stay. Also, we were going to be put on soldiers' rations. No more butter or coffee, they announced sternly, and that made me laugh because it was almost the start of the Great Fast, when we never ate butter anyway. And we all drink tea, not coffee.

Intolerable, we whispered among ourselves—but we had to tolerate it.

One of those let go was my dear Shura. Gilliard arranged for her to move out of her cubicle in the fish merchant's house and into a small apartment nearby. I think it was an arrangement they both liked, and of course we teased them mercilessly. Shura promised to come to see us every day, but we quickly learned that was forbidden.

A new rule was imposed. No one in the fish merchant's house could go anywhere unless accompanied by a guard. "The guards dislike it and sometimes refuse," Gilliard told us. "I have to bribe them to take me to see Shura."

"If we're going to be rescued, I hope it happens soon," Alexei said one evening.

That's what we'd prayed for, and Mama believed that our prayers were about to be answered. Her maid, Anna Demidova, repeated a rumor that she'd heard whispered in one of the shops: A man named Boris Soloviev who had married Rasputin's daughter was raising money to arrange a rescue—armed guards hired, a riverboat or several sleighs secured, depending on the time of year, to take us to a train that would also have to be secured, to carry us all the way to Vladivostok. That it was Father Grigory's son-in-law in charge of the plans convinced Mama we were soon to be saved.

We waited tensely. The days dragged on. We heard nothing, but Mama's faith didn't waver.

The cold deepened. I could hardly wait to rush back inside at the end of the hour we were allowed for outside exercise. At least inside the governor's mansion it was slightly above freezing. Still, despite the privations, we were all fairly healthy—even Alexei—although everyone was bone-thin except *me*, the dumpling on legs.

Every day Dr. Botkin came to look at our throats, take our temperatures, and listen to Mama's heart. He looked weary. His elegantly tailored blue suits hung on his large frame, his immaculate white shirts were frayed and yellowing, and he had apparently exhausted his supply of French cologne that had always been the clue that he was somewhere nearby.

We asked if he had brought another story about Mishka Toptiginsky and more of Gleb's paintings, and sometimes he had. I waited for the doctor to say something, anything at all, about Gleb. I was glad when Mama asked about him.

"I have spoken again to him about entering the priesthood, once this situation has come to an end and we leave here," he said.

Mama beamed. "Such a lovely boy!" she said. "So good and pure! I believe he's well suited to become a priest. He would minister well to those who were in his care."

"But now he claims to have changed his mind about it. He seems to have become more interested now in pursuing the life of an artist," said the doctor. He reached in his medical bag for the pills Mama took for her heart. "Or perhaps there is some other reason that he hasn't mentioned."

I felt my face grow hot—even in that freezing room. Was I the reason? That was too much to hope for, but the one thing I had clung to during the dark weeks of our imprisonment was the notion that Gleb might care for me as I cared for him.

I wondered if he thought of me, and I had to believe he did.

When I sometimes caught a glimpse of him, after staring for an hour or two through a small opening I'd melted in the thick frost covering the window, I imagined the conversations we might have as we walked along together. We would talk about art, of course, and share our memories of Livadia, the *Standart*, the beach at Peterhof where he found the sea glass as green as his eyes. And maybe we'd even talk shyly about our dreams of the future. But these conversations existed only in my mind.

Alexei hadn't been bleeding for some time, but there was a wildness in him that could not be controlled. He took it into his head to try using one of Kharitonov's metal trays as a toboggan and the staircase as a toboggan slide, now that the snow mountain had been destroyed. No one saw what he was up to until it was too late. We heard the clattering as he made his first run, and then his cry when he fell off. The bleeding started inside his body, and the pain increased until it must have been unbearable. It was like the terrible time at Spala all over again. I stopped my ears against the sound of his screams, but Mama never left his side. The two doctors did what they could, but there was no Father Grigory to perform a miracle. Eventually, though, the pain eased, and slowly Alexei got better. Mama said our prayers were responsible.

The news from beyond our prison got worse. When Papa learned that the new Bolshevik government had signed a peace treaty with Germany, he broke down in tears. "A disgrace!" he sobbed. "Suicide for Russia, the death of my beloved country!"

Moscow was now the capital instead of Petrograd, and a

new commissar was coming to take the place of the two who'd been dismissed. We speculated who this new commissar would be—Papa thought it might be Leon Trotsky, who was running the Bolshevik government with Lenin. Then one day, when the spring thaw was turning the frozen ground to muddy slush, a government official rode into Tobolsk escorted by dozens of horsemen. We watched them pass, their horses and their uniforms covered in mud, and a little later Vasily Vasilyevich Yakovlev sent a message asking if he might have tea with Mama and Papa. We studied him carefully as he arrived. He was tall and strong looking, dressed in a clean uniform and polished boots, and he made a good impression by bowing and addressing Mama and Papa as "Your Majesty." They took him to meet Alexei, and he seemed truly concerned when he saw that my brother wasn't able to bend his leg.

My parents were nervous about this man. He didn't tell them why he had come. Every change seemed to be a bad omen, and not knowing what was about to happen kept us on edge.

"Vasily Vasilyevich speaks well," Papa said. He was nervously smoking one of the last of his cigarettes. "He seems like an educated man."

"I don't trust him," Mama said. "I don't trust what he's been sent here to do. There is a shifty look to his eye that I don't like." She turned to Tatiana. "Perhaps you girlies can find something to do in your room while I discuss matters further with your father."

Tatiana, Marie, and I rose obediently and started to leave, but Olga didn't move. For months Olga had said little, dispirited and sunk in her own dark thoughts. Now suddenly she rebelled. "We want to know what's happening," she announced. "We are no longer children. We might have been 'girlies' in Tsarskoe Selo, but we are not 'girlies' in Siberia—not any of us, neither Tanya nor I, and not Mashka, and not Nastya, either. And Lyosha, too, must know—he's not 'Baby.' These months as prisoners have made us adults."

Mama looked shocked. "All right," Papa said, and smiled wanly. "I agree. We will keep nothing from you. Yakovlev brought a telegraph machine with him and a telegraph operator who keeps him in direct communication with Moscow. His orders come from there. I believe he has come to take us to Moscow and put me on trial. But so far he has told us nothing."

Mama sighed. "We must have faith that God will see to it that we are rescued. Our fate is in His hands."

One day when sleet pounded relentlessly against our windows and we decided to forgo the hour of outdoor exercise, Yakovlev came again to the governor's mansion. This time he was blunt. He had received orders to take our family from Tobolsk to an undisclosed destination, but because Alexei still could not walk and was clearly an invalid, only Papa would be taken. "The rest will stay behind."

"I refuse to go," Papa said. "I will not be separated from my family."

Yakovlev tried to reason with him. "If you do not go willingly, you will be taken forcibly." He didn't call Papa "Your Majesty" this time, but he did promise to be personally responsible for Papa's safety. Then he added, "You may take anyone with you that you wish, but you must be ready to leave at four o'clock tomorrow morning."

As soon as Yakovlev had gone, Papa sent for Kobylinsky. "Where do you think they'll take me?" he asked.

Kobylinsky shrugged helplessly. "I have been told only that the journey will take four or five days."

"Moscow, then?"

"Perhaps."

I had never seen Mama so upset, so torn. On the one hand, she felt compelled to go with Papa, to be with him for whatever he faced. If he was to be put on trial in Moscow, then she wanted to be at his side. On the other hand, Alexei was still unable to walk and was far from well. How could she bring herself to leave him?

"For the first time in my life, I don't know what to do," she said, burying her fingers in her hair—it had turned completely gray in the past months. "I've always felt inspired by God in making a decision, but now I simply can't think!"

Olga, Marie, and I sat close to her, weeping helplessly, but Tatiana—always the strong one—immediately took charge. She ran downstairs and returned with Monsieur Gilliard.

He kissed Mama's hand. "Alexei's crisis is past," he assured her. "Go with your husband with the complete assurance that I will take responsibility for the care of your son."

Mama gazed at Gilliard for a moment or two, and then her face became calm. "Yes," she said. "Yes, you're right. I'll go with Nicky, and you will stay here." She looked at each of us thoughtfully. "One of you must come with me."

"But which of us, Mama?" I asked. My head was spinning. I did not want to go, but I also did not want to be left behind.

"Decide among yourselves," she said.

We looked at one another. I thought it should be Olga, because she was the eldest. But she seemed to know what I was thinking and shook her head. "Tanya," Olga said. "Tanya should go."

"No," Tatiana said. "No, I think it best if I stay here to oversee the household and help Zhilik with Lyosha. Mashka is the most cheerful of the four of us, the most reliable, and therefore best able to be helpful to Mama. She should go."

I agreed with Tatiana's choice. "Yes, it must be Mashka."

Marie closed her eyes. "All right then," she said when she'd opened them. We each nodded. "Of course I will go."

More decisions were made. Anna Demidova, Mama's maid, would accompany them, although she was plainly terrified. So would Papa's valet, Trupp.

Dr. Botkin, Prince Dolgorukov, and General Tatischev came to take tea with us, as they did every evening, and listened as Papa explained the plan they'd agreed upon. Dolgorukov immediately announced that he, too, would go, and Papa gripped his hand gratefully.

"Certainly I will accompany you," Dr. Botkin said quietly, and I stopped crying into my handkerchief long enough to stare at him. "Dr. Derevenko will remain here as Alexei's physician."

Mama was surprised, too. "But your children? Gleb and Tatiana? You will leave them?"

"I will make arrangements for them. My duty has always been with Your Majesties."

What arrangements? I wanted to ask, but I dared not.

• • •

The hours passed much too quickly. Clothes were packed and repacked, last-minute instructions given, good-byes said, rivers of tears shed. We still didn't know where they were being taken, or when we would be able to join them. Yakovlev shouted orders, directing people into the clumsy peasant carts lined with straw swept up from a pigsty. Mama was bundled in Dr. Botkin's fur coat, and someone went to fetch another coat for him. Marie was to ride with Mama. Papa was ordered into an open carriage with Yakovlev. Prince Dolgorukov, Dr. Botkin, and the others were directed to carts. Guardsmen mounted on restless horses waited for the order.

A signal was given and the carts jolted forward and clattered away, leaving the street deserted and eerily silent. We climbed upstairs, numb with fear. I remember hardly anything about the rest of that day, but the following day I read this in Olga's notebook:

> *The world is a dark, dark place. Our family now wrenched apart, parents and one sister taken away, who knows to where, for what purpose? Tanya stands ready to keep us going here until the next terrible thing happens. She's so much stronger than I am. Even Nastya is stronger. Father and Mother continue to cling to the belief that we will be rescued, somehow, by someone, but who? I have no hope of rescue. I have no hope of anything good happening. The only hope I have is that I am wrong about everything.*

PART

V

Fate,

1918

CHAPTER 23

Love and Fear

obylinsky himself delivered the telegram from Mama. They've been detained in Ekaterinburg, somewhere on the eastern slope of the Urals. No explanation. We discuss it, wondering why there and not Moscow. Even Kobylinsky seems puzzled. But now we know where they are.

At Easter our sad little household gathers to worship together. We can't help remembering how it used to be, the glorious midnight service with candles and incense and a choir singing, and the magnificent feast afterward. Kharitonov somehow procures a few eggs and a little cheese and makes a *paskha* for us, and we weep with gratitude. Tatiana and Olga have grown thin as knife blades—Alexei, too. Even I am no longer "round as a barrel" or "a *pirozhok* on legs."

Since Mama's instructions to "dispose of the medicines,"

282 · C A R O L Y N   M E Y E R

we've been working diligently. Sometimes we sing songs or tell stories to try to keep our spirits up, while we sew the jewels into our corsets or wherever else we can think to conceal them. We brought chests of jewels with us from Tsarskoe Selo— not to wear, but to provide the money we'll need when we are finally rescued. No one bothered to search us, but Mama and Papa were taken away from here so suddenly that there was no time to hide the jewels in their clothes. We may not be so lucky next time.

Then a letter came from Marie, describing how they were searched when they arrived in Ekaterinburg:

> *We weren't allowed to unpack our suitcases until hours after we arrived, because they went through everything, including the medicines and candy. Prince Dolgorukov was arrested almost as soon as we arrived when it was found he was carrying thousands of rubles. We have not seen him and don't know what's happened to him.*

We have constructed "double brassieres," sewing two together with jewels wrapped in cotton batting from Dr. Derevenko's medical supplies and stitched between the layers. We try on these strange garments and double over with laughter at the big bosoms we have suddenly developed. It's been a long time since we've had something to laugh at.

"Do you remember, Tanya, when I didn't yet have a *bosom* and you insisted I must not use that word but say 'figure' instead, because it was much nicer?"

"I was simply trying to make you more ladylike," she says.

"Well, you failed miserably," I tell her.

• • •

This type of sewing is boring. It occupies my hands but gives me too much time to think. Mostly I think of Gleb. He and his sister are alone across the street, their father in Ekaterinburg with our parents. Before he left, Dr. Botkin brought two more of Gleb's paintings of Mishka the Bear to show us, but he took them back again. I wish that I'd been allowed to keep one of them—something of Gleb's to have, besides the piece of sea glass.

It's impossible to guess what is going to happen next. Soon we will be leaving here to join Papa and Mama and the others. I wonder if Gleb and his sister will be permitted to come with us. I wish I could see him again, even for just a few minutes. Sometimes when I can't sleep, or when I'm tired of "disposing of the medicines," I stand at the window, hoping he'll pass below and that he'll look up at the right moment and wave.

If he does, I will blow him a kiss.

A kiss. I have never kissed Gleb, and that's what I have begun to wish for: *one kiss.* If I told Olga and Tatiana, they would certainly laugh at me, or tell me how foolish I am even to think of such nonsense. Yet I can't help thinking of it. I awaken in the night thinking of it, and I think of it while I stitch jewels into my clothes.

We have almost finished disposing of the medicines. Two days ago I unstrung the diamond and pearl necklace, jewels given to me on each birthday and name day, and I have concealed most of them in my corset. When just one pearl was left, I had an idea. It's a dangerous idea, but it won't go away. I turn it over and over in my mind, examining it from every angle. I drop the pearl into my pocket. It will be easier to sell than a diamond.

I think of Anton Ivanovich, the guard who has a crush on Marie. Anton's crush is on my sister, not on me, but I wonder now if I can persuade him to help me. It would be a grave risk to offer Anton the pearl as a gift. Suppose he accepts the pearl and then reports my attempt to bribe him to his commanding officer? Or doesn't accept, and still reports me?

Anton Ivanovich is not my only problem. What if Olga or Tatiana finds out? Olga probably wouldn't care; she might even be sympathetic. But Tatiana would no doubt be horrified.

I decide to risk it all. I will do anything to be with Gleb, if only for a few minutes.

The guardhouse where Anton is on duty is by the front entrance of the mansion. I wait and watch for an opportunity. Three days pass. Then one day when we're in the salon, about to go down for luncheon, someone knocks and shouts up the main stairs that he has a letter for us.

"It's that guard who's in love with Mashka," Tatiana says.

I'm already on my feet. "I'll go and see," I volunteer, and run out of the salon and down the stairs.

"Good morning, Anastasia Nikolaevna," he says politely, and holds out a letter.

"Yes, yes, thank you, Anton Ivanovich." I steer him toward the door, open my hand, and show him the gleaming pearl. "Something for your trouble," I add in a whisper. "And I need to ask you a favor."

He stares at the pearl cradled in my palm and then at me, shaking his head. I'm afraid he's going to refuse me outright, or say something so loudly that we'll be given away before I can even explain what it is that I want.

"What?" he says softly, but he still hasn't taken the pearl.

"I need to have a conversation with Gleb Evgenievich. A *private* conversation—do you understand? Not for long—just for a few minutes. In the guardhouse, perhaps?" Anton is still gaping at me rather stupidly, and I know that I have to convince him quickly, before my sisters descend and put an end to my plot, which, I can see plainly, is weak and far from foolproof. "I want to say good-bye to him, and I may not have another chance, because I believe we may soon be separated and never see each other again." I'm close to tears, and I plead, "Oh, Anton, please! Have you ever been in love? Surely you must understand what I'm asking!"

I see his features go through a shift, from puzzlement and suspicion, then veering toward understanding. "I do understand. And I hope you understand that I'm an honorable person, and if my mother and my sister were not in such great need, I would not consider taking what you are offering me."

"You'll do it, then?"

He hesitates, reaches out his hand, and I drop the pearl into his palm. His fingers close around it.

"When?" I ask.

My sisters are coming down the stairs, followed by Gilliard carrying Alexei. "Nastya?" Tatiana calls. "Nastya! Luncheon is being served! What are you doing?"

"I have to arrange it. I'll speak to you later." The door slams shut behind him.

"Whatever was that about, Nastya?" Olga asks curiously.

"Oh, poor Anton!" I say, laughing. "He asked what we've heard from Mashka."

The letter he brought is from her. Tatiana reads it aloud while we eat.

> *Everything here is in a terrible state. Dirt and filth everywhere, everything disturbed and destroyed. They have gone through everything we have with their dirty hands—even the paper I'm using to write to you has been soiled. Everyone who comes into the house inspects our rooms and goes through our things. It's impossible to write about anything cheerful, because there is no cheerfulness here. But God does not abandon us. The sun shines, the birds sing, and this morning we heard the church bells ringing. Oh, my dearest ones, how I do long to see you!*

We avoid looking at each other. Olga sighs, and finally Tatiana says, "We must be strong."

"Bastards," Alexei says, and we all stare at him, surprised. Alexei has never been heard to use crude language. Mama would be appalled! I expect to hear a lecture from Tatiana, but I'm wrong.

"Yes," she says. "Bastards."

It is all I can do to stay calm until I hear from Anton. There is still the chance that he will simply keep the pearl and do nothing. Or that I have asked him to perform something that is clearly impossible. I have no idea how he'll get the information to me— will we have to wait until there is another letter to deliver?

But I have underestimated Anton. When he comes to unlock the door to the exercise yard, he has a drawing for Alexei Nikolaevich, sent by Gleb Evgenievich. This is unusual—I can scarcely believe that it has been allowed. But it has: I see the commissar's official stamp on the little sketch. A mouse wearing a chef's hat and apron stands in front of a kitchen stove. A clock above the stove shows hands pointing to one o'clock, and a calendar page on the wall is turned to tomorrow's date.

"See?" Anton says. "One o'clock. He must be preparing luncheon."

Alexei points out the crescent moon shining through a tiny window. "It's not luncheon. It must be a late-night tea."

"Well, there you are," says Anton, glancing quickly at me.

"How strange," Olga remarks when Anton has again taken up his position by the door and is staring blankly into space. "I wonder why Gleb has sent this?"

I shrug and turn away so that she won't see my face.

Marie's bed next to mine is empty. I miss her. If she were here, I might tell her about my plan—or I might not. I lie awake, my eyes wide open, and I hope that my sisters are sleeping soundly. If anyone stirs, I will explain that I'm going to the lavatory. Sometime after midnight I slip out of bed and creep down the service stairs to the little hall next to the pantry. The outside door opens to the fenced-in yard, with a path leading to the kitchen building behind the house. This door is kept padlocked from the outside except when the servants are carrying our meals from the kitchen to the pantry. I try the door. It's still locked. Anton has not come to unlock it. My hands shaking, I try again. Minutes pass, but it feels much longer. Something has gone wrong. I fight back tears of disappointment.

Then I hear a click and a snap, sounds of a padlock being opened and removed. The door opens easily and I step out into the yard. There is no moon. A cold wind blasts, and the path to the kitchen building is slick with ice. I struggle to keep my footing, shove hard on the door to the kitchen, and nearly fall through when it flies open.

Gleb pulls me inside and closes the door. We stare at each other, our eyes getting used to the dark. I'm grinning like a fool. He reaches out and touches my cheek. I take his hand, bring it to my lips, and kiss his fingertips. "You arranged this, Nastya?" he asks.

"I wanted to see you," I tell him. "It's such a long time since we've spoken—not since last summer on the *Rus*."

"I'm afraid we won't see each other even now," Gleb says, and I can hear the smile in his voice. "Anton says we must not even strike a match." He tucks my hands inside his coat to warm them. "Have you heard from your parents?"

"We're being taken to Ekaterinburg soon to join them. And you, too?"

"My sister and I have been told that we won't be granted an entry permit at Ekaterinburg, and we're likely to be put in prison if we go. I'm willing to take the risk, but she believes we should stay here."

I lean my head against Gleb's chest. I can hear his heartbeat, slow and steady. "We may never see each other again." My voice is shaking. I don't want to spoil these few minutes we have together with tears.

Gleb's lips brush my brow. "I know. But we have so little time, and there is something I wish to say to you before we part. I love you, Anastasia Nikolaevna, and if it is ever possible, I will ask your father's permission to marry you. He will surely refuse, but that will not stop me from loving you, now and always."

I smile through the tears I can't hold back any longer. "And I love you, Gleb Evgenievich, now and always."

Gleb's lips find my mouth and he kisses me, and I return the kiss. It's as sweet as I knew it would be.

There is a light tap on the door. "It's Anton," I whisper. I don't want to move out of Gleb's arms.

He holds me tighter. "We must go. He's risking everything. He could be shot for allowing us to be together."

The knock on the door is more insistent. "God be with you and protect you," I whisper close to Gleb's ear. "Now and always."

"And with you, dearest Nastya." Gleb makes the sign of the cross over me and pushes open the door. "Now and always."

I step out into the black night and follow Anton. How is it possible to feel so happy and so terribly sad at the same time?

Colonel Kobylinsky is gone with no explanation. This frightens us, because we have no idea what will happen now, and no one to ask. Every change frightens us, because it's never a change for the better.

A beast named Nikolai Rodionov takes Kobylinsky's place. He says that he is the soviet commander in the Urals, and he makes it clear that he hates us. Rodionov is not tall, but he is broad-chested and strong, with thick, stubby fingers. He doesn't believe that Alexei is still not well enough to travel. Rodionov sees my brother lying in bed, but later he sneaks back and surprises us, probably thinking he will catch Alexei up and walking around. He must have been disappointed.

Rodionov does whatever he can to make us as miserable as possible. He orders the locks removed from our doors. All of them.

"I shall not be deceived!" he bellows. "I must be able to come here whenever I wish, to make sure none of the prisoners has escaped!"

It would be enough to make me laugh if it were not so stupid. If only escape were possible! Even Monsieur Gilliard says the chances of our being rescued now are next to nothing.

I know that I will never again have a chance to speak to Gleb, and I play our few precious minutes together over and over in my head, like a scene from the cinema. But still I wait by the window in our bedroom and hope that Gleb will pass by, and that he will look up for just a second or two and I will see him smile and, if no one is watching, wave to me.

This morning I was at my window, hoping as I do every day for a glimpse of Gleb, just to know that he is still here, still alive. And there he was! He did glance up—as I knew he would—and I raised my hand and pressed it to the glass. Gleb raised his hand, too, and for a moment we gazed at each other. Our bad luck, though, was that Rodionov stepped out of the fish merchant's house just then and saw us. He shoved Gleb into the muddy street, shouting, "It is forbidden for any person to look into the windows and to signal to another person! Anyone who does so will be shot immediately!"

I gasped and took my hand away. Gleb picked himself up, ignoring Rodionov, and made a little bow in the direction of where I stood. I blew him a kiss that he couldn't see and watched him as he continued down Freedom Street toward the river and vanished from sight.

The snows have melted and the ice is gone from the river. On Papa's birthday in May, we are told to be ready to leave the next day. Mama and Papa and Marie have been at Ekaterinburg for five weeks, and no matter how awful it is there, we are glad to be going. We spend the day preparing. We are not allowed to take much, but we put on the double brassieres and all the clothes we can and carry the pillows in which we've hidden jewels—minus only one pearl. I wonder about that pearl. I haven't seen Anton since the night he allowed Gleb and me to have our short time together, and I wonder if somehow Rodionov found out about it. If he did, it would not have gone well for Anton. I hope that whatever fate has come to him, he somehow got the jewel to his mother and that it will help her and his sister.

At noon we are escorted between rows of soldiers to the river steamer, *Rus*, that brought us to Tobolsk months ago. We have our dogs with us. We board the *Rus*, and I think of last summer when Gleb and I linked our fingers on the rail of this boat and I felt sure our lives were somehow joined. I was right, but this is not at all like last summer.

My sisters and I are shoved into a dark, dank cabin and told that we may not lock the door at any time. A guard shuts Nagorny and Alexei in another cabin and padlocks the door.

...lliard complains to the horrible Rodionov, reminding him that Alexei is sick and Dr. Derevenko needs to be able to get to him when he's needed.

Rodionov says nothing, but only sneers. The door remains locked.

After two days the steamer arrives at Tyumen, where sentries herd us onto a waiting train. Gilliard is taken to a car somewhere at the end. The train rumbles out of the station, headed west toward the Urals and Ekaterinburg. Heavy clouds close in, and rain begins to fall in gray sheets.

We are offered a little food during the journey, but none of us wants to eat. Eventually I fall asleep, and when I wake up, we're no longer moving. Daylight leaks in around the window curtains, which we're not allowed to open. I open them a little anyway and peek out. We seem to be near a town, but the train has not pulled into the station. This must be Ekaterinburg. Soon we'll be reunited with Mama and Papa and Marie, and that cheers me, because I've missed them so much. But then I begin to worry what will happen next. My stomach aches.

The rain still falls, and mud thick as pudding is everywhere. Several carriages have drawn up beside the train, and Rodionov barks orders: We are to gather up our belongings, get off the train, and board the carriages. My sisters and I do as we're told, sinking deep in the mud that sucks at our boots. Mine are leaking. Tatiana tucks Ortino under one arm and drags a valise, staggering through the mud. My spaniel, Jimmy, splashes after me. Nagorny carries Alexei, with a thoroughly filthy Joy following them at the end of his leash. I look around for everyone who came with us—Gilliard, Countess

Hendrikova, dear Trina, General Tatischev, and the servants—but I don't see them.

A soldier prods me painfully in the ribs with a rifle butt, but the thought that our family will soon be united keeps me going. Tears wash down Olga's face. I make a feeble joke: "I do hope I have a clean pair of white gloves in my luggage."

Tatiana stares at me as though I've gone mad. "You must be crazy, Nastya," she says dully.

"Just trying to make you smile," I explain.

"I doubt we'll ever find anything to smile about again."

My sisters and I crowd into a carriage, two soldiers—one tall, one short—squeezed in with us and our piles of luggage and the two dogs that gaze up at us helplessly. Nagorny and Alexei and his poor little Joy are being shoved into another carriage with Kharitonov and Lenka, and two more soldiers. But where are Gilliard and the others? The first two carriages pull away, and I assume the rest will follow.

Olga sits opposite me. She looks ill. "I have something to tell you, Nastya," she says, and her feverish eyes gleam in her gaunt face. "I've destroyed the secret notebook that you found so fascinating." She watches me with a ghost of a smile. "I'm not joking."

I stare at her, my mouth opening and closing. "You know?" I manage to gasp.

"Of course I know! I've known for quite a long time. Why do you think I've made it so easy for you to find?"

My thoughts are scrambled; I can't think what to say. I've been reading her secret notebook for years, since she first fell in love with Lieutenant Voronov. In that time, as I've grown up and changed, I've watched my oldest sister also change—from a beautiful, talented, carefree young girl into a disappointed woman filled with bitter disillusionment.

"I don't know," I mumble. "Why did you?"

Olga shrugs. "I'm not sure. I suppose I wanted you to share something of my *real* life. To show you that things are not quite so perfectly ordered as Mother and Father always wanted us to believe."

Tatiana is looking from one to the other of us like someone in shock. "What on earth are you two talking about? *What* secret notebook?"

"Just some notes I made," Olga explains, "besides our regular diaries that anyone could read, although I don't know who would want to, they're always so dull. This was just for me to read. But Nastya found them, and when I realized she was reading them, I decided that maybe, since she's the youngest, she might have more choices in her life than I did, or you, or even Mashka. But as it turns out, none of us have any choices at all."

"Don't say that, Olya!" Tatiana orders. "You must not say such a thing! We must have faith that everything will turn out as it should. Our fate is in the hands of a gracious God!"

Olga shakes her head and says nothing.

The soldiers glare at us. "Speak only Russian!" growls the short one.

CHAPTER 24

The House of Special Purpose

I t is still raining when the four carriages draw up in front of a large white house surrounded by a high wooden fence with a sentry stationed every few paces. We clamber out of the carriages and rush up the stairs. Alexei and Nagorny follow from the second carriage, but the other two carriages do not arrive. What happened to the others—General Tatischev, Countess Hendrikova, and Trina Schneider? Dr. Derevenko, Baroness Buxhoeveden, Sydney Gibbes? And where is Gilliard?

There is no time to think about that now. We are caught up in the sweet joy of being a reunited family, even in the reality of our new prison. The two-story house is on a hillside in the middle of the city. The first floor has been made into guardrooms, and the second floor converted into a series of cells: the doors to the rooms taken off, and the windows nailed shut and then whitewashed so that we can't open them or look out. It belongs to a merchant named Ipatiev, but they've named it the House of Special Purpose.

There are five rooms and twelve people to share them—OTMA in one room and Mama, Papa, and Alexei in another, the rest finding beds in other rooms. All of our baggage has been taken away and put into a room on the first floor—"for safekeeping," they tell us, grinning. We can guess what that means. Marie has hung a sheet over the doorway to our room.

Three men carrying revolvers lounge outside the rooms and watch us. These men are terrible human beings. They will not allow us even to use the lavatory without one of them following us. They have made crude drawings on the walls and smirk and tell us to be sure to look at them. It is too embarrassing for words.

In charge of our prison is a swine named Alexander Avadeyev.

"Ah, so these are the daughters of Nicholas the Blood-Drinker!" he roared when we arrived. It seems that he is always drunk. Or maybe he is always obnoxious.

We have been trying to find out what has happened to our friends and relatives. Most of the news we get is very, very bad: Mama's sister, our aunt Ella, was imprisoned in Perm, not far from Ekaterinburg, and so was Papa's brother, Uncle Misha. Two of his uncles and several cousins are being held in the Fortress of Peter and Paul. In the midst of this wretchedness is a single bright spot: our beloved Aunt Olga has a baby boy and is managing to survive—very happily, she wrote—somewhere in Crimea.

Now Kharitonov must take whatever food is sent over from a community kitchen and prepare our meals from it. We have tea and black bread for breakfast, and that seems to suit Papa. Occasionally Kharitonov performs miracles and makes *pirozhki*, delicious dumplings, stretching a little meat with potatoes and vegetables. Sometimes he does so well with what little he has that the soldiers help themselves to it first, and we get whatever is left. Avadeyev is by far the worst of them. He dips his filthy hands into our food, deliberately drips it on Papa, and says, "You've had enough, blood-sucker."

But we are grateful for small blessings. Alexei and the fourteen-year-old kitchen helper, Lenka, play checkers and card games when Lenka has a little free time. Alexei is teaching him to play the balalaika, although he had to leave all but one behind at Tobolsk, and the one he brought is now missing a string.

One bleak day Kharitonov asks my sisters and me if we would like to learn to make bread. It turns out to be quite interesting—measuring the flour, mixing the yeast and water, and then the magic of watching the dough rise, and the delightful feel of sinking one's fingers deep into the dough and kneading it. Even the horrible guards behave more like human beings when the odor of baking bread wafts from the oven, and they beg for a piece of it before it has a chance to cool.

We wash our own clothes, a chore that at least gives us something useful to do, but where to put our underthings to dry that the brutish guards won't make obscene remarks about them? Mama says we must always wear our double brassieres and corsets with the jewels stitched inside, or they will be found—the guards go through everything. The garments are very heavy, and the weather is growing hotter every day.

Avadeyev has hired a couple of young girls from town to scrub the floors, which are always a mess from the guards tracking in muck and mud on their boots. It would not occur to them to take them off and leave them at the door, or at least to clean them off before they come upstairs. What pigs!

The girls, Elizaveta and Irina, were shy around us at first, but when we ask about their families they become eagerly talkative. Elizaveta's brother is a guard at the prison, and she lets it slip that three of those who traveled with us—General Tatischev, Countess Hendrikova, and Trina Schneider—are now prisoners there. We are shocked to hear this, but we dare not ask questions, because the guard we despise most is waving his revolver around and Avadeyev appears to be drunk, as usual.

When there is a chance, I whisper to Elizaveta, "What about the others?"

"Don't they tell you anything?" She shrugs. "I guess it doesn't hurt to tell you that—unless I get caught." She jerks her head toward the guards. "They're living in the railroad car," she whispers.

The railroad car? We hope for more information, but it will have to wait. The guards are singing some filthy song to shock us. Elizaveta shouts something crude to the swinish guards, and they shout back and bray with laughter.

And so it goes. The guards enjoy taunting us and sneering at Papa and thinking of obscene things to say in front of us and Mama, to see if they can get us to react. Nagorny did not disguise his loathing for them, and now it has come to a very bad end. My brother had a gold chain hanging near his bed with some holy medals attached to it, and one of the worst of the guards decided to take it. "What does a filthy rich boy like you need with another gold chain?" he snarled, and that was too much for Nagorny.

"You will not take it," Nagorny told the man. "It is not yours to take."

"I'll take what I damn well please," the guard growled.

Nagorny seized him by both arms. "And I said you will not."

"Arrest him!" the guard shouted, and the other guards stepped forward and forced Nagorny down the stairs.

We have not seen him since, and Alexei cannot stop crying. Papa tries to reassure him that Nagorny will surely be released, but Olga says under her breath, "They'll shoot him."

I hope Olga is wrong, but I'm afraid she is right. Now, every morning when we are allowed a half hour of exercise behind the house in the bleak space they call a garden, it's Papa who carries Alexei down the stairs and puts him in a chair, where he watches with big, sad eyes as we walk back and forth, back and forth, until the thirty minutes are up. His great pleasure is when Lenka comes to visit and plays checkers with him.

On my seventeenth birthday I find *The Adventures of Anastasia Mouse* and kiss the pictures Gleb drew for me a year ago. When I remember the conversations we once had, I am comforted. I remember the promise we made, "now and always," and find joy in knowing that he loves me and I love him. But that joy vanishes like smoke when inevitably the reality closes in around me and I know that I will never see him again. When I'm frightened—that's most of the time now—I retreat to happy memories and try not to *think*.

Then Papa receives a letter—he's not sure who wrote it— asking which windows are ours, how many armed guards there are and where they're posted, and advising us to be ready at a moment's notice. Papa replies with the information, along with where the guns are mounted and how many men are guarding us. Mama believes that Father Grigory's son-in-law, or possibly someone else, has organized a rescue, and our hopes are raised—everyone's but Olga's.

Days pass, nothing happens, and our hopes fade one more time. Having no news of any kind of the outside world makes the unknowing even worse.

Our only source of information is Elizaveta, who comes once a week to mop the floors and occasionally passes on some scrap of news. She tells us that Dr. Derevenko, Gibbes, and Gilliard, along with Sophie Buxhoeveden, who have been living in the fourth-class train carriage, were ordered to leave Ekaterinburg. She thinks they returned to Tobolsk.

Suddenly the drunken, loutish Avadeyev is gone and his drunken, brutish guards with him, replaced by a new group. We're not sure who these men are. Their leader is Yakov Yurovsky. He is not drunk, his behavior is quite proper, but Papa doesn't like him at all. "This is a specimen lacking a heart," Papa says. He thinks they're members of Cheka, the secret police.

Marie says, "When we are rescued—" and Olga interrupts, "We are not going to be rescued, Mashka."

"Don't say that, Olya!" Tatiana orders. She's twenty-one now, still OTMA's bossy "Governess."

Marie bursts into tears, and then we're all crying.

I have finished my prayers and am falling asleep when someone taps on the doorframe. I hear Dr. Botkin's voice on the other side of the sheet Marie hung there. "Get up and dress quickly."

"Maybe we're being taken somewhere," Tatiana guesses.

I put on my corset and the double brassiere under a dress and jacket with jewels hidden inside. At the last moment I pick up the piece of green sea glass that Gleb once gave me and drop it into my pocket. Jimmy barks, and I pick him up.

Papa is already in the hallway. He's carrying Alexei, still half asleep and clinging to Papa's neck. Papa looks haggard, his kind eyes tired and sad. Mama, her expression grave, mouth set in a severe line, leans on Anna Demidova's arm. The maid carries a pillow with jewels stuffed deep inside. Trupp and Kharitonov appear, nervously smoothing their hair and adjusting their jackets. Dr. Botkin's glasses glitter in the lamplight.

"Where's Lenka?" Alexei asks sleepily.

"Yurovsky sent him this morning to visit an uncle in the country," Kharitonov explains.

"But if we go without him?"

"Don't worry," the chef assures Alexei. "They tell me he'll be back tomorrow."

Papa looks us over and nods. "Come, then," he says.

Marie clutches my hand, and we follow our father down the stairs to whatever fate awaits us.

Epilogue

ANASTASIA'S FATE

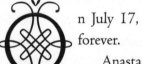n July 17, 1918, Anastasia's voice was silenced forever.

Anastasia and her family, their loyal friends, and the family dogs were ushered into a small room on the ground floor and told to wait. When Nicholas asked for chairs for Alexandra and Alexei, Yurovsky called for chairs to be brought, and the three sat down, with the others standing behind them, arranged as though they were posing for a photograph. Moments later Yurovsky returned with the Cheka squad, a dozen soldiers armed with revolvers. The commandant offered a short statement:

"Your relatives have tried to save you. They have failed, and we must now shoot you."

The soldiers began to fire. Nicholas was killed almost at once, and so were Alexandra and Alexei, but Anastasia and her sisters in their jewel-stuffed corsets and clothing that acted as bulletproof vests were not so easy to kill. The soldiers fired round after round until, at last, all were dead. Anastasia was the last to die.

The bodies, wrapped in sheets, were carried off in a truck, dismembered, burned, and soaked in acid—a process that took three days—and the remains were hastily buried in a shallow grave in the forest. The murderers were convinced that they had gotten rid of all traces of the Romanov family. But they were wrong.

Years later, in 1991, the bones were dug up, and DNA testing proved the identity of some of the victims. When more bones were found nearby in 2007, the rest of the victims were identified. Eighty years to the day after the murders, a funeral was held and the remains reburied at the Cathedral of Saints Peter and Paul in St. Petersburg, where Romanov tsars have been buried since ancient times. Bells tolled and a nineteen-gun salute rang out.

On the same day that the tsar and his family were murdered in Ekaterinburg, the tsarina's sister Ella and several uncles and cousins were thrown into a mine shaft and grenades tossed in after them. The tsar's brother, Mikhail Alexandrovich, had been shot a few months earlier. Several other Romanov uncles and cousins were executed by firing squad the following January.

General Tatischev, Countess Hendrikova, and Trina Schneider, who had traveled from Tobolsk to Ekaterinburg but then were removed from the train and imprisoned with Prince Dolgorukov, were all shot in September 1918.

Nicholas died without knowing that the United States had entered the war as an ally of England and France in April 1917. In November 1918 the war ended with the defeat of Austria and Germany. The armistice was signed November 11, four months after the murder of Anastasia and her family.

Not everyone perished. Sydney Gibbes and Baroness Buxhoeveden crossed Siberia to Omsk, which was controlled by the British and the White Army (which opposed the Bolsheviks). The baroness finally reached England safely, and lived the rest of her life there. Gibbes remained in Omsk and worked with the British for a time before they were forced to withdraw to China, where he lived and worked for a while. In the late 1920s he returned to England, and eventually he converted to the Orthodox religion and became a priest. He died in 1963.

Pierre Gilliard stayed in Siberia for three years, married Alexandra Tegleva—Anastasia's beloved Shura—and eventually managed to leave Russia by way of Japan, then to the United States, and at last to his native Switzerland, where he became a professor of French at the University of Lausanne. He died in 1962.

Prince Felix Yussoupov and his wife, Irina, escaped to Paris.

Anya Vyrubova, who was taken from Tsarskoe Selo with Lili Dehn, was first imprisoned in the Fortress of Peter and Paul for five months, then released, and then imprisoned repeatedly, until in 1920 she escaped from Petrograd and fled to Finland, where she died in 1964. Lili Dehn, who was briefly imprisoned with Anya, was released and placed under house arrest to care for her son, Titi. Later she and her mother and

Titi escaped on a ship bound for Greece, eventually reaching England, where she was reunited with her husband.

Anastasia's Grandmère Marie could not keep her promise to celebrate her granddaughter's sixteenth birthday in Paris. The dowager empress, who last saw her son Nicholas at the time of his abdication, fled to Crimea with other Romanov family members. She occasionally received word of the family's ordeal and their imprisonment in Ekaterinburg. Her sister, Dowager Queen Alexandra, mother of King George V, persuaded Dowager Empress Marie to accept the king's offer to send a ship to take her to safety in England. She chose to return to Denmark, where she'd been born, and died there in 1928 at the age of eighty. She never accepted the terrible story of the murder of her son and his family.

Grand Duchess Olga Alexandrovna, Nicholas's sister, who had finally found happiness in her marriage to Nikolai Kulikovsky, somehow survived the Revolution in Crimea. Olga and her husband were taken there by train with her mother, Dowager Empress Marie, and her sister, Grand Duchess Xenia, and Xenia's husband, Sandro. They lived under house arrest at Sandro's estate. Olga's son Tikhon was born there while the family was under a death sentence from the local revolutionary council; another son, Guri, was born two years later, after the family had managed to escape and gone to join Dowager Empress Marie in Denmark. There they lived, not entirely happily, with Olga's domineering mother. After her mother's death, Olga and her family moved to a farm. After World War II ended, they emigrated to Canada, where they farmed until they were too elderly to continue. Olga lived out her final years in a simple apartment in Toronto; she died in 1960. Throughout her long life Olga continued to earn money from her paintings.

And then there were the children of Dr. Botkin, Tatiana and Gleb. When their father chose to accompany the Romanovs from Tobolsk to Ekaterinburg, Rodionov told Tatiana and Gleb that they could go with the others as far as Ekaterinburg but he would not grant them an entry permit and they would be arrested. They made the decision to stay in Tobolsk. When they learned of the murder of their father along with the tsar and his family, Gleb and his sister fled from Tobolsk. That fall, Tatiana married a Ukrainian officer whom she had known at Tsarskoe Selo and who had become involved with an anarchist movement. She and her husband escaped through Vladivostok and made their way to France. Tatiana's son, Konstantin Melnik-Botkin, attended the funeral service for Anastasia and her family at the Cathedral of Saints Peter and Paul in 1998.

After fleeing from Tobolsk, Gleb initially found refuge in a Russian Orthodox monastery. He once again considered becoming a priest but ultimately rejected that idea. He met and married Nadine Mandraji, daughter of a Russian nobleman and widow of an officer killed in battle in 1915. Like his sister, Gleb and his wife and her three-year-old daughter escaped through Vladivostok. Then their paths diverged: Gleb went to Japan and finally to the United States, where he worked as an illustrator.

A common theme that runs through many of these survivors' stories is the possibility that of all those cruelly murdered on the seventeenth of July, there was one who somehow managed to escape: Anastasia. In 1922, the story of a young woman claiming to be Grand Duchess Anastasia Nikolaevna began to circulate and capture the imagination of the public.

A woman calling herself Anna Tschaikovsky turned up in a psychiatric hospital in Germany, claiming to be Anastasia. One of the first of the survivors of the Bolshevik revolution to visit Anna was Baroness Buxhoeveden, who declared there was no resemblance. Eventually Pierre Gilliard and his wife, Shura, came to visit, and they too were quite firm in their assertion that this was definitely not Anastasia. Anastasia's aunt, Olga Alexandrovna, denied that the woman could be her niece. The tsarina's brother, Ernst, Grand Duke of Hesse, hired a private detective and reported that the woman was actually a Polish worker named Franziska Schanzkowska. Even Prince Yussoupov, who had participated in the murder of Rasputin, and his wife, Princess Irina, Anastasia's cousin, denied any possibility. So did Charles Sydney Gibbes, Anastasia's English tutor. When Dowager Empress Marie died in October 1928, a dozen Romanov relatives gathered at the funeral in Copenhagen and signed a document attesting that Anna was an impostor.

But not everyone was so sure. Lili Dehn thought this was the real Anastasia. Tatiana Botkina-Melnik thought she saw a resemblance. Her brother, Gleb, was sure of it: This was truly Anastasia.

Ten years after the murders, Gleb hired a lawyer to investigate Anna's claim that the tsar had secretly hidden a large fortune in England. That turned out to be false, but it didn't change Gleb's mind about Anna. For a year or so Anna lived as the guest of a wealthy woman in New York, but when her mental condition began to deteriorate in 1932, Anna went back to

308 · CAROLYN MEYER

Germany. She lived on the grounds of a mental hospital for some time.

The years passed. In 1939, Germany, under the leadership of Hitler, invaded Poland, France declared war on Germany, and World War II began. Kaiser Wilhelm—Cousin Willy—died in the Netherlands in 1941 after two decades in exile, and six months later, Germany declared war on the United States. World War II devastated Europe, just as World War I had.

Meanwhile, Gleb Botkin still believed Anna's claim. This was surely his dear friend. In 1968—had she lived, Anastasia would have been sixty-seven—Gleb and a wealthy and eccentric friend, Jack Manahan, a history professor in Virginia, paid for Anna's passage to return to the United States. Just before her visitor's visa was to expire at the end of six months, Anna and Jack Manahan were married, with Gleb as their best man. Manahan was twenty years younger; it was strictly a marriage of convenience. A year later Gleb died. A few more years passed. Anastasia Manahan, as she was then legally known, was in poor health and mentally unstable, and she was again put in a mental hospital. That was in 1983. She had been in and out of mental hospitals for more than sixty years. A few months later she died of pneumonia.

DNA testing has demonstrated that Anna was not related to the Romanovs but to the Polish family Schanzkowska. Grand Duke Ernst's private detective had been right. One can't help wondering whether Gleb ever had the slightest suspicion that this woman was not the lovely young woman to whom he had once lost his heart, "now and always."

SUGGESTED READING

Many books make good reading about the Romanovs, as well as about Russia in the early twentieth century, the outbreak of World War I, and the rise of communism, and the terrible end of Anastasia and her family. Among my favorites are *Nicholas and Alexandra*, by Robert K. Massie (New York: Atheneum, 1967), written nearly a half century ago, and the much more recent *Alix and Nicky: The Passion of the Last Tsar and Tsarina*, by Virginia Rounding (New York: St. Martin's Press, 2012). Both are clear, informative, and engaging. I desperately wish *The Romanov Sisters: The Lost Lives of the Daughters of Nicholas and Alexandra*, by Helen Rappaport (New York: Macmillan, 2014), had been available when I was working on my own book.

The most beautiful book is surely Peter Kurth's *Tsar: The Lost World of Nicholas and Alexandra* (Boston: Little, Brown, 1995), with gorgeous photographs by Peter Christopher. On a smaller scale, *Anastasia's Album*, by Hugh Brewster (New York: Scholastic, 1997), features many candid Romanov family photographs with an emphasis, of course, on Anastasia.

A charming book written by Anastasia's friend, Gleb Botkin, and illustrated with his paintings, *Lost Tales: Stories for the Tsar's Children* (New York: Villard, 1996), is more difficult to find but worth the search. I especially like the inclusion of a photograph of Gleb, handsome and soulful, taken in 1917.

Naturally, multitudes of websites exist relating to the

Romanovs, but one stands far above the rest: the Alexander Palace Time Machine, accessible at www.alexanderpalace.org/palace. There you'll find four principal categories to explore: palace archives, personalities (with eyewitness accounts), resources, and palace tour, each offering many fascinating subcategories.

I'll also mention one more book: *Anastasia: The Last Grand Duchess, Russia, 1914* (New York: Scholastic, 2013), part of the Royal Diaries series; I wrote it fifteen years ago with younger readers in mind, and it was recently reissued in paperback. In 2012, I began to write *Anastasia and Her Sisters* in order to explore in greater depth the emotional life of Anastasia, including her relationships with her older sisters and younger brother and with Gleb Botkin.